PRIMEVAL

SHADOW OF THE JAGUAR

Coming soon in the *Primeval* series:

THE LOST ISLAND
By Paul Kearney

EXTINCTION EVENT
By Dan Abnett

PRIMEVAL

SHADOW OF THE JAGUAR

STEVEN SAVILE

TITAN BOOKS

Primeval: Shadow of the Jaguar
ISBN-10 1 84576 692 X
ISBN-13 9781845766924

Published by
Titan Books
A division of
Titan Publishing Group Ltd
144 Southwark St
London
SE1 0UP

First edition March 2008
2 4 6 8 10 9 7 5 3 1

Visit our website:
www.titanbooks.com

Did you enjoy this book? We love to hear from our readers.
Please email us at readerfeedback@titanemail.com or write to us at
Reader Feedback at the above address.

To receive advance information, news, competitions, and exclusive Titan offers
online, please register as a member by clicking the "sign up" button on our
website: www.titanbooks.com

A CIP catalogue record for this title is available from the British Library.

Printed in England by Mackays Ltd, Chatham.

For Sarah and Lee
Consider this a 'get out of Christmas and Birthday presents' free card
For the next... ooh... five years.
With love
Bruv

ONE

The animal's lonely voice haunted the mountainside. The melancholy sound rolled across the canopy of wet leaves and dripped down the trailing vines, all substance lost long before it reached the brothers' ears. It did not matter.

The rainforest spoke with the tongues of Peruvian devils, a thousand sounds competing for attention, and beneath them a thousand more just as eager to be heard. The place was alive with the constant chittering of insects; the deep-throated rumbles of the yellow-backed toads; the raucous caws of the colourful birds as they preened and strutted on the high branches; the scuttle of tuco-tuco, sloths and opossum through the thick vegetation; the slithering of the *lachesis muta* through the thick grasses; the soft susurrus of the leaves and the silken rush of the rain falling down between them.

Even at dusk, everything was vivid and alive. But night was coming on fast beneath the thick, leafy canopy.

It was hot. Unbearably so. The cotton clung to Cam's flesh. He plucked at it with sticky fingers. There was nothing comfortable about the cloying humidity. He ran his fingers through his hair. They tangled in a greasy knot that he couldn't tease through.

"I'm telling you, Jaime, it was like shards of ice spinning lazily in the air." Cam shook his head, knowing the words couldn't come close to describing what he had seen.

"Right," his younger brother said, a wry grin playing over his lips.

"Clouds of ice in the middle of the rainforest, and you still say you've not been on the whacky baccy?"

"Give it a rest, Jaime. I'm serious. It was weird."

"You're telling *me*." Despite his words, Cam could tell Jaime was intrigued. "Did you try and touch one? I mean, what was it like?"

It was the obvious thing to ask. It was precisely what *he* would have asked, if their roles had been reversed. Even so, he didn't have an answer.

Cam peered across the fire at his brother. How could he admit that the strange phenomenon had actually scared him shitless? He played the big tough guy, but the thought of reaching out and actually *touching* that eerie light sent a chill running the length of his spine.

"No," he admitted, a part of him hoping that would bring an end to Jaime's questions.

He picked up a stick and stirred the fire. The flames had almost guttered out, and they sprang back to life, throwing weird shadows across the small enclave within the trees. It quickly burned low again, its fuel reduced to charcoal. The shadows shrank, becoming hunched and cadaverous as they ghosted across the encroaching foliage.

Beyond them lurked thicker clusters of darkness; the stones of the ancient Incan temple they'd discovered. It was a loose term, *discovered*; it wasn't as though they were the first humans to set foot in the place, but with the isolation and lack of anything approaching a beaten track it still felt that way.

With dusk drawing in they'd decided to hold off on exploring the ruin until morning. Without the luxury of electric lights, the risk of injury outweighed their curiosity. So they had bivouacked down for the night, with the promise of adventure waiting for them the next day.

In the fading light, they had gone to search for enough dry wood to start a fire — more as a deterrent to the insects than as a source of heat. That was when Cam had seen the peculiar light.

He picked up a piece of charcoal, which broke and smeared across his fingertips. It was potent stuff, the essence of life and death in one crumbling stick. As he stared at it, it appeared so mundane, and yet everything around him, even his brother, could be reduced down to this simple dust of carbon, and without it nothing could live.

He shook his head.

Jaime grunted, obviously far from satisfied with his brother's evasiveness, but equally familiar with it.

"You weren't in the least bit curious?" he pressed. "That's not the Cam Bairstow I know and love. Hell, you almost sound like the old man. Gearing up for a career in politics, are we?"

"God forbid," Cam replied, matching his brother's grin. He brushed away the dirt at his feet and jammed the stick into the ground. Then he rooted around in his pack for his water bottle, uncapped it, and drained a long swallow of warm water. He missed the simple luxury of ice.

"I'm going to take a leak," Cam said as he pushed himself to his feet and dusted off his hands on his shorts. "Try not to burn anything down while I'm gone."

Away from the fire the air was thick with the hum of mosquitoes. One brushed against his face. The tickle of its wings reached his lips before it disappeared. A week ago he would have squashed it or swatted it away. A rash of bites later he'd wised up to the fact that dead mosquitoes only drew more. Now he was content to let it explore the warmth of his face and move on in its own good time, trusting the mosquito repellent to live up to its name.

Cam pushed aside a trailing branch and the leaves closed around him as he moved further away from the safety of the fire. Within a dozen paces the trees became so thick that the night lost all definition, and turned black. The deadfall on the ground crunched beneath his feet as he blundered forward blindly, reaching out until he found a thick-trunked tree. He unbuttoned his shorts, grunting contentedly as he relieved himself against it.

For a long moment Cam felt inconsequential beside the sheer size of the Amazonian giant. It was a lovely moment of role-reversal — now he was the mosquito, grateful that the tree couldn't squash him.

If a man urinates in the rainforest and there's no one around to hear it, does it make a sound? He chuckled at the thought. His mind had started running off on so many bizarre tangents recently; a symptom, no doubt, of being a million miles from civilisation, with only monkeys, tree rats, and his brother for company. After a month in Madre de Dios, an ecology reserve in the heart of the Peruvian rainforest, he ranked all three on roughly the same level of the evolutionary scale.

One by one the natural harmonies of the rainforest fell silent, until there were only the sounds of the rain in the high leaves and his urine puddling at his feet.

Cam buttoned up.

Something was wrong.

He knew it instinctively. Some primal part of his brain responded to the sudden silence. The rainforest was a living thing. For it to suddenly fall still could only mean one thing: there was something out there in the dark that had scared off the fauna.

"Jaime?" Cam called.

His voice cracked. He shook his head, smiling at the silliness that had him spooked by simple silence.

As though in answer, he heard a brief rustle of movement, the tangled scrub shifting as something heavy prowled through the darkness. He turned in the direction of the sound, but there was nothing to see. Blinded by the darkness, he tried to follow the sound with his ears instead.

"Jaime, stop playing silly beggars. It isn't funny."

Though he was hopeful that it was his brother, Cam couldn't bring himself to raise his voice. Something told him that wouldn't be a good idea.

This time, a low-throated growl rumbled close to his ear. It was a predatory sound filled with the resonances of the hunter stalking its succulent prey. Cam spun around, certain the animal was at his shoulder, but it was nowhere to be seen.

Off to his left, the sharp crack of breaking deadfall snapped his already shredded nerves. He peered frantically at the layers of darkness that lay beyond the leaves.

"Jesus," he muttered, breathing hard. "Pack it in, Jaime."

His heart hammered against the cage of his ribs. Warm beads of perspiration trickled down the curvature of his spine. It didn't matter that he couldn't see anything; he could *feel* it. He wasn't alone.

And he knew it wasn't his brother.

There was a distinct rhythm to the movement, like something moving on all fours, close to the ground. He was put in mind of a cat, circling its prey; which made him the mouse.

Cam cursed himself for not bringing a torch. Suddenly the safety of the fire felt a long way away.

He dared not move.

"Jaime," he said, very quietly, willing it to be nothing more than his brother, playing the fool.

The animal moved through the darkness slowly, its passage a threatening whisper as it brushed against the vines and leaves.

And then it was gone — the beast moved on. He was alone with the oppressive silence.

Strangely, that was worse. At once the rainforest felt incredibly claustrophobic, the towering trees and dragging branches pressed in on him, heightening the sound of the rain on the canopy of leaves. It lent the night a nightmarish quality. The chill of dread settled beneath the trickles of sweat pouring down his skin.

"Jaime?" Cam called again, but there was no answer.

Suddenly the darkness erupted with the sounds of violence. And he heard his brother begin to scream.

Cam started to run, blundering through the trees blindly, feeling as if he was moving in slow motion. He pushed aside branches that clawed at his face, ducking beneath the sting of barbs and thorns. His brother's shrieks were sickening.

Worse, though, was the sudden hush that followed them.

"*Jaime!*" Cam shouted, bursting out of the trees.

The campfire lay scattered, faggots of wood smouldering, barely casting enough light to hold back the night. Still, it showed too much.

His brother lay on his back amid the ruin of the fire, dark stains all across his body where his flesh had been torn open by tooth and claw. The savagery of the attack was writ in blood and shadow. Cam took an unsteady step forward, unable to wrench his eyes away from the sight of his brother's broken body, all thoughts of Incan ruins suddenly far, far away.

Before he could take a second step a huge muscular creature hit him, the sheer momentum of its attack hurling him into the underbrush as huge teeth snapped and snarled at his face.

TWO

The call came in at midnight, the voice on the other end of the line summoning James Lester to the Under-Secretary's residence. He knew better than to question the venue or the hour: the more powerful the man, the less he slept.

Lester dressed quickly, adjusting the lie of his bespoke waistcoat and teasing the knot of his plain silk tie. Appearance was everything. He shrugged into his jacket and then into his topcoat, and walked out to the waiting car.

Miles, his driver, nodded and opened the rear door for him. The interior was pleasantly warm against the chill of the night; Miles had obviously set the heater running while Lester had dressed again.

"Where to, sir?"

"The Under-Secretary's in Belgravia."

"Very good, sir."

London might not sleep, but it most certainly dozed, Lester thought as the car left the South Bank, swept over the Thames and turned onto the Strand. The quiet street was bathed in the yellow glow of the lights. The legal district was dead, though some of the usual tourist spots were still isolated hives of life.

Peering out into the night, he was sure some pseudo-scientist must at that very moment have been studying the social strata of the city, and drawing the same conclusions as the anthropologists studying the apes of deepest darkest Africa. Man was, after all, a beast. The city at night showed just how little the species had truly evolved. And of course, it boasted other denizens, populating the darkness that surrounded the pubs, clubs and restaurants.

It was a different breed that came out after dark. The street people, invisible during the day, could be seen huddled in their doorways wrapped in blankets and newspapers while the twenty-four-hour party people danced, drank and acted as though they owned the city. They had all the rituals of their jungle counterparts, banging their chests to attract a mate.

It was all quite pitiful, really.

The car negotiated the kinks around Charing Cross and took the turn onto Pall Mall. Here the street retained much of the dignity it must have known in the days of Gentlemen's Clubs and hansom cabs. Even this late at night the immaculately tailored doormen stood beside the gleaming porticoes, playing guardian to the last bastions of entitlement. Behind those doors lay other worlds of charm and old money. Those portals were, Lester thought wryly, every bit as paradoxical as any anomaly that opened into the Permian. Polite society had its own magical rifts that only a certain class of traveller was allowed to enter, where the hoi polloi were about as welcome as a plague of locusts.

They turned right on St James and entered the heart of Belgravia.

Sir Charles Bairstow's residence was a three-storey Edwardian townhouse in a narrow mews. Within a hundred yards it was as though they had driven into the land that time forgot. Everything was transformed, right down to the faux-gas street lamps and the planters dripping colourful lavender bougainvilleas, their petals like tissue-paper flowers.

Miles pulled up to the curb, and kept the car idling while Lester clambered out. Standing on the pavement, he looked both ways, not really sure what he expected to see.

The street was empty.

He walked up to the door and rapped on it, using the lion-headed brass knocker. The noise was shockingly loud in the quiet residential street, like the report of a gun, or a car backfiring. Lester winced, half-expecting a dozen curtains to twitch in response.

He heard someone fiddling with the security chain, and then the latch, before the door opened.

Bairstow's housekeeper peered myopically out into the dark street.

"James Lester to see Sir Charles," Lester said, adjusting the knot of his tie. "I'm expected."

"Yes, yes, come in, Mr Lester. Sir Charles has retired to the smoking room. He is expecting you. May I take your coat?"

Lester entered the warmth of the old house, wiping the soles of his shoes on the mat despite the fact that he knew they were immaculate. He gave his topcoat to the old woman, who said, "Second door on the left, on the first landing." She nodded toward the narrow stairs.

Before proceeding, Lester took a moment to look around, taking in the impracticality of the thick champagne pile of the carpet, the ostentation of the heavy chandelier, and the delicacy of the armoire. Several large oil paintings lined the stairs, the familial resemblance obvious in each, from the current Sir Charles at the foot of the stairs all the way back through the generations to wigged ancestors along the landing.

Another anomaly.

Lester nodded to the housekeeper and went up.

A night-light illuminated the landing. The second door was slightly ajar. He pushed it open and entered.

The old man was sat in a wing-backed Chesterfield armchair with his eyes closed. Logs crackled and spat in the open hearth, the fire providing the room's only light. This chamber was the living embodiment of Victoriana, with antique maps and leather-bound books decorating the walls, the bookcases augmented with a variety of mounted animals and other curiosities. A glass-fronted cabinet contained various lepidoptera specimens, their thin membranous wings providing a splash of colour to the dour setting.

Lester coughed politely into his hand.

Sir Charles Bairstow was as much a throwback to those quintessential times gone by. He sat beside the fire in his plush smoking jacket, a thick cigar clutched between equally thick fingers. Ash gathered in the small silver tray balanced on the arm of the chair. He had silver-grey hair and thick bushy mutton-chops. All of his sixty-one years were etched deep into his face as he opened his eyes.

"Ah, James, come in, come in." The old man gestured toward the second empty armchair.

"Sir Charles," Lester said, joining him beside the fire. Bairstow looked tired; more so than the hour accounted for. This was a weariness that had been ground in over days. He recognised the symptoms of insomnia in Bairstow's eyes and the pallor of his skin. Dark shadows followed the line of his jaw, suggesting that it had been more than a day since he last shaved. Still, he maintained an air of dignity, despite his exhaustion.

"Care for a snifter?" Sir Charles unstoppered an ornate crystal carafe filled with amber brandy, and poured himself a finger's worth into his equally ornate glass.

"It's a little late for a social call," Lester observed.

"Indeed, but we are civilised men, James. We can conduct our business with a modicum of decorum, no?"

Lester inclined his head in agreement.

Sir Charles filled a second glass and pushed it across the table. Lester picked it up and cradled it in his hand, swirling the rich liquid gently against the sides of the glass before lifting it to his nose and inhaling. The fumes alone were intoxicating. He sipped the brandy and set the glass aside.

"I take it there is a reason for the hour, and the location?" he ventured.

"Indeed," Sir Charles said, leaning forward in his chair. "It's all very clandestine, I know, but I would ask a favour of you." The way the old man said "favour" left Lester in no doubt that he was about to be asked for the sort of favour he could not refuse.

"Do you have children, James?" Bairstow asked.

"Three," Lester said.

"Ah, then you will understand, I am sure. I have two sons, Cameron and Jaime. They are of that age, idealistic, with a fire in their bellies. You know how it is." Lester nodded. "We had them late, spoiled them completely, of course, like most old parents. They were our little miracles." Sir Charles' focus seemed to drift into nostalgia. There was obviously something he wanted to say, and it was equally obvious that he didn't actually want to say it.

"Cameron recently graduated in archaeology from Cambridge, Jaime is about to enter his final year. In this day and age, even an honours degree is not a guarantee of a job, and archaeology is not what anyone would call a lucrative career, so Mae and I thought it wise to give the boys a leg up. It is all about experience, after all. A man is no more than the sum of his experiences, and all that."

"Absolutely," Lester agreed, savouring another sip of the ludicrously rich brandy.

"Do you know how fiercely competitive it is, this digging up of old bones? And for what, exactly? The opportunity to sleep in a tent and live on ramen noodles?" He said it in that 'boys will be boys' manner adopted by fathers the world over.

"Quite," Lester said. He glanced at his watch; then tried to mask the gesture a moment too late.

"Ah, I'm boring you," Sir Charles said. "My apologies. I'm an old stick-in-the mud, I'm afraid. I don't understand all of this fascination with bones and broken stones."

"Something about those who don't understand the mistakes of history being doomed to repeat them, perhaps?" Lester offered. "Now, tell me about this favour." His only hope for sleep was to get the old man back on track.

"Yes, yes, of course." Sir Charles looked pained that the conversation had steered itself back around. "We arranged for the boys to travel to Peru. They flew into Lima, and then moved on to Cuzco. They travelled from there to the rainforest in the region known as Madre de Dios — the Mother of God. It's a nature reserve, one of the few in the world that harbour so many truly endangered species, as well, of course, as fabulous Incan ruins."

"Sounds like a dream holiday," Lester said. But the expression on Sir Charles' face indicated that he did not agree.

"James, it's been six days since anyone has heard from either of them, and nothing is being done about it." His voice was low and firm. "The Peruvians are being deliberately pig-headed. No one will tell me anything, and as far as I am able to ascertain, there are no search parties out looking for the boys. Madre de Dios is rife with poachers; ruthless men who hunt these dying species and sell their hides to the highest bidder.

"I will *not* allow my boys to simply disappear off the face of the Earth, I may not have been the best parent, but I am still their father."

"And you think the boys might have run afoul of these poachers? Surely there may be another explanation. As you said, boys will be boys. Perhaps they found themselves a nice pair of *señoritas*, and are holed up in a hotel in Trujillo drinking pisco sours and dancing the nights away."

"No, I don't believe that for a moment. It isn't like them to be out of touch. They know how much their mother worries."

"Nevertheless, I don't see how I can help you, Sir Charles. Surely you'd be better off talking to someone in the Foreign Office. Strings *can* be pulled."

The old man leaned forward in his chair, his expression suddenly intense as he steepled his fingers. The gesture was somewhere between a prayer and an act of begging.

"Anything official becomes a diplomatic incident, James. You know how the system works. The Peruvians are investing more money than they can afford in promoting the region as an eco-resort. If anything threatens those investments, they're likely to bury the truth, whatever it may be, and Number 10 won't stand for too many waves: the entire eco-resort is being underwritten by British Insurance firms, and financed by a conglomerate of British banks. We're talking bad business, James. No one wants adverse publicity.

"If something has happened to the boys..." He let the possibility hang there, not wanting to finish the thought.

"Still —" Lester began. But Sir Charles cut him off.

"There must be a way for your department to help me, James. Your men are scientists. I was thinking that you might mount an expedition? No need for political red tape, doesn't arouse suspicion at home or abroad to have a few scientists doing research, and therefore much easier to get the necessary visas from the Peruvians."

"That's out of the question, I'm afraid," Lester said, shaking his head. He didn't even want to consider the ramifications of what the Under-Secretary was asking.

"Please." The old man stared at him.

"Sir Charles, we have no remit for work overseas, and mercifully no proof that our research has any relevance beyond the natural boundaries of the British Isles."

"Then you will not help me?" The shadows beneath his brows seemed to deepen.

"I'm sorry. You should talk to your counterpart in the Foreign Office, sir. Perhaps we have operatives in the area, or close by. I can't imagine the Prime Minister would countenance such heavy investment from our own economy without at least a few eyes watching the pot. Eyes everywhere, and all that."

The old man seemed to deflate in his chair, the stiff upper lip crumbling visibly.

"I could order you," Sir Charles said then, a last ditch gambit.

"If that were true, we wouldn't be meeting like this. We would be in Whitehall." Lester rose from his chair, setting the empty glass on the table. "Goodnight, Sir Charles. I hope you hear from your sons soon. I truly do."

"But you won't help." It wasn't a question, so Lester didn't answer.

He left the old man by the fire, well aware of the fact that by saying no he had almost certainly made his life more difficult.

It was a little after two when he clambered back into the waiting car. That left him with less than four hours sleep. Instead of returning home, he had Miles drive him to the Anomaly Research Centre. He could catch an hour or two in the ARC lounge, if needs be.

Professor Nick Cutter was woken by the electronic voice telling him that he had mail.

He rolled over groggily.

Cutter had fallen asleep on the couch in his office. It still didn't feel like his office, though — he was used to the clutter he had accumulated over years of study and hoarding. This place felt more like a laboratory than a place for thoughtful contemplation.

He yawned and knuckled the sleep out of his eyes before he forced himself to sit up. Everything ached.

The ambient light replaced the passage of time with a constant illumination; it was never night in the Anomaly Research Centre.

He stood and stretched, working the kinks out of the muscles in his shoulders and lower back. Though only in his late thirties, and reasonably fit, he still felt joints popping. *Sleeping on the couch is for a younger man*, he thought wryly.

His stomach grumbled. He had no idea what time it was, he realised, or how long it was since he had last eaten, and even then it had only been a slice of Apple Danish washed down by a cup of tepid coffee. Deciding the email could wait, Cutter went in search of sustenance.

His footsteps echoed hollowly as he walked across the cement floor of the loading bay, the quality of the echo changing as he entered the corridor of offices and laboratories that led down to the team's rec room.

He caught a glimpse of himself in the glass of the vending machine, and ran his hand through the dark blond rat's nest he called hair, trying to bring it to its normal sense of order. Then he fed a handful of coins into the machine and punched in the code for a multigrain nutritional meal supplement bar that sounded both healthier and tastier than it was, and a diet caffeine-free low-sodium soda that was essentially fizzy water. Collecting his bounty, Cutter headed back toward his office.

Re-entering the loading bay from the other side, he saw that the light was on in Lester's office. The man was a bureaucratic machine. Cutter watched a shadow move against the wall, but didn't see Lester himself. Shrugging, he wandered back through to his own office, peeling back the foil on his multigrain treat and eating half of it before he sat back behind his desk.

The computer screen had fallen asleep. *Lucky bastard.* He pushed the mouse to wake it.

He opened the mail box and saw that he had three messages flagged as new, one from Lester, another from someone distinctly fictional promising increased length and girth for only ninety-nine dollars, and the last one from someone called Nando Estevez. Cutter recognised the name in that vague *I've met you at a function or somewhere* kind of way.

He popped the tab on the can and drank a mouthful of too-cold soda.

Opening the email, he read through it twice; then sat back in his chair.

Even with evidence in black and white, it took him a moment to associate "Nando" with Fernando Estevez, a student of his from almost ten years ago now. *All sorts of ghosts come back to visit, sooner or later*, he mused darkly. But he remembered Fernando well, a short, serious young man, gifted with a fearsome intelligence that was only held back by his blatant disregard for grammar and spelling. That, at least, seemed to have improved marginally over the years that had passed since he had last read his student's essays.

But this was no essay, and even a third reading left him with a growing sense of concern.

From: Nando Estevez <NandoE@MadredD.com>
Date: May 17, 2008 4:44:28 AM GMT+01:00
To: Nick Cutter <Nick.Cutter@arc.gov.uk>
Subject: Behaviour and Bones

Dear Professor Nick Cutter,

It is me, Nando Estevez!

I am sure you remember me. It has been a long time for both of us, but how could you forget old Nando?

I would ask for your help in something. I think, perhaps, you will find it very interesting, and very mysterious.

After graduating your class I took a job along with Esteban, my half-brother. We worked for a few years off the coast of Trujillo on a marine expedition. It was fascinating work, though I must admit it was mainly to impress the girls! But all good things come to an end, they say, and recently we began working in the new nature reserve at Madre de Dios. The work is sadly less impressive with the ladies, but it is far more interesting for us!

There are things happening in the reserve that I do not understand. In fact, they make very little sense when I think about them.

It is my job to identify the various species that dwell in the reserve, to tag them and follow their movements and record their habits. We have a great variety of rare animals like the capybara, *Hydrochoerus hydrochaeris*, and the giant river otter, *Pteronura brasiliensis*. It is a zoologist's dream!

Now, to the crux of the matter, the animals have been behaving strangely, you see. Their patterns no longer match our expectations, even considering for the increase of poaching and the threat of mankind. All I can think is that something else is causing this peculiar behaviour.

Only this week I have identified several tracks that should not be here. I am confused by them, yet I do not wish to mention this to anyone for fear they will think I have gone mad. These are tracks and bones that do not make sense. There is no one I can trust with the secret I believe I have found. For I have checked all of the books, and the only conclusion I can find makes no sense.

Who could I show the bones to? Who would believe that these fresh bones are also old bones? Who would believe me if I said I thought they were from the Plio-Pleistocene perhaps, or even earlier, but show no signs of fossilisation? The marrow in the bones is fresh.

It seems absurd to me that these strange bones and wrong tracks would be here now, and with my animals behaving so strangely. I fear I am losing my mind! My number at the resort is 84235151, with the Peruvian prefix, 0051 from England. Please call me, Professor Nick!

Your old student,

Nando Estevez

Cutter set aside the soda can and stared.

His first instinct was to dial the number and press his old student with a dozen questions about the nature of these tracks, and his suspicions about the behaviour of the indigenous fauna. Cutter felt a tingling thrill of excitement at the possibility that what he was looking at was proof of the first anomaly off the British mainland.

The implications were massive.

His second instinct was to call the team in and share the excitement. However, he didn't succumb to either urge. Instead, Cutter opened a web browser and entered 'Madre de Dios' into the search function.

A lot of the pages the search returned were either religious in nature, illuminated with iconic images of the Virgin Mary cradling the baby Jesus, or they were written in Spanish. Refining his search to provide English-language results only, Cutter trawled through the rest for the better part of an hour, finding miniscule maps he could barely read and spectacular scenic photographs of the Amazon rainforest and the misty peaks of Machu Picchu.

The first non-religious hits were all for the same sort of stuff: trail tours for Incan ruins, Kon Tiki rafting trips and dream vacations in the Andes, and they were followed by virtual tours and the wiki page for the region. 'Biobridges.org' provided him with a list of the research stations such as the one to which Nando and his brother had been assigned.

Deeper into the search he found a host of Inca ruins, some so breath-taking they looked like oil paintings of imaginary places. He wasn't particularly interested in the old stones, though — it was old bones that piqued his curiosity.

Since the rest of the ARC team wouldn't arrive for quite some time, he had time to kill, and ran various searches on South American fauna using a variety of keywords, one being 'Plio-Pleistocene'.

The results were even less encouraging than the initial search, though more Darwinesque than intelligent design: *hominin* evolution in the Amazon basin, climate change and glacial shifts, volcanic history of the region, geological abstracts on the Madre de Dios River and the clay strata, and even a paper which promised paleomagnetic evidence of a counter-clockwise rotation of the Madre de Dios archipelago in Chile.

He paused for a moment and glanced at the clock in the top corner of the computer screen. It was barely a quarter to six — which, according to the time and date function on the computer, meant that it was almost midnight in Lima. Too late to call Nando, and it would still be a couple of hours until the others rolled in. So he contented himself with printing off any articles that seemed even remotely promising. There were times when he still preferred paper to electronic files.

He tried a blog search next, using one of the many web crawlers that trawled through the inanities of the world's everyday lives. Most were glorified diaries for public consumption, and they were very much the modern disease, reflecting the Average Joe's need to prove that his life had genuine meaning, and that had its advantages. But every now and then there were hidden nuggets of gold to be found in the blogosphere, so once again Cutter ran through a number of keywords, looking for anything that even vaguely hinted at a South American anomaly.

Every one drew a blank.

He didn't know whether or not to find it reassuring. After all, that didn't mean there wasn't an anomaly out there — only that no one had seen it.

So he left the computer and wandered across to the window that looked onto the loading bay. There were no windows opening out of the ARC into the world at large — more to stop people from looking in than to stop the staff from looking out — and it lent the facility an oppressive feel. He braced himself on the sill.

It still seemed so alien.

There were times when it was difficult to reconcile himself with the fact that evolution had taken the slightest of nudges, and drifted askew just enough for this pseudo-military government establishment to exist. Stranger yet, everyone else seemed to feel so *natural* with it.

The world around him had changed without anyone realising it. Anyone but him.

Cutter clenched his fists.

Thinking about it just left him feeling frustrated and angry, and not a little guilty. He had stepped out of the rift with Helen, thinking... what? Cutter laughed bitterly. Thinking just brought it all back, and for however long he thought about it, it didn't matter that the affair had happened a decade ago.

But that way lay madness. So many ifs, buts and maybes. Cutter pinched the top of his nose, furrowing his brow.

He was hungry again — or rather, hungry still. There was a greasy spoon not so far away, and he could do with the air and to stretch his legs. The email would still be there when he got back.

There was smoke rising through the trees. It was thick, black, cloying stuff that carried with it the reek of cooking meat.

Cam Bairstow staggered down through the smothering vegetation, tripping and stumbling along a path that wasn't there, his eyes fixed desperately on the one sign of civilisation he had seen after days and nights alone in the jungle. The smoke meant hope. He was dizzy from dehydration, exhausted and weak from blood loss, but his cuts had begun to clot. Now it was all about food and water.

The fragrance flavouring the smoke was irresistible.

Cam stumbled on blindly.

While he was lost within the trees, time had become a meaningless concept. There was no day or night, only shadows and darker shadows. His heart hammered erratically now, and his vision swooned as he hit the bole of a thick trunk. The flair of pain in his shoulder reignited the fire in a dozen of his wounds, and a croaking cry escaped his swollen lips.

He couldn't remember anything of the last few days. He had woken into a world of blood and hurt. He hadn't moved for the longest time, allowing the pain to own his flesh. There had been sounds all around him as he opened his eyes, and he had thought that odd. The last thing he remembered had been silence. Complete and utter stillness.

But that couldn't be right. The forest was never still. Never silent. It was a living thing.

Then he remembered the screams.

Somehow he had staggered away from the ruined temple, but he had been too weak to risk the rope bridge, and instead had slipped and fallen and skidded and slid down the side of the long mountain toward the ravine, his eyes fixed on the crystal blue water. The trees offered him some protection from the elements, though a mist had risen thickly to engulf the world around him, leaving Cam to blunder down until he reached the bottom.

Images of death formed within the curls of mist, and faces formed in the thick white. He saw again and again the last few seconds before the creature's attack. It brought back the pain with a shocking clarity. And the pain brought something else in turn, a hollowness at the memory of Jaime's body lying there, a mess of blood in the dirt of the forest floor.

His foot caught on a ragged spur of root.

The plant snagged Cam.

He fell sprawling into the dark loam of the forest floor.

He lay there on his back, too bone-weary to move, knowing that if he didn't locate that reserve of strength needed to carry him to the village, they would be finding his bones. Nothing more.

Above him a stripe-faced monkey swung through the canopy hand-over-hand in a looping, easy motion, working its way down through the branches. The animal was skittish, swinging quickly from perch to perch and leaving rustling leaves in its wake. Cam watched it, wishing for a moment that his life might be that uncomplicated — but it was in a way. It had been reduced to the most basic of elements — stand up and walk, or lie there and die.

He didn't move because death didn't feel like such a bad place to be.

Then the scent of the smoke — ugly and abrasive — entered his lungs, seeping down his throat, but it was also a glorious sensation, one filled with hope. The meat that was flavouring it was sickly sweet. The odour clawed at his empty belly, reminding him how desperately hungry he was.

He pushed his hands beneath him and tried to stand. He was like a new-born calf, struggling to balance on shaky legs as he rose and stumbled on between the trees. More than once he was forced to use their trunks for support.

The smell of burning meat grew more and more aromatic as he neared the source of the smoke, until it became so strong that it stung his eyes. It was too strong, he realised, to be some haunch of lama basting on a cooking fire. And the flavour was all wrong. He tasted something else in the air, salty on his tongue, like the crackling of pork rind.

It was more than a simple cooking fire. He knew that much instinctively, and some primordial part of his brain recognised the stink. But he had no idea how much more than a cooking fire it was until he lurched out of the shroud of trees and saw the smouldering remains of a huge funeral pyre in the centre of the clearing.

Five women stood weeping at the fireside, watching their loved ones burn. Cam stumbled forward, his hands held out before him as though begging for mercy, until he saw the fear in their eyes. His hands fell to his sides then. He felt the sting of the smoke in his throat, his bile rising, and he felt the bite of the fire's heat on his face, tightening his raw skin as he walked into it. He couldn't begin to understand what had happened, even as he began to make out the limbs that were visible within the dying flames.

One woman hissed something at him, waving her hands, and another screamed as though he were some mindless corpse staggering out of hell to claim her. It was a soul-wrenching sound.

Cam lurched forward, his legs buckling beneath him, and then fell to his knees. He couldn't see beyond the flames. There were so many bodies within them. So many shapes all piled one atop another. It was only as the branches shifted, breaking as the fire robbed them of their strength, and one of the blackened bodies rolled out of the pyre that he saw the death wounds, and understood.

The creature that had killed Jaime had found these people, as well.

Death had come disguised within the shadow of a huge black jaguar.

Cam stared at the burning men, unable to move. He tried to form words. To say something. But nothing would come. What words could match the horror trapped within the dancing flames?

Coincidence?

Lester had no time for coincidence. In his opinion, it was a word that had no place in a rational man's vocabulary.

Cutter walked into his office a little before nine carrying a sheaf of papers and proclaiming that they needed to talk.

Against his better judgement, Lester listened, and for the second time in less than twenty-four hours heard the words "Madre de Dios".

"Thus the gods do conspire," Lester muttered, steepling his fingers almost exactly as Sir Charles had in his smoking room just a few hours before. But that was where the similarities ended. This conversation was a very different one, and Nick Cutter wasn't remotely like the old civil servant.

"What if we've been wrong all along?" Cutter was saying.

"How so?" Lester said.

Cutter was dishevelled, more so than usual. The academic scruffiness had given way to a lack of grooming which smacked of slovenliness.

"What if we started from the wrong supposition? We've been working under the assumption that these anomalies were localised on our side, following some heretofore unknown law of physics. But what if they're not? What if rifts are opening in the Arctic, or on the Siberian Tundra? Just because there is no one to see them doesn't mean they don't exist."

"Like the proverbial tree falling in the rainforest," Lester said, leaning forward on his elbows. "I assume you are going to blind me with science now." He eyed the sheaf of papers still clutched in Cutter's hands.

"Research," Cutter said. Lester had noticed that the more passionate the Professor got about his work, or an idea at which he was worrying, the more pronounced his otherwise mild Scottish burr became.

"I've been contacted by an old student working in Peru." Cutter continued. "His job is to monitor the behavioural patterns of various endangered species, and he's noticed some peculiarities there, including disturbed migratory patterns among the indigenous animals, and, more importantly, he believes he has found bones from the Plio-Pleistocene."

"Hardly evidence of an anomaly, Cutter. Tell me, has an anomaly actually been sighted?"

"Well, no."

"And have these bones been carbon dated, or positively identified in any way, Professor?"

"No."

"Then I would suggest you are reading your own agenda into the evidence. May I remind you that foreign jollies are well beyond our remit. We do not follow hunches based upon 'jumped to' conclusions."

"I thought our remit included tracking the anomalies and preventing the rewriting of the evolutionary chain," Cutter countered. The look on his face made it clear that he didn't want to let this one go.

"Well, yes, but within reason," Lester said. "The British government does not act arbitrarily on foreign soil. There are protocols that must be observed. A few bones are not reason enough to breach them, Cutter. That's just the way of the world. Bring me hard evidence, and then we'll talk, but until you do, the answer to the riddle is no, if a tree falls in the rainforest, and there is no one to hear it, it does *not* make a sound."

There was a polite knock on the glass door and the team's public relations specialist, Jenny Lewis, poked her head around the corner.

"There's a call for you on the secure line, Lester," she said, smiling cheerfully. "Sir Charles Bairstow."

Lester rolled his eyes.

"I'll take it," he said to her. "We're done here," he told Cutter. "If you would excuse me..."

Lester picked up the phone before Cutter was halfway out of the office.

"Lester," he said into the mouthpiece.

"James? Good man." Sir Charles sounded unsettlingly confident, given the way their previous conversation had ended. "There is news that I think might interest your team." He paused, clearly waiting for someone to tell him to continue.

Lester left the silence hanging a moment longer than was polite.

"Go on?"

"Word has come through from my man on the ground in Peru. A little after nine this morning our time, a young British tourist matching my son Cameron's description crawled out of the jungle. He has been taken to a hospital facility in Cuzco. No one will allow me to talk with him, so I am missing vital information. He is apparently delirious and suffering the effects of some serious trauma." He paused, then continued.

"I want my son back, James, and if — God help me — Jaime is still out there by himself, I want him found and brought home. Do I make myself clear?"

"Crystal," Lester said, "but what exactly do you expect me to do, Sir Charles? We are not in the business of Kidnap and Rescue, after all."

The voice on the other end of the line turned cold and distant.

"This is no longer a polite request from one father to another, James. I have spent the morning making calls. As of ten o'clock this morning you and your team have been assigned to assist me, under the auspices of a scientific investigation. You, of course, will receive confirmation of this imminently. I suggest in the meantime that you prepare your people for a journey, to cut back on wasted time. Bring my boys home, James. That is all I ask. Needless to say I would much rather we had come to an amicable agreement last night, but in the cold light of morning it matters little to me whether you are a willing ally or a co-opted one."

"Indeed," Lester said stiffly, not appreciating the position the senior Civil Servant had angled him into. "Hello Mr Rock, welcome to the Hard Place."

Sir Charles did not laugh.

"My man seems certain it is Cameron, and is doing all he can to get close to him, but the Peruvians have got their security tied up tightly and we are being blocked at every turn from ascertaining the truth. It is, needless to say, a delicate situation, James. Regardless, I want my boys home."

"I can appreciate that, Sir Charles, but in all honesty we cannot mount a military expedition to bring your sons home. It is quite out of the question. There are protocols that must be observed."

"The question has changed, James. In fact I would go so far as to say it has become a statement. These things you will do: you will make preparations for your team to travel to Cuzco. You will take three men of my choosing from the Regiment who will assist with the recovery of my son and aid with on-the-ground activities. They'll be fully briefed — we can't let sheer ignorance jeopardise the mission, so I'll expect you to fill in the details concerning your... ah... *unique* activities. And most important of all, you will bring my boys home. I don't care how you do it or what excuses you concoct, but if you wish to have a desk to sit behind, you will make it happen. If I were you I would stop thinking about what is out of the question, and start thinking about solutions to the problems you face."

With that, the Permanent Under-Secretary severed the connection and left Lester holding the phone.

Lester placed the handset in the cradle, and buzzed Jenny through.

"Fetch Cutter and the others," he told her.

***

She was his own personal ghost, and this was his own personal hell. Jenny Lewis knocked on the glass door of Cutter's office.

"Lester wants to see you," she said with Claudia's voice.

Nick Cutter glanced up at the woman who appeared so much like Claudia she might have *been* Claudia, were it not for the slightly darker hair and her perpetual air of confidence. It was difficult to look at her and not see the woman he had allowed himself to love. Difficult because he kept thinking there was a history between them, a connection that she did not share, and he found himself taking it for granted at the strangest moments, in the stupidest of ways.

"What does he want now?"

"What does Lester ever want?" Jenny replied, raising her eyebrows and grinning. It was a moment of familiarity that might easily have been shared with her ghost.

Then she spun on her heels and left him.

Cutter took his time.

When he finally walked up the spiral ramp to Lester's office, the rest of the team were already assembled. Connor Temple and Abby Maitland sat like naughty school children on the long leather banquette against the far wall, her short-cut platinum blonde hair in stark contrast to his dark, unruly mop and five o'clock shadow. Stephen Hart leaned beside them, close to Abby. Jenny stood beside Lester's desk, while Lester sat back in his leather chair, seemingly content to wait forever. The Spartan warrior's mask rested on the desk between them. *No, not content*, Cutter thought, seeing the wrinkled crow's feet around his eyes and the strain that lurked behind them. *For want of a better word, he looks haunted.*

"Close the door behind you," Lester said. That in itself aroused Cutter's curiosity; like most modern managers, Lester chose to operate an 'open door' policy. It was meant to make him seem approachable, but in actuality it allowed him to see all and hear all, like two of the wise monkeys rolled into one.

Cutter closed the door.

"What's this all about, Lester?"

"In economic terms, they call it a double coincidence of wants," Lester said.

"And what, precisely, is that supposed to mean?"

"It means that what you want and what I want are no longer mutually exclusive, Professor Cutter. Considering our conversation this morning, this should amuse you no end. Word has come down from on high that you are going on a little holiday."

"What are you talking about?"

"The short version is that Sir Charles Bairstow's two sons have gone missing in the Madre de Dios region of Peru, which I believe is the same region where your former student was reporting those peculiarities. We have been... requested to aid in their safe return."

"We're going to Peru?" Connor blurted, his dark eyes flashing. "Cool."

"That's the spirit," Lester said.

"Wait a minute," Cutter interrupted, "this morning it was out of the question, now suddenly it's a done deal?"

"As I said, a double coincidence of wants. Answering the call for assistance from your colleague provides a legitimate cover for the government's exfiltration of Sir Charles' errant children."

"I don't like the sound of this."

"You don't need to," Lester told him smoothly. "You get to satisfy your curiosity about the possibility of an anomaly in the region, subtly of course. There will be three more members of your team, from the Regiment. They will oversee the recovery of the boys. You need not get your hands dirty with anything apart from Peruvian loam. Consider it a case of getting what you wanted, but not perhaps how you wanted it — or why.

"Your cover will be relatively straightforward, since the best lies are always close to the truth, after all. You will be investigating the migration of certain endangered species out of the region. More socio-science than the pure stuff, but interesting to the British government nonetheless as we look to protect certain species of our own from dying out. I suggest you begin making preparations, you ship out in the morning."

His expression made it clear that they were dismissed.

Cutter wasn't about to argue; Lester was right, he had got precisely what he wanted, no matter how uncomfortable the means of its procurement left him feeling.

"Come on, then," he said to the others.

"One last thing," Lester said, as Cutter opened the door. "Jenny will be accompanying you — the last thing we need is a public relations nightmare. There's a lot you need to know about the region and the obstacles you are likely to encounter. I'm putting you in charge of this operation, so let's do our best to keep both feet out of our mouths for once, shall we?"

THREE

It was still too early to call Nando Estevez, and would be for some time yet, but that didn't mean he couldn't make preparations. There were a thousand things that needed to be put in place for a legitimate scientific expedition, and almost none of them could be done overnight. Still, they had to be done.

Cutter corralled the team into his office, mentally sorting out the best way to divvy up responsibilities.

He looked at them looking at him, and wondered what they saw. Sometimes he had difficulty recognizing the man he saw reflected in their eyes, seeing instead a distorted image in a fun-house mirror. He recognised the features, the lines and bone structure, that was all intimately familiar to him, but the flesh did not make the man. The sum of his experiences did. Memories shaped a man's life and gave it purpose and meaning.

They had their memories, and he had his, and even when they were of each other they were different. Cutter hadn't lived through many of the experiences they thought they shared between them. It was a peculiar thing to think about: a wrinkle in time.

He needed to think about something else. Time to throw himself into his work.

They had resources now, he reminded himself. The ARC was a long way from his disorganised academic haven shunted away on the far corner of the university campus. They had money at their disposal, and they even had access to the strings that needed to be pulled.

He could probably have left them to their own devices, said something like: "Suit up and be ready for the morning," and they would have been. But he preferred to be on top of things, even if it was akin to teaching his grandmother to suck eggs — an expression that had never made that much sense to him.

"I feel like I just stepped through the looking glass," Cutter began, peering beyond them at his reflection in the glass door. "Now I'm trying to believe in five impossible things before breakfast, and I think my head is going to explode."

"Six," Connor corrected.

"What?"

"It's six impossible things."

"Right. And that's meant to help prevent my head from exploding?" Cutter scratched at the stubble on his cheek to hide his slight grin. "Okay, so let's review the situation from our end." He turned to Stephen. "Was Nando Estevez in your seminar group?"

Stephen shook his head. "The name doesn't ring any bells. Sorry."

"Ah, well, Nando is an old student of mine. He contacted me last night to report something potentially very exciting. He's a ranger in an eco-reserve in Peru. Part of his job is to study the behavioural patterns of the 100-plus endangered species that can be found within the rainforest. Recently, he's noticed a lot of strange activity, including tracks he doesn't recognise, and bones that are out of time. Reading between the lines I think he suspects they are from a supposedly extinct creature. By themselves they prove nothing, though they do raise a lot of questions, and coupled with some peculiar migratory patterns he has observed in the species, I think it means a prehistoric creature has been introduced into the ecosystem. Perhaps more than one. This could be our first solid evidence of an anomaly outside of the British Isles."

He paused, and allowed that to sink in for a moment. Connor, of course, was the first to speak up.

"Do you know what that means?" he said breathlessly, as his mind raced to catch up with all of the possibilities. This was a conspiracy theorist's dream... and nightmare. "It doesn't have to be the only one, does it? I mean, there could be anomalies all over the world. Everywhere."

The implications of it hung there, just waiting to be voiced. It was

Abby who spoke up next.

"Oh, God," she said, shaking her head. "What does it mean? If anomalies could begin opening everywhere, the past and the future breaking through, is time itself coming undone? Life's supposed to be a straight line, from birth to death, not twisting and turning across the millennia."

Then her specialty kicked in.

"How can we survive if bacteria from the Permian are suddenly let loose, and we're not there to contain it? We have no vaccines. No resistance. Look at bird flu. What if it's not natural? What if it appeared just because a bird in Eastern Europe fed on some Jurassic faeces? Look how it's spread, what it's done to livestock..."

She sat back and muttered, "Oh, God."

All of this had occurred to Cutter, and more. The threat to humanity didn't have to come from the past, either. Seeing Abby's troubled face, he chose not to voice his fears.

"You think something has come through, then? Some sort of predator?" Stephen asked, bringing them back, ironically, to the present.

"I don't know," Cutter admitted. "But that would be the logical conclusion. The rainforest ecosystem is a finely balanced mechanism. Sudden changes are uncommon, and when they do occur it's almost always because something has unsettled the balance. A new predator is the logical extrapolation of the facts."

Stephen nodded.

"It's hardly new, though, surely?" Connor said. "What about El Chupacabra? South American territories are rife with stories of mysterious predators and mystical devil dogs going back centuries. Iconographically, even their gods are based upon incredible monsters. Take Quetzalcóatl, the bird serpent."

"True," Cutter said. "There might still be unidentified species in the region."

"Any ideas what we're looking for?" Jenny asked.

"Could be anything, literally. We've got all of history to contend with. Predators were common on the South American pampas." He stopped, wary of letting them get carried away with endless supposition.

"So, this morning I was told in no uncertain terms an investigation was out of the question, and this afternoon we're packing our bags for

Peru. As much as I hate the political ramifications of what Lester is asking us to do, this is a pretty unique chance for us to see what's out there. Let's not waste the opportunity.

"With that in mind, we're going to need to make some pretty serious preparations in a very short period of time. I'm going to contact Nando and arrange for a welcoming committee, once we reach the reserve. Connor, I want you to sort out the technical side of things, go to the stores, work out what we're likely to need to do this properly.

"Abby can you handle the practicalities: tents, dry bags, first aid supplies, salt pills?

"Jenny, if this is meant to be a legitimate expedition, we're going to need transport both to get there and once we're on the ground — and it has to be of the non-military variety. Let's distance ourselves as far as possible from anything official. Get onto the airlines, find out the nearest airport, arrange the hire of an All Terrain Vehicle. I'm sure there are a stack of permits we'll need to have in place before we touch down."

"Already onto it," she said briskly.

"Great. Stephen, we're going to need supplies in situ: food, water, dietary supplements. We're not going to be in a position to wander into the nearest supermarket once we land, and certainly not once we're in the wild. We're going to need maps too. I don't want to leave anything to chance."

"Maps? Maps? We don't need no stinking maps," Connor said, doing a fairly miserable Bogart impression. "We've got the GPS trackers, satellite hook-ups, pin-point accuracy. All the mod cons for us, Prof. None of this splashing around in the mud trying to read soggy paper."

"Right, and they're all well and good, but how exactly do you plan on charging them up on day two? We're going to have to do it the old fashioned way, I'm afraid."

"I don't suppose..." Connor paused, looking around the room hopefully. "You know... What about guns?"

"What about them? Should we plan on smuggling them across international boundaries? Last time I looked 'gunrunner' wasn't in the job description."

"We could use diplomatic pouches," Connor offered.

"Do you really think I'm going to let you run around in the jungle with an AK47?" Cutter asked. And his face made it clear that it wasn't really a question.

Connor shrugged. "Worth a try."

"Who knows, one day I might weaken," Cutter said. "But I wouldn't bank on it."

Alejandro Inatuzi was a simple man. His life consisted of simple things. The simplest of which was the dream of going home to sleep. The Médico Clinica Cuzco operated on a three-shift system — at least in theory. He had worked eighteen hours straight, with three more to go, and needed a cigarette if he was going to make it through.

He snuck out, nodding as he passed the ward sister who was hunched over patient charts working out doses of medication for the night shift. Pills of all colours were laid out in white paper drinking cups, waiting to be taken through to the wards. She smiled up at him as he walked by her desk. Her deep brown eyes were manna from heaven. There was beauty, he mused, the young, pretty kind that was brushed on with makeup, and then there was *real* beauty, the lines of the face, the curves of the body, ample and rounded, of a proper woman. Sister Maya Vennasque was a proper woman in every sense of the word. She had the kind of beauty that would have made painters weep and plead for the chance to immortalise her.

Hell, Alejandro wanted to paint her, and there wasn't an artistic bone in his body.

He mimed smoking a cigarette and she shook her head. So he shrugged a kind of rueful *can't blame a guy for trying* shrug, and pressed the button for the elevator.

The corridors exuded that ever-present ammonia and antiseptic smell. The floor tiles were scuffed and worn, any kind of lustre long since trodden into submission by countless feet over the course of too many years to remember.

The elevator arrived, and he went outside for his smoke. Alejandro rolled his own licorice-paper cigarettes, adding a little smoothing extra to the tobacco in order to wake him up during the interminably long shifts. He savoured the smoke as it filled his lungs, finished cigarette, then wandered back up to finish the chores on his duty roster. He had six rooms left to visit before he could go home.

Maya smiled her heart-stopping smile as the elevator doors opened up again.

"No rest for the wicked," he said, leaning up against the desk, "and no use pretending I'm not the wickedest."

"Alejandro Inatuzi, what would your wife say if she knew you spent your nights flirting with another woman?"

"She'd threaten to cut bits off of me, I am sure," he replied, grinning. "So let's keep it our secret."

"You're incorrigible," Maya chuckled.

"I try to be."

"Take these in to the Englishman would you?" she said. "He needs to take three on the hour." She handed him one of the small pill cups.

He wandered back toward his steel cart, which was still up against the wall where he had left it an hour ago. That was one thing about the night shift, generally it was calm — at least once it was past three a.m., that is. That was one of the curiosities he'd discovered working in the hospital — more people died at three in the morning than at any other time of day. They joked about the Death Hour, but they all believed it. 'El Diablo's Time', they called it.

He checked his watch. It was five minutes to four. Five more minutes, then he was home free. He laughed quietly at himself and started whistling as he walked.

The Englishman was in the last room off the corridor, sharing it with Paco, an emphysemic who hadn't said a word since he lay down in bed, six weeks earlier. Paco had been brought into the hospital to die, left there by a grandson who had no wish to care for the old man. Sometimes people disappointed Alejandro; there was honour in caring for your elders. It went back to tribal times; the men gave their lives for the tribe, and when they could no longer hunt or fish or fight, they were cared for by the beloved they had spent their lives feeding and protecting.

This new generation, with their flat-screens and their fast cars, left a lot to be desired when it came to humanity. With that thought, he turned to enter the darkened room.

There was a man standing over the Englishman's bed.

It took Alejandro a moment to realise that he didn't recognise him.

"What are you doing?" he asked. A superstitious part of his brain began screaming that he had walked in upon El Diablo, come to claim the Englishman for himself. Inwardly, he cursed himself for a fool.

The man turned to face him, but said nothing.

For a moment it seemed as though he had no face. There was no shape to it; no features, no colour. Alarmed, Alejandro reached for the switch and turned on the overhead lights.

The stranger was wearing a mask, and he held a needle gun, which he had stabbed into the morphine dispenser. Alejandro watched as he depressed the trigger again and again and again, administering dose after dose.

"Get away from him!" the orderly cried in alarm.

The stranger let the dispenser drop and stepped away from the window-side bed. The saline drip was shot through with a ribbon of red: *blood*, Alejandro realised sickly.

Still the stranger said nothing. He reached behind his back for something as he walked slowly toward the door. His hand came back holding a snub-nosed revolver.

Alejandro threw up his hands, pleading, "Don't shoot me. Please. I did not see anything. The Englishman died in his sleep. It happens. Please, do not shoot me. I have a wife and three boys. Please."

The stranger came close enough that the foul stench of his breath was sucked back into Alejandro's lungs as he swallowed air.

He didn't pull the trigger. Instead he raised his hand and hammered the hilt of the gun into the side of Alejandro's skull with a sickening crunch of bone. The orderly fell, sprawling out across the freshly disinfected floor. He could see his own face reflected in the white tiles, and the blood-red rose that seemed to flower at his temple.

The stranger stepped over him, his footsteps echoing hollowly in the antiseptic quiet of the ward.

Alejandro did not dare move until the steps had faded to nothing. Only then did he struggle back to his feet. He stumbled across to the Englishman's bed and pulled back the blankets. He wrenched the needle out of the patient's arm, cutting off the supply of whatever drug the stranger had administered.

The flesh had already turned bruise-purple around the central line. Poison? There were a hundred lethal drugs in the supply cabinets, and no way of knowing the toxicology of what was in the Englishman's blood without testing the bag from the drip itself.

The rhythmic beep of the heart monitor beside the bed faltered, and stopped.

Alejandro hit the alarm.

A minute later the crash team came running.

The call came in a little before six in the evening.

"Lester," he said, answering the phone himself. As the voice spoke on the other end, however, he sat up straight in his chair.

Cameron Bairstow was talking.

Sir Charles' man had made it through the wall of protection ringing the hospital by posing as a hospital orderly.

"We've had word." Sir Charles' aristocratic burr was stretched painfully thin by a mix of grief and the muted telephone line. "It is Cameron they found, and Jaime is dead."

"I'm sorry for your loss," Lester replied, surprising himself because he actually managed to sound as though a part of him meant it.

"I don't want your sorrow, Lester, I want you to bring my boy home. That is all that matters to me."

"I understand, but surely Cameron is safe now, and at the risk of being insensitive, there's nothing we can do for Jaime. There is no longer the need for our little charade. And I'm sure the Foreign Office can assist with the arrangements..."

The silence on the line was long and drawn out, the rasp of breathing the only hint that Sir Charles was still there. Finally, he spoke.

"Cam is far from safe. There was an attempt on his life tonight. He was drugged in his bed, Lester. Someone broke into the hospital and tried to kill him while he slept. God only knows why. I won't lose him, Lester. I have instructed my man to post armed guards at his bedside twenty-four seven, until your people arrive to collect him. It is only by the grace of God that he is *not* dead, twice over." Again there was silence, and then he spoke again.

"Listen to me, and listen to me well. I have lost one son. I will not lose another, Lester. I do not trust these people."

And despite that shocking truth, there was something in the way Sir Charles spoke that hinted there was still more to this than he was telling. That rankled.

"I would very much like to contact your man," Lester remarked, fastening onto the old man's evasiveness. He wasn't about to let this go. If there was one thing he hated, it was people hiding things from him.

"There are questions I need to ask, for my team, and no disrespect, but it would be best to hear from him, rather than through your filter."

"Are you suggesting that I would lie?"

"Not at all, sir, not at all. You have nothing to hide, I'm certain, so why should I think you are being anything other than 100 per cent truthful? I understand you are concerned that any indiscretion might make your son's situation worse — loose tongues cost lives, and all that — but I assure you my team will act with the utmost tact. We *will* bring him home, but we really need to talk to your man to assess the situation properly. We have questions that need answering. Fools blunder in, Sir Charles, and none of us like to think of ourselves as fools, do we?"

"Very well." Sir Charles said. "I am trusting you with my boy's life, Lester. Don't let me down." Then he gave him the com-sat co-ordinates, call signal, a list of contact times, and the frequency that would allow Lester to reach his man on the ground.

"A simple telephone number would have sufficed," Lester said dryly.

This time the silence on the line was absolute. Sir Charles had broken the connection, leaving Lester holding the phone.

He sat back in his chair as he worried over what *hadn't* been said. It was far more telling than what had. Lester cracked the bones of his knuckles, one at a time.

Sir Charles wanted his son back, there was no denying that, but he wanted it done quietly, with the minimum of fuss, because for whatever reason he didn't want Cameron's story splashed across the front pages.

Was he just protecting his son? There was nothing untoward in that, if he was. No sinister purpose. Cameron had almost certainly witnessed his brother's killing, and that someone had attempted to murder him before he could talk added a sense of urgency to the situation. That intrigued Lester, he had to admit. But then murder was often fascinating.

So what was it, an eye for an eye? Had Jaime's killers come looking for Cam to finish the job? If so, what had he seen that could possibly frighten them into murder in such a public place?

He had to impress Sir Charles' urgency onto Jenny. He had given his word. That meant that they *would* bring him home.

And not in a box, if it could be helped.

***

The storerooms were an Aladdin's Cave of gadgets. Connor Temple scratched the scruff on the side of his face and tapped through the various menus looking for anything and everything that might be of use.

Every item he could possibly need or want was represented by a small icon, which led to a description detailing precise dimensions, weight, and function. Despite what Cutter had said, he fully intended to fill up one of the Personal Digital Assistants with every scrap of data he could find on Peru, including flora, fauna, maps, political climate, hot zones, traditions and culture. They could jury-rig extra juice from a spare battery cradle that would give them twenty-four hours continuous use, and considerably more if used sparingly. Sometimes the holes in Cutter's understanding were frightening. When it came to technology, it was as though he were trapped somewhere back in the eighties with his transistors, eight-track players and LEDs.

"Practical, think practical," he muttered to himself, resisting the urge to get carried away and requisition stuff for every eventuality.

As an afterthought, he patched through to Jenny on the intercom.

"Stupid question, but what sort of baggage allowance have we got?"

She laughed at him. It wasn't cruel laughter, though — far from it. There was genuine affection in the sound. He could imagine her smiling into the intercom.

"We aren't flying British Airways, Connor. And we can't exactly drop in on a Hercules, so just this once we're travelling in style. I've chartered a private jet from a government contractor."

"Nice." He was impressed.

Moments later, Connor was compiling the playlist for his MP3 player in his head, and he had it complete by the time the first of the steel coffins rolled in on the conveyor belt. It was all about the mood, matching the spirit of adventure with the mellowness demanded by fifteen hours cramped up in a tin can hurtling through the sky. Augustana, Aimee Mann, Breaking Benjamin, some Foo Fighters and Everclear to kick-start the journey. He could imagine Dave Grohl singing 'Next Year' as the wheels left the ground, followed by something more grungy as they climbed to altitude, The Levellers' 'England My Home' with its discordant fiddles, and Pearl Jam's 'Black' with its melancholic melody. Throw in some Snow Patrol, Billy Corgan, Neil Hannon, and Mike Doughty and some old classics like Black Dog and 2112, and that was the first hour pretty much sorted.

The second hour, well, that had to be mod classics like Madness' 'Must Be Love', Adam Ant's 'Prince Charming' and The Specials' 'Ghost Town', then shake it up a bit with 'It's A Kind of Magic', 'Mirror in the Bathroom' or Bowie's 'Ashes to Ashes' to follow. With any kind of mix, the success was down to how well the individual tracks flowed — it wasn't about how great they were individually. There needed to be just the right amount of juxtaposition and continuity between bass lines and vocals to make it interesting, but not jarring.

He broke the seals on the coffins to make sure everything he had chosen was safely stowed inside. Once he was satisfied all was as it should be, he locked them up again and struggled to drag them through to the loading bay. He muttered the refrain from a Stone Temple Pilots song as he wrestled with the steel boxes, not that anyone would have been able to recognise the words between huffs and puffs.

It was a huge amount of equipment, but then, he had tried to think of every eventuality.

Connor went through to the rec room. A re-run of *Robot Wars* was playing to itself on the flat-screen. He sank down into one of the bean-bags across from the sofa and fired up the laptop someone had left on the table. The ARC was on an integrated network. Within a few minutes he was browsing the music files on his own machine and recreating the playlist from scratch. It took him the best part of an hour.

It was an hour in which his curiosity got the better of him. He went back to the virtual server that linked the various machines up, and tapped in a string of commands. He hit a wall immediately, *But*, he thought to himself, *what are walls for if not climbing?*

He tried another string, hit another wall.

Then he went back to his own file directory and pulled out a spider program, and set it running as he returned to the wall. In five minutes he was through and looking at the main server, completely free of any filters or barriers.

"Well, well, well," he said to himself, cracking his knuckles. Six more keystrokes had him in the personal files. Four more and he was reading the name Abigail Sarah Maitland on his screen. It was all there, everything that was known about her, and he couldn't stop himself from reading until he heard footsteps in the corridor outside.

Connor slammed the laptop case down and tried to pretend that he was minding his own business. He was whistling a mangled Nirvana tune when Abby's pixie-like face peered around the doorframe. Seeing Connor, she stuck her tongue out, grinned, and then hurried away, her heavy boots clattering along the corridor.

He blushed and, sighing with relief at his narrow escape, fired up the laptop again. He killed the connection to the personnel database.

He spent the rest of the day filling three PDAs with everything remotely Peruvian that he could find, and it really was a case of anything and everything: restaurant addresses in downtown Cuzco, emergency service numbers, embassy contact details, festivals, ceremonies, custom and costumes, religious practices, poisonous plant life, six-months-worth of newspaper articles. By the end of the day he had compiled an electronic oracle.

"Ask it a question, anything you like," he challenged Abby the next time he saw her.

"Oh, I don't know, how about the meaning of life, the universe and everything?" Abby said, smiling.

"That's too easy." Connor tapped out a couple of commands, and the number forty-two appeared on the screen. He held it up to show her.

"You are such a geek."

"But a loveable one, right?"

"Not the first word I would have chosen."

"Tread softly," Lester said, handing Jenny Lewis the contact details for Sir Charles' man on the ground in Peru. "There was an attempt on young Bairstow's life last night. He's still with us, and we need to keep it that way.

"Needless to say," he continued, "Sir Charles is most upset by the whole affair. I promised him you would take care of it. There are armed guards assigned to the hospital now. You are to get Bairstow out of there. Understood?" She nodded.

"Minimum of fuss. Sir Charles is leaning on me to get his boy home, which is all well and good, but on top of the whole attempted murder thing, we've got an actual murder to worry about, of a Peer of the Realm's son on foreign soil. Like it or not, we're talking a political minefield.

"Sooner or later, the press are going to get wind of Jaime Bairstow's death. They always do. Someone in Births, Deaths and Marriages will sell them a copy of the death certificate, or one of the baggage handlers at the airport will let slip about the coffin he carried off the plane that morning. We don't need a diplomatic incident here, Jenny. It's all about damage limitation. We need to keep our stories straight."

Jenny read through the contact information.

"What am I supposed to do with this?" she asked quizzically.

"Make the call, ask the right questions. That's what you're good at, after all. Make the necessary arrangements to bring the boy home."

"There's something you aren't telling me, Lester," Jenny said, laying the paper aside. "What is it?"

Lester shrugged.

"I don't know. Just a feeling. I'm really hoping we're talking about poachers here. Perhaps the boys stumbled across some of them *in flagrante delicto*, so to speak. God forbid Cutter's paranoia rubs off on me, or Connor's conspiracy theories, but I can't help thinking there's something Sir Charles doesn't want us to know — and my money's on the fact that that something is tied in with Cameron's recollection of the attack. First Cutter comes into the office talking about anomalies in Madre de Dios, now this. I'm not a huge believer in coincidence, if you catch my meaning."

"It's rather hard to miss."

"Good. Let's be blunt here, if it turns out young Bairstow has seen an anomaly, we're going to need to make sure that part of the story never makes it out for public consumption."

When the next contact time arrived, Jenny took the details down to the Communications Centre on the main concourse. She had a technician relay one of the handsets through the com-sat on the right frequency, and retreated into the privacy of an empty lab.

"Little Gods," she said into the handset. "Little Gods, are you receiving me?"

A burst of static answered her.

She repeated the call sign every twenty seconds for five full minutes before a disembodied voice crackled back.

"This is Little Gods, over."

"Little Gods, this is the ARC calling. Over."

"What can I do for you, ARC? Over."

"Our mutual friend suggested we contact you before we fly in. We have some questions about the lie of the land. Over."

"Ask away. Over."

"We've been led to believe you have spoken with Cameron? Over."

"Yes, I have. Over."

"What can you tell us about the attack on his brother? Over."

That was met by a grunt of what sounded like laughter. She hoped it was a quirk of the broadcast.

"Nothing that makes any sense, I'm afraid. Over."

"Try me, Little Gods. Over."

"His recollections are patchy at best, though he does recall being stalked by a big cat. Over."

"So it wasn't poachers? Over."

"No. He's adamant that it was an animal. A jaguar perhaps, but huge. He kept saying that. The cat was huge. That's about the only coherent part of his story. Over."

"Don't make me drag it out of you, Little Gods. Over."

More laughter greeted that.

"He talked about diamonds in the air, as well. Diamonds that swallowed his attacker. Over."

Jenny paused a beat, and wished she hadn't heard correctly.

It was a concise and credible description of an anomaly, but she wasn't about to let Sir Charles' man know that his words meant anything to her.

"I see what you mean," she said. "It makes no sense. Over."

"Trauma plays tricks on the mind. It's a miracle the lad is alive, after everything he's been through. His wounds are terrible to see. Over."

"Indeed. I am assuming one of them was a head wound? Over."

"Multiple blows to the head, resulting in severe concussion, all of which would account for the disturbed vision and so-called floating diamonds. Not very exciting, I'm afraid. Over."

This time it was Jenny who laughed. Breaking protocol, Bairstow's man continued.

"Our friend tells me I am to meet you at the landing strip. I hope you are as beautiful as your laugh, ARC. Over and out."

Jenny sat there for a few moments, letting the implications of what she had heard settle in. *Diamonds in the air.* Cameron Bairstow had described the shimmer of an anomaly. There was nothing else she could think of that could possibly account for what he had seen. Not even a concussion would lead him to that precise a description.

The revelation posed an entirely new set of problems, but it did not begin to answer why someone would try to kill him.

She needed to talk to Lester.

"Well, that *is* most disturbing," Lester said. He had his back to her, and stared at the wall as though gazing out through a window that wasn't there. "Are you sure that's what he said?"

"Positive," Jenny confirmed. "At least that's what Little Gods reported."

"So what do you suggest we do now?"

"Cutter should be made aware of the situation, for a start."

"I'm not entirely sure he should. The last thing we need is Indiana Cutter thrashing through the jungle with a machete, in search of diamonds in the sky."

"But what's the alternative?"

"In-and-out, that's the remit. Keep Cutter away from the Bairstow boy. Keep the Bairstow boy away from the press. Basically keep everyone away from the anomaly, and bury this non-story dead."

"You make it sound simple."

"It's why we pay you the big bucks," Lester said without the slightest trace of irony in his voice. As he turned, she saw that he was smiling. Far from being pleasant, it was an almost predatory expression. "Do your job, manage the situation, Jenny. Go there. Get the boy. Bring him home. I don't want to be reading about any of this in the newspapers. No anomaly lasts forever, we know that much. So we keep it quiet, bide our time, wait it out. It will decay and disappear. It might already have done so, for all we know. The fewer people who know about what's going on, the better."

"Standard governmental operating procedure," she said, before she could stop herself. Lester didn't appear to catch the cynicism in her voice; he was far too preoccupied with fighting imaginary PR fires in his head.

"Quite. Least said, soonest mended. It is not as though people are going to stumble upon a temporal rift in the middle of the rainforest."

She resisted the temptation to point out that it had already happened once.

FOUR

Connor hurled aside the garishly covered book he was reading in disgust, nearly hitting Stephen.

"Sorry," he said sheepishly.

"What's wrong? They kill your favourite character?"

"No. It's this bloody stupid rule that says all superior officers have to be fat, corrupt, and incompetent. Just once I'd like to read a military novel where the arch prelate wasn't a back-stabbing son-of-a-bitch with his own agenda instead of God's, and the Captain of the Guard wasn't some bloated power-hungry moron who'd gut his own mother for a chance to advance."

Connor looked across at the three soldiers spread out in the row behind him. Gesturing, he got their attention.

"Tell me your Commanding Officer is a fat, bloated, slug of a man, and I'll scream," he said, eliciting strange looks from each of the trio.

"It's an occupational hazard." Jack Stark, one of the three men who made up their covert military support, explained, "Bosses get fat and they get stupid, forgetting everything that made them ruthless enough to rise through the ranks in the first place. That's just the way it goes."

Connor shot him a look of disgust. Andy Blaine, the second of the three, grinned at Stark.

"Remind me to let the Sarge know your thoughts on his waistline when we get home," he said. Then he nodded at the discarded novel. "You not reading that then, sunshine?"

"No, not any more."

"Mind if I do?"

"Be my guest."

Connor plugged his headphones in, leaned back, and screwed his eyes closed.

Across the row, Abby turned away from the exchange that had just occurred. She was quietly impressed with the way the soldiers were taking to the mission. It wasn't every day you were told about rifts in time, and learned that prehistoric beasts walked the earth. In many ways, the hardest part had been explaining that the anomalies reached both backward and *forward*.

Yet they didn't seem phased.

Her attention was drawn back to the window. There was nothing quite like the bird's eye view of flight to make one appreciate the sheer immensity and raw beauty of nature. The difference between London — with its precision geometry of streets and roundabouts that intersected like cogs on some vast clockwork mechanism — and the barrenness of Cuzco, which for as far as the eye could see was nothing more than sand-blasted stone and dehydrated trees, was as extreme as the world had to offer.

Coming out of London City Airport, the view out of the window had quickly degenerated into thick clouds that had thoroughly obscured England's green and quite unpleasant land as far as the coastline, giving way to the deep blue of the ocean.

Then for more than a thousand miles she had been able to see the curves and lines of water trailing in the wake of oil tankers and cruise liners and fishing vessels, the ships themselves skating on the meniscus curve of the Atlantic.

Coming down over the east coast the vista had been replaced by snow-capped mountain peaks, and then bare expanses of farming land with cities dotted in between. The world hadn't truly become green until their flight path took them over the Amazon basin.

Here the heat shimmered on the horizon. It was a peculiar phenomenon, considering the chill of the pressurised cabin's air-conditioner, but it offered a good indication of the weather conditions they were flying into.

Glancing over, she decided that Connor was probably fantasising about being Flash Gordon, skimming over the surface of Arboria. She chuckled at the thought, though a moment later she realised the implications of it: her lodger's geekdom was rubbing off on her. Six months ago the word 'Arboria' wouldn't have meant anything to her, outside of some vague conjugation of plant life. Shuddering at the thought, she turned her attention again to the window.

The verdant greens of the rainforest had given way to sand and soulless stone. The plane juddered again, the rocking no more severe than a carriage's jounce on the underground, but vastly exaggerated by the sensation of falling.

Abby loved flying. But she saw Connor's knuckles whiten as his fingers dug into the faux-leather armrest of his chair, not sharing her passion.

Stephen had his head buried in an extreme sports magazine, the glossy pages filled with photos and accounts of wingsuit flying, ice climbing, storm chasing, bungee jumping, and other death-defying activities. He had stared at the same pictures at least a dozen times during the long flight.

Cutter sat in quiet conversation with Jenny, though Abby noticed that he never seemed to look the woman in the eye.

There were three other men on the plane with them, and not one of them had the look of a scientist about them. They were uniformly over six feet, with broad shoulders and a lithe musculature which spoke of hours of punishing exercise. But more telling was the coldness about their eyes, and an alertness that shouldn't have been there. They all shared it. Even now, fifteen hours into a cramped flight, these three men had not relaxed. It wasn't that they were tense, but more that they were incredibly aware of the world around them.

Abby found their presence reassuring, given the uncertainness of what awaited them.

Viewed from above, the single concrete runway of Velazco Astete Airport looked like a gash in the earth. The small plane banked, adjusting its approach as it bumped down through the thermals toward landing.

The Captain's voice came over the loudspeaker, instructing them to take their seats for a landing that would take place in ten minutes.

The plane banked again, the left wing dipping toward the earth, and came around to line up with the concrete strip. Abby watched the terminal building, a low, flat single-storey structure, come into view. She could see red letters on the side of the terminal, and she assumed they said 'Welcome to Cuzco' in both Spanish and Quechua, the two official languages of the country.

Through the metal of the hull, she felt the landing gear engaging, the reverberations shivering up through the bulk of the plane and into her chair. Squeezing her hand over her nose, Abby popped the pressure that had built up inside her ears during the gradual descent.

She fastened her seatbelt, sank back into the leather, and closed her eyes, waiting for the bump of the wheels on the ground.

Esteban Estevez heard screams.

He was out in the rainforest with his fellow rangers Rafe and Joaquim. They had stumbled into another one of those peculiar cones of silence, only this time the silence had not lasted.

The screams were gut wrenching. He pushed through the trees, fighting back the thick leaves that had grown across the track.

A few minutes later three women burst out of the smother of branches, shrieked at the sight of the rangers, and fled to one side even as Rafe tried to calm them. He marked the fear in the women's eyes, and a glance at the other two men told him that they had seen it, too. They weren't the first people the rangers had encountered.

There was a settlement less than half a mile from their location, he knew. It didn't take a genius to put two and two together. He unclipped the walkie-talkie from his belt and radioed in to the reserve office.

Esteban was at the very limits of the radio's reception. It took him a few moments to find a place where the crackle of static was reduced sufficiently for him to hear his half-brother on the other end.

He told Nando what they had found.

"There are a number of peculiar tracks all over sector echo twenty-seven. They appear to be leading down toward the village of Helevuia. I don't like it, Nando." He removed the fedora from his head and wiped away the sheen of sweat that clung to his brow. "There's something wrong here. We hit one of those silent patches again a little while ago. This time it isn't the animals that are fleeing; it's the tribesmen. A dozen women and children have fled past us in the last five minutes. We are less than half a mile from the settlement. I am going to take Rafe and Joaquim and investigate.

"I don't like this, little brother," he continued. "I saw fear in those women's eyes. I swear it was as though they had come face to face with El Diablo himself."

"Be careful, Este."

"When am I not?"

"I can think of plenty of occasions. Just be careful."

"Worst comes to worst, we are armed. We can take care of ourselves."

"Keep your eyes open."

He turned the radio off and joined the others.

"Ready?"

They were.

Together the three rangers trekked toward the settlement of Helevuia.

A short time later, they walked into a slaughterhouse.

It was beyond eerie; they walked in utter silence. Even the crush of deadfall beneath their feet, which gave way to dirt and gravel as they emerged from the trees, seemed to dampen in deference to the carnage. Esteban walked slowly along the path that led to the houses.

He understood the screams now.

There were bodies sprawled in the dirt, bloodied and torn. It wasn't the dead that drew his eye: it was the huge cat prowling amongst them.

Suddenly the beast stopped, inclining its head as it scented the intruders on the air, then it turned to look Esteban square in the eye. It growled once, low in the throat. This was the first sound he had heard since the screams. A heartbeat later the growl was answered by a roar that seemed to rumble all around them.

Esteban fumbled for the radio and dropped it even as he tried to unholster his service revolver. His hand shook so violently that he could barely drag it clear without dropping it.

Gunshots rang out as the great dark beast charged toward them. Echoing his fellow rangers, Esteban raised the revolver, the muzzle roving wildly with his trembling hand as he squeezed off a round, then another. The shots flew high and wide. He stared horrified, enraptured by the huge blood-soaked fangs bared as the cat roared its death-challenge, and pulled the trigger again and again.

There was at least one hit; he saw the spray of blood as the metal slug buried itself beneath thick hide.

It wasn't enough.

The huge animal slammed into him, pinning him down and delivering a fatal bite to his throat, even as he fired off another shot.

Stephen Hart was the last man off the plane.

The heat hit him like a physical blow as he stepped out onto the shaky metal stair the ground crew had pushed up against the side of the small jet. Every muscle of his body ached from being cooped up on the cramped aircraft. He stretched, knuckling his hands into the base of his spine, then ran a hand through his short but unruly brown hair. By the time he was at the bottom of the stair, sweat had already begun to trickle down the side of his face.

The flat-baked concrete finished twenty feet beyond the steps and gave way to tarmac. The asphalt-like stuff was hot and sticky beneath his feet. The temperature must have been up in the mid-thirties; he felt the raw heat in the air on the back of his throat as he inhaled.

They had a welcoming committee: a large black SUV with tinted windows was parked fifty feet away on the hardstand. There was a small cavalcade of vehicles lined up behind it. A man in a wrinkled off-white linen suit leaned against the SUV's bonnet. He was unshaven, tanned to an almost olive complexion, his well-defined physique showed through the thin material. He moved with an economy of movement and grace that betrayed military training.

He greeted Cutter with a laconic smile and an outstretched hand. This was obviously Sir Charles Bairstow's 'man on the ground'.

They exchanged words Stephen couldn't quite hear, then the man made a slight bow before Abby. He took her hand and raised it to his lips. Before he could repeat the move with Jenny, she shifted her grip and shook his hand briskly.

"ARC, I presume," he said. His voice was that classic nasal Etonian that reeked of old money.

"Little Gods," she responded. The exchange made no sense to Stephen.

"I prefer Alex Chaplin, and only my mother calls me by my full name."

Jenny laughed at that. But as he turned away, Stephen noticed that she gave him a strange look. *She doesn't like him.*

Chaplin inclined his head toward Stephen and Connor.

"Damned good to have all of you here. Sir Charles has said good things about you."

"He's said almost nothing about you," Cutter replied.

"The old man can be a little tight-lipped, I'm afraid. It's a throwback to a Cold War mentality most of his generation haven't been able to shuck. All right, then, first things first. You're booked into the Hotel Del Prado in the main city for the first two nights of your stay. I'll take three of you in my car, the rest of you will go with Fabrice in the second one. Your gear will follow in the remaining vehicles. I imagine you're tired, but I suggest trying to stay awake for a few more hours before you turn in for the night. It will make the jet-lag less intrusive tomorrow."

"Thank you," Cutter said, starting to walk toward the first car. Over his shoulder he said, "Jenny, Stephen, you're with me. Abby, Connor, you take the second car along with Jack, Sean and Andy."

"It'll be a bit of a squash, I'm afraid," Chaplin said.

"That's fine — just means we have to cosy up," Connor said. His glance at Abby said he didn't mind at all.

"I don't think so," Stark said, resting a friendly hand on Connor's shoulder. His hands were like ham-hocks. Stephen grinned, while Connor writhed.

"Yeah... erm... no, that's not what I meant," he mumbled, much to the amusement of the other two soldiers, Sean Lucas, and Andy Blaine.

"Oh, I don't know, Stark, it might be fun," Blaine chuckled, slapping the bigger man squarely on the back.

"I'd squash you like a bug, Blaine."

"What about customs?" Stephen asked, shifting the focus away from a squirming Connor. "Passport control? Surely we can't just drive off into the sunset."

"Hah! Hardly. The agent will be waiting at the security gate to check your documents. The situation is a bit sticky out here. It all looks very polite on the surface, but scratch a bit deeper and, well, I wouldn't advise trying to skip the security checkpoint without showing your papers. They're likely to shoot you in the back. It's a little different from Heathrow."

"No kidding," Connor said, tugging at his collar. Sweat already stained the material around his throat. "Mind you, they'd probably try and shoot you at Heathrow these days."

Behind them, the ground crew opened the seal on the hold door and went to work unloading the equipment.

"Looks like you guys plan on settling in for the duration," Chaplin observed, watching the steel coffins slide out of the plane.

"If this is going to look like it's being done properly, it might as well be done properly," Cutter said, opening the SUV's passenger door.

"Agreed," Chaplin nodded, getting in on the driver's side.

Stephen climbed into the back seat and closed the door behind him. He had hoped for air conditioning, but inside the SUV was hot and stuffy. Jenny climbed in the other side.

"Buckle up," Chaplin said.

"Don't tell me, they'll shoot you for not wearing your seatbelt," Cutter said as Chaplin gunned the engine to life.

"No, but I drive like a clumsy Lewis Hamilton. I'd hate to have to explain to Sir Charles how you fell out the passenger door and rolled down the side of a mountain because I turned a corner a tad too sharply."

They pulled away from the hardstand and drove slowly towards the terminal building, following yellow lines painted onto the tarmac. The dark tint to the windscreen and side windows leached the colour from the world around them. The sun glinting off the huge plate windows of the terminal building was reduced from a dazzling light to a series of white spots, like stars that had gone supernova.

As they approached the gate, Stephen took his passport from the breast pocket of his shirt.

The car was surprisingly loud, a third sound throbbing beneath the caged power of the huge v8 engine and the annoying whir of the air-conditioning fan. It took him a moment to realise that the sucking sound was the rubber of the wheels sticking to the road beneath them.

"So what do we need to know?" Cutter said, cutting straight to the chase.

Chaplin turned slightly in his seat. Stephen watched his eyes through the rear-view mirror.

"The official story is that young Cam staggered out of the jungle five days ago, delirious and near death. He had no identification, and no idea who he actually was or that half of the British government was looking for him. His only coherent words were: 'They're all dead.' Not the most reassuring thing to say to the authorities.

"He now claims he and his brother Jaime were set upon by some sort of wild animal while they were out playing explorer in the Madre de Dios. His wounds seem to back up the story." Chaplin sounded dubious.

"You don't believe it?" Cutter asked.

"I don't get paid to believe, Professor. There are a lot of wild stories floating out there. My personal favourite is that the boys were the victims of El Chupacabra, and that greedy government officials have brought the curse of the beast down upon the region because of their plans to turn the rainforest into a tourist trap. The vengeful Chupacabra, they say, won't stand for that sort of nonsense."

"Are we sure it wasn't poachers? Perhaps his injuries were caused by dogs."

"We aren't sure about anything," Chaplin admitted, slowing the SUV to pull up beside the customs gatehouse. A flimsy wooden barrier barred their way. A short, grim-faced guard, clutching the distinctive muzzle of an Uzi 9mm to his chest, stepped up to the side of the car and rapped on the tinted glass.

"Papers?" he said in pigeon-English as the window hummed down. The nametag pressed up against the glass read 'Cristóbal'.

Chaplin collected their passports and handed them across to the guard, who examined them slowly, then leaned in through the window to match each of the photos to the passengers.

"What is your business in Peru?" he demanded.

It was a straightforward enough question, but what exactly were they supposed to say? That they intended to smuggle a British citizen out of the local hospital before the local killers got to him?

Hardly.

"We're scientists," Cutter said, leaning toward the open window. "We're here as part of an expedition within the Madre de Dios."

"You have papers for this?" the guard asked, the muzzle of his sub-machine gun rattling against the side of the SUV, as if to remind them all that it was still there.

"Yes, of course. Jenny?"

She leaned forward, holding out a sheaf of paperwork. The officious little guard took them, thumbing through them page after page as though they made a lick of sense to him. Stephen would have laid down a decent-sized bet that the man couldn't read half of it, and was just looking for a stamp and a scribbled signature that would make it someone else's responsibility.

A moment later he seemed to have found what he needed to reassure him, and handed the papers back into the car, then returned the passports, each with a ninety-day visa stamped into them.

"Thank you," Cutter said, taking them back from the man.

The guard stepped back and signalled to someone inside the guardhouse. The barrier rose, then he waved them through. A short time later they were on the open road.

The 'open road', however, was hardly fit to bear the name. Every dozen or so yards the concrete was broken, causing the SUV's suspension to judder alarmingly. Chaplin changed up through the gears, easing through the traffic of flatbed trucks and paint-flaked Fiats, the regular dub-dub-dub of the cracks sounding like an erratic heartbeat.

The air-conditioning was broken, Chaplin explained apologetically, and it was sucking the hot air of the outside into the compartment and heating it in the process. Whereas the tinted glass had kept out the sun before, now they found it preferable to open all four windows to let the wind blow through. Stephen felt as though his eyeballs themselves were sweating.

"Now, you were saying, you don't think it was poachers?" Cutter said, speaking loudly as they merged with the faster moving traffic in the outside lane. Driving on the wrong side of the road was unnerving, especially since flatbeds with rattling tailgates and bald tyres were bouncing along barely in control beside them. Crates of produce were stacked up and tied down, along with people crushed and clinging on for dear life as they sped down the uneven roadways.

"Not having examined the boy's wounds too closely myself, I can't say for certain," Chaplin responded. "But no, I don't think it was."

He told them a little more of what he knew: Jaime Bairstow's body had yet to be recovered, but his brother's description of the slaughter left no room for hope that the boy might still be alive.

"I was only able to talk with Cam for a moment, but he described their attacker as a sleek powerful big cat. That doesn't sound like poachers *or* dogs."

"A puma or jaguar perhaps?" Cutter offered.

"Anything is possible," Chaplin agreed. "Between you and me, he is hardly the most reliable witness. Three times he mentioned seeing diamonds in the sky."

"Really?" Cutter said, a look passed between him and Stephen as he looked behind him. It was the first conclusive proof they had found that the two stories were linked. He felt a small thrill of triumph. It disappeared quickly when he noticed the lack of surprise on Jenny's face, and made a mental note to ask her about it later, in private.

"They've got him dosed up on morphine right now, so I wouldn't take anything he says as the gospel truth, especially the notion that he found some air that was filled with crystals and diamonds that glittered and shone and made all these beautiful colours as they refracted the light. It sounds more like a drug-induced hallucination," Chaplin concluded. But three of the four people in the car knew better. He was almost certainly talking about the first anomaly to be found off British soil.

That gave them plenty to think about on the long drive from the airport. And a welcome distraction from the cloying heat.

"So you think he's lying? Covering something up?" Jenny shouted, leaning forward between the seats.

"I wouldn't bet against it," Chaplin said.

"How so?"

"There could have been a falling out, the boys coming to blows. One thing leads to another, and suddenly we have black cats and hallucinations. It isn't impossible.

"And further more, it would be a damned sight more convenient for the Peruvian authorities to declare it the truth. Much better to have a couple of tourists trying to kill each other, rather than have to try and explain away either poachers or wild animal attacks in their precious eco-reserve."

"I can see that," Cutter agreed. "But I don't see how that would account for the attempt on his life in the hospital?"

"Well, that was almost certainly down to a terrorist faction like Shining Path or some such guerrilla group, trying to make a point by killing a privileged foreigner. It happened soon after Cam's story started to spread. It makes him a wonderful target for these supposed 'freedom fighters'."

Cutter nodded. Watching their host, Stephen was unsure whether or not Chaplin actually believed what he was telling them.

"So," Cutter said eventually, "is poaching really such a huge problem here?"

"Put it this way," Chaplin said, "we're talking *big* business. The smuggling of endangered species generates billions of pounds a year. Only slightly less than drugs, and far more than armaments."

"Jesus," Stephen said, the scale of it far beyond anything he had imagined.

"The worst thing is that it really doesn't matter if the animals are alive or dead, so that means these bastards catch the animals and keep them in conditions of intolerable cruelty. It's all about the ivory and the penises, the pelts, skins and meat. Nothing gets wasted. Not the marrow from the bones, nor the fat insulating the skin. They even grind the sexual organs up to make aphrodisiacs for horny businessmen. They promise that the livers will cure cancer and other rubbish. People are willing to pay outrageous amounts — the rarer the creature, the greater the value. Can you imagine the price a dodo breast would command? Millions."

"So these people would definitely kill to protect their business."

"Oh, hell, yes," Chaplin said, signalling to leave the main flow of traffic.

The first thing Stephen noticed about Cuzco itself, as they began to drive down the dip into the town proper, was that it was very much a single-storey community of white stucco houses and clay roofs. More than once he saw steel rebar struts sticking vertically out of the walls, as though the buildings were unfinished. He asked Chaplin about this.

"Curiously enough, it is meant to be a sign of hope. The builders want to give the illusion of prosperity. It's all a game, though. They want you to believe that one day they might have the money to add a second storey. They aren't fooling anyone, of course — not even themselves."

"Ah," Stephen said.

His shirt clung uncomfortably to his back. He didn't want to sit back in the leather seat because the sticky wetness made his skin creep. Instead he leaned forward in his seat and watched the countryside roll by.

The transition from rural to urban was every bit as distinct as anything he would have expected to see in London or any other European city. At first the roadside was dotted with sporadic trees, the colour bled from their leaves by the sun, and the occasional building. The stucco was invariably either cracked and broken or only part-finished, leaving the guts of the stone to hang out, bleeding red dust.

Sallow-skinned men sat on plastic beer crates outside open doors, watching the cars go by. They smoked thin roll-ups and wore battered cowboy hats pulled down low over their sad eyes. Then, further into the city, the colours returned. Sprinklers kept the trees moist, in turn keeping the leaves green. Here the grass beneath could easily have been lifted from a Wimbledon lawn, and was shockingly green against the painted yellow curbs.

Battered bicycles with rusted frames leaned against walls, their kick stands propping them up on flat tyres.

The nature of the traffic changed as well, as bigger, newer gas-guzzlers dominated the wide roads, their lacquers bright and shiny.

The pedestrians were a curious mix of locals, dressed to meet tourist expectations, mingled with the tourists themselves. The ruins of Machu Picchu were close by, and the Inca Express could be seen leaving for Lake Titicaca, the Pisac fortress, the Nazca lines, the puma-shaped Sacsayhuamán fortress and the tiers of Moray — all of which were also nearby. Cuzco was the ideal staging point for the holiday-of-a-lifetime adventures sought by the rich and the curious.

Finally they reached the urban centre. Set in a basin of surrounding hills, the Incan capital was a stunning fusion of old and new, the architecture like something out of medieval Andalusia. It was a city of statues and fountains, its structures built around wide, open plazas, like the Plaza de Armas, which was the beating heart in the body of Cuzco.

Stephen wasn't sure what he had expected, but the opulence of the Cathedral, with its glorious cupola and twin bell-towers, wasn't it. The architecture was spectacular. Their SUV slowed to a crawl as pedestrians wove back and forth across the busy road amid the blaring of horns. Chaplin took them around a huge two-tiered fountain supported by what appeared to be water nymphs, and drew up alongside the curb outside their hotel.

"This is it," Chaplin told them. "I'll pick you up at ten tomorrow to take you to the hospital."

"I'd rather go straight away," Jenny said. "Time really is of the essence, and frankly, if there's been one attempt on his life already, I'd rather not leave anything to chance. Stark and I can pick him up and bring him back to the hotel, where we can keep an eye on him."

Chaplin made a face.

"Really not the best of ideas. At Sir Charles' behest, I have two armed guards, both ex-special forces, on watch outside his room. Two more are located on the lobby level of the hospital. He is safer there than anywhere else in the city."

Jenny wasn't convinced. But Chaplin wouldn't be swayed.

"I appreciate your concern, Miss Lewis, but honestly, angels would fear to rush in. Your expedition has raised a few eyebrows in certain official circles, and you are no doubt going to come under some rather intense scrutiny. I would therefore strongly suggest that you act like scientists and, of course, tourists. Running to the hospital now would immediately tip our hand. It's all about appearance.

"I don't need to teach you how to do your job, I'm sure, but this place isn't like London. We have factions, governmental and what are euphemistically called 'freedom fighters', like the Shining Path I mentioned before. When a new factor comes into the equation, something that might unsettle the precarious balance, a lot of eyes become very interested.

"So, tomorrow we can make arrangements to slip you out from under the watchful eye of whoever, after you've spent this evening doing exactly what every other visitor to this fair city would do. I suggest you get your bearings, and take a little wander around. There's plenty to see, and you really want to work up an appetite."

Jenny couldn't really argue with him, though her expression said that she was far from happy at being told what to do, and especially by this man. There was something about Chaplin that didn't sit right. It wasn't the brylcreem smile or the *Our Man In Havana* shtick. Stephen couldn't put his finger on it.

"Peruvian cuisine is rather distinctive," Chaplin went on, convinced the argument was won. "I feel duty bound to point out that you're unlikely to get cow or pig, so if you see a steak advertised, it's liable to be alpaca, or lama meat. Guinea pig is quite popular as well."

"Abby will be pleased to miss out on those delicacies, I'm sure," Cutter said, clambering out of the car.

"You might want to try crema de tarwi or chalona. Traditionally, you'd be served alpaca, but most restaurants serve lamb instead. Wash it down with a nice Inca Cola, that'll give you the complete Peruvian experience."

"Thanks, I think."

"No problem. I'll see your equipment is brought to the hotel later."

Stephen closed the car door behind him, and stood on the side of the road. Again the sheer physical force of the heat hit him. The window across the way advertised Cusqueña in painted letters. He assumed it was beer, though it might equally have been the name of the bar itself.

Chaplin hadn't been lying. Even from that vantage point, there was plenty to see, the most noticeable thing by far being the two armed militia members leaning casually against the hotel wall, sub-machine guns dangling at their sides. They fit every preconception Stephen had ever harboured about the military junta stereotype. Neither man acknowledged them as they entered the lobby. The others hadn't yet arrived, no doubt delayed in the chaos of traffic.

The hotel itself was curious, and not at all what he would have called 'luxury', with clay pots and grotesque statuettes dominating the lobby. The floor was a chequerboard of terracotta tiles, some rubbed smooth by the passing of bags and feet, others still rough with their rustic charm. The colours were bright and mismatched. Woven tapestries hung in place of pictures behind the reception.

Stephen followed Cutter and Jenny up to the desk, where Cutter collected their keys.

"We're short of rooms, so we're going to have to double up. Jenny can you share with Abby? And Stephen, you can bunk in with me."

"No problem."

"Let's go make camp then, shall we?"

Their rooms were on the fourth floor, the beds hard as boards. Stephen pulled off his shirt and flopped down onto the one closest to the window, closing his eyes. It was all he could do not to fall straight to sleep.

He heard the key in the lock of the next room, then the slam of another door, and assumed the others had arrived — which meant they needed to go downstairs to collect their gear.

He opened his eyes. A ceiling fan spun lopsidedly above his bed, the rhythm of its rotation just slightly wrong. Watching it was hypnotic.

Cutter went through to the bathroom. A moment later Stephen heard the spray of the shower running. He waited for Cutter to finish up, then followed him through to rinse off the grime of the flight and the sweat from his skin with soap that refused to lather. He ducked his head under the shower nozzle, massaging his scalp vigorously as he tried to wake himself up.

He towelled dry and pulled on his boxers and jeans, then picked up the shirt, and dropped it again. The thin material was as thoroughly soaked as it would have been if he had still been wearing it when ducked under the shower. So he rummaged in his backpack for a clean t-shirt and pulled it on over his head.

It felt good to be clean again.

"You notice our friends downstairs?" Cutter asked.

"A little hard to miss."

"We're not in Kansas anymore, Toto," Cutter said. "Come on then, let's go get the gear. The sooner we start, the sooner we finish."

It took the best part of twenty minutes to drag their equipment up to the room, and the effort left them as sweaty and uncomfortable as they had been before their showers.

When everyone was done, they gathered in the lobby, then went out for a reconnoitre, taking in the vicinity. They were centrally located, close to most of the tourist traps. The gun-toting guards were still at their station, as disinterested as ever. A lama grazed on the grass across the road.

"You don't see that every day," Stephen said to Connor as they left the hotel.

"Unless you're Jeff Minter."

"Sometimes you're just weird, Connor."

"Killer Trivial Pursuit player though," Connor said with a grin.

The hour in their room and lugging the luggage had taken the worst of the heat of the day. The first thing Stephen noticed as he stepped out onto the street was the gentle kiss of the breeze. There was a tall pole in the centre of the main square, the colourful ribbons that dangled from it blowing in the soft wind.

They crossed the grass, walking slowly and turning in circles, trying to take everything in. Stephen saw the spray of two small fountains on the roof of a neighbouring building, which struck him as just plain peculiar. The others talked and walked and gawked. He looked over his shoulder to see Stark's eyes narrow. It was a marginal thing, something he wouldn't have noticed if he hadn't been less than five feet away.

Stark nodded once and, reading his silent intent, Stephen turned away.

It didn't take long for Stark to catch up with Stephen and match his leisurely stride for a dozen paces before saying, "Your shoe lace is undone. You better tie it up, I'll wait for you."

Stephen looked down at his trainers. Neither lace was loose. Without a word, he went down onto one knee and pretended to fasten them properly.

"We've got eyes on us. Three sets I can see. One in the nearest bell-tower, another pretending to read *The New York Times* beside the fountain in the garden, and the third making a pig's ear of following us."

"What do we do?"

"They want to see tourists, let's give them tourists," Stark said matter-of-factly.

FIVE

They led the watchers on a merry dance around the landmarks of Cuzco, making a show of pointing at this and that, pausing to read every plaque and admire every statue. Performers in garish local costumes were busy untangling the ribbons from the pole when they returned to the main plaza.

"Let's watch for a minute," Cutter said, putting his arm around Connor's shoulder, then barely vocalised a second instruction, "How good is the camera on your phone, Connor? Good enough to take a few photos of our uninvited guests?"

"Five megapixels, boss."

"I'll take that as a yes, then. Just be careful, make it look like you're taking a few holiday snaps."

"No problem."

Connor reached into his pocket, pulled out a neat little camera phone, and proceeded to take a couple of photographs of the Peruvian acrobats limbering up with the ribbons, then a few more of them in full flight as they ran clockwise around the pole, jumping and clinging to the rope as they did, so that their momentum carried them higher.

It was quite something to see, as they wrapped their muscular calves around the ribbons and hung upside down while others ran and leapt and pivoted, the display becoming faster and faster the higher the first rank of acrobats ascended.

Connor casually switched from still images to video, and turned in a full circle as though trying to take everything in all at once. He scratched at the side of his head and turned back to watch the acrobats for a few minutes longer. He let the camera run; the memory on the thing was enough to record an hour's worth of video. He would dump it onto the PDA later for a closer look.

The acrobats formed a pyramid, six men on the lowest tier, running for dear life, three men seemingly running on their shoulders, and one final acrobat forming the pinnacle. Each tier moved at a different pace from the next, clockwise and counter-clockwise, their bodies in constant motion.

But Connor wasn't watching them. He was looking beyond the streaming ribbons at the man who sat beside the water fountain, folding the copy of yesterday's newspaper and laying it down on the bench beside him. The bloke was utterly nondescript, average in every way. Mousy hair, thin face, not too tall, not too short, he was the Goldilocks of spies.

Connor chuckled at the thought.

It took him a moment to realise that he was staring, his imagination wrapped up in thoughts of James Bond and Spy vs. Spy, he quickly looked away.

"My stomach thinks my throat's been cut," he said to no one in particular.

"Fancy a lama burger?" Stephen asked, coming up to stand behind him. The man could move with unnerving quiet when he chose to.

"I was thinking more alpaca steak and chips, to be honest." Connor's grin was infectious. "Come on, let's go eat."

They found a small restaurant on a side street off the Plaza de Armas, that promised a fusion menu of genuine Andalusian, Italian, and traditional Peruvian food. Despite the shabby exterior, the aroma drew them in.

There were eight small tables for two lined up alongside a long faux-leather banquette, and six more tables in the centre of the small room, each covered with a red and white chequered tablecloth and a stout wine bottle that had been turned into a candlestick. Wax of a hundred colours had run and hardened around the fluted stem of the bottle. And each table was empty. The restaurant's walls were decorated with Incan masks and fertility symbols. The whitewashed walls and low ceiling gave the impression that they had just entered some kind of grotto.

A craggy-faced woman smiled in welcome as they walked through the door. She dusted her hands off on her apron and said something in Spanish that Connor didn't understand. When no one said anything, she ushered them toward the banquette, chittering away like an excited mynah bird, her voice spiralling up through the octaves the more animated she got.

"Do you speak English?" Cutter asked, and the old woman shook her head briskly. Her reaction was almost comical.

Connor sat across from Abby — his back to the wall — and beside Andy Blaine. Stephen sat on his other side. He noticed that the three soldiers positioned themselves so that each faced in a different direction, with a different vantage point. He assumed it wasn't paranoia but some sort of training on their part that had become instinctive. *Then again, maybe healthy paranoia isn't such a bad thing after all.* He could see the logic of not allowing your enemies to sneak up behind you when you were eating.

The old woman hovered over Abby's shoulder, lighting the candles one at a time as she moved down the tables. Her hands shook, causing the flame to waver. She needed three tries to light the wick of their candle.

"Water?" Connor asked, miming the act of taking a drink as the old woman handed out menus. "Aqua Minerale? Frizzanti? Vattan?"

"Agua, por favor," Blaine said to the woman in flawless Spanish, much to Connor's surprise.

She nodded. The rising light from the candles transformed her face from old to ancient, bringing out the depths of the creases in her cheeks and chin. For a moment he thought he saw the skeleton beneath, picked out in shadow and shade.

"You were just making words up, weren't you?" Abby teased Connor, moving the silverware slightly so she could rest her elbows on the table. He shot her a mock look of chagrin, but she was already looking around the room. "I can't believe we're here."

"I know, it's completely mad, isn't it?"

"And aren't *you* the dark horse," she said, turning to Blaine.

"I spent sixteen months in the Basque region, so some of the words are still up there," he said as he tapped his temple.

"What were you doing in Spain?"

"Ah, if I told you, I'd have to kill you," Blaine said, winking.

The woman bustled around the table, with Blaine translating the drink orders, before disappearing into the back room. A moment later what sounded like piped Pavarotti drifted into the small room. *Nessun Dorma.*

"And there's the final nail in the coffin of history," Cutter said.

"How so?" Stark asked, his expression curious.

"Here we are, a million miles from what the West would call civilisation, and what are we listening to? Bottled opera watered down and made palatable for the masses, be those masses Italian, Chinese, or in this case, Peruvian. Globalisation is killing individuality across the world, my friend. We ought to be listening to the music of the Andes, pipes and chimes and all the things that make this part of South America unique. Instead we've got dead Italians to entertain us in the blandest of ways.

"It's the end of history. We're turning the Earth into one big conglomeration of chain stores and brand identities. The Third World War's been going on silently for years, and the corporations have already won it. I wouldn't be surprised if we find the golden arches of a certain fast food giant waiting around one of the corners, and see locals riding Vespas and wearing Levi jeans and Nike trainers. The world is going to hell, and our obsession with fine things is helping it on its way."

"And you get all this from one Pavarotti song? You're a bitter and cynical man, Professor Cutter," Stark said, shaking his head.

"At least it isn't James bloody Blunt," Connor joked. "Now that really *would* be hell."

"Well, we may be on our way to a global empire, but we're not there yet," Jenny said. "I tried to use my mobile phone to call home, and can't get a signal. It's downright irritating." With that, she turned her attention to the menu.

Connor took one glance at the offerings, and looked disappointed that there weren't pictures to make his decision easier. Rather than ask for Blaine's help, he reached into his pocket for a PDA. He quickly translated some of the meals and their ingredients, and opted for something that ought to have been braised lamb with fried potatoes, but turned out to be baby goat.

He didn't care, he said, since the meat was so soft and tender it almost melted against his tongue.

Midway through the main course the newspaper reader came through the door and took one of the tables in the centre of the room.

A few minutes later a woman came in to join him, and like any other lovers in any other restaurant, they ordered, ate, and shared small talk, and for a moment Connor wondered if Stark wasn't just being paranoid.

That notion was dispelled when they returned to the hotel.

Stark stood in front of the door to the room he shared with Connor, his hand on the handle, but he did not open the door.

At least not at first.

"Something's wrong," he said. "Get behind me, and keep quiet."

Connor nodded. He had no idea what had spooked the SAS man, but he wasn't about to argue. Then he saw the paperclip lying on the floor. Stark had slipped it into the jamb as he closed the door when they left.

Someone had been in the room.

Connor felt a coldness steal beneath his skin. This was a different world from the one he usually occupied. Guards with sub-machine guns, watchers in the street, and now this. He looked left and right along the landing.

Blaine and Lucas were likewise stood in front of one door each, Abby and Jenny behind Blaine, Cutter and Stephen behind Lucas. Stark gave the signal, and all three burst into their respective rooms.

Stark reappeared a moment later, shaking his head.

"Empty," he said.

He turned on the light.

Connor looked over his shoulder into the room. It had been thoroughly ransacked. Their gear was tossed everywhere. Whoever had done it hadn't been bothered about being found out. Clothes were strewn all over the place, the steel equipment crates open, the contents rifled.

"Anything missing?" Cutter asked. They had gathered in the room he shared with Stephen.

"Not that I can tell," Jenny told him.

"So what the hell did they want?" Cutter fumed, stalking the cramped room.

"No idea."

"Whatever they wanted, they didn't get it," Stark said.

"How do you figure that?"

"The mess. If they had found something, they would have stopped looking. *Everything* was tossed. They didn't find whatever it was they wanted, trust me."

Cutter nodded — that made sense.

"So what do you suggest we do?"

"Business as usual, for now," Stark said. "There's not much else we can do. Like Chaplin said, they're watching our comings and goings. They'll expect us to react to their invasion. If we bring in the local police, what are they going to do? Nothing is missing. Complaining to the hotel isn't going to get us anywhere, either. This wasn't down to bad housekeeping."

"So we just sit tight?"

Stark nodded.

"We get some sleep, and in the morning we start to deal with things. They'll still be watching us, only now they know that we know they are. It changes the nature of the game. More than ever, this needs to look like a genuine scientific expedition, Professor. You need to make contact with your man, and make arrangements to transport your stuff to the eco-reserve, and while you're doing that — and making sure our watchers are seeing what we want them to see — Miss Lewis and I will make a trip to the hospital to see Bairstow.

"And before you object, they *will* be watching you. I'm just a grunt, as far as they're concerned, but I'm a grunt who knows how to make himself invisible, which is a handy skill when you're being followed. From your team, Miss Lewis is the logical choice of companion. She's here as public liaison. Chaplin is an embassy man, so her meeting up with a government official is unlikely to raise too many eyebrows.

"You — on the other hand — need to be seen gearing up for whatever it is you intend to do out in the jungle.

Cutter didn't like the idea, but he couldn't find a decent argument.

"Are you okay with that, Jenny?" he asked.

She nodded.

"But Cutter," she said, "if they hit us already... what about Cam in the hospital? We need to find out he's safe."

"Well, then I guess we need to use the telephone. Not ideal, but beggars can't be choosers."

Connor took Cutter to one side.

"Do you think they were after this?" he asked, holding out the PDA.

"Why would they be?"

"I don't know, but I'm trying to think of what we have that wasn't in our rooms, and this is all I can come up with." Connor shrugged.

"Again, why would they be interested in a PDA? What's on it that's worth breaking into our hotel rooms to recover?"

"Nothing, just stuff from the Internet. Anything and everything I could find out about Madre de Dios, the eco-reserve, food, culture, superstitions — nothing that isn't available in any decent library."

"Then I think you've just answered your own question. Good night, Connor. Try to get some sleep."

Jenny made the call in to the hospital, and spoke in her schoolgirl Spanish to a ward sister who refused to give her any details about Cam. She did, however, sound quite unworried, so it seemed unlikely that there had been a murder committed. Jenny had to content herself with that.

It didn't occur to her until the middle of the night that the woman dealt with death every day, and would hardly have been reduced to a weeping mess, no matter what had occurred.

The hours until dawn stretched on, shredding her nerves.

He slept like the dead and the damned, but that didn't stop Cutter's body clock from waking him abruptly at four in the morning. It jarred him out of a dream.

He couldn't fall back to sleep because his mind was racing. Instead, he lay on his back, the bedclothes uncomfortably damp with sweat, the sheet tangled around his legs where he had kicked it off while he slept. He watched the blades of the fan turn in and out of the shadows on the ceiling.

The trace memories of his dream still lingered.

He had been tormented by thoughts of Helen, reliving again the moment when he had stepped out of the anomaly and asked Lester, "Where's Claudia?" He had dreamed the dream every night since he had lost her. But the familiarity did not make it any more bearable. On the contrary, it brought back the sense of grief and loss all the more intimately. Her face and her smile and the taste of her lips all the more real, the more of a ghost she became.

She was never coming back. Jenny Lewis' existence proved that. It wasn't as though she had simply stepped through an anomaly like Helen, all those years ago. She had been removed from history itself, reformed as another woman, given a new life and new memories from the same primordial clay of life. Jenny was so similar, and yet so different at the same time.

He lay awake for hours, taunting himself with memories that he could no longer be sure were even real. Memories that only he possessed.

It had been different with Helen. Finding her had become an obsession, but it had been an obsession he could share with others.

Yet he didn't want the dreams to leave him, because as long as he dreamed them they stopped Claudia Brown from dying.

Watching the lazy cycles of the fan, he couldn't bring himself to let go. Not yet.

Come sunrise he felt like one of Romero's walking dead. It was as though he didn't fit within his own skin; his flesh crept and crawled as though infested with bugs. He watched the sun drape shadows on the floor, and felt its warmth as it slowly moved across the room, across his body, bringing with it the beginning of the new day.

Cutter rose quietly, so as not to wake Stephen, and dressed. He pulled on a light white cotton shirt and a pair of cargo pants. He caught his reflection in the full-length mirror and saw a washed-out middle-aged tourist looking back at him. He slipped out of the room and went downstairs, deciding to go for a walk to stretch his legs.

He needed to pull himself together. It was one thing to grieve, but it was quite another for it to strangle his life. He had a team that looked to him for leadership, and that needed his wisdom and guiding hand. He had to be the father to this motley little crew.

The walk would clear his head. When he got back, he'd freshen up and put on his braver face.

The two sentries were no longer guarding the hotel door, a fact which made him wonder if they had been stationed there with no other purpose than to observe his team. Perhaps after the rooms had been ransacked, they had left, having fulfilled their duty. It wasn't out of the question.

Someone didn't want them here, that much was certain, but why that might be was far from clear.

He needed to start thinking straight. Jet-lag had left him muzzy and lethargic. Cutter crossed the plaza, then took to the side streets, moving away from the touristy areas into narrower and narrower alleyways and passages. Mangy cats, all slack skin, fur and bone, followed him along the low rooftops. He felt the moisture being baked out of the air as the sun rose.

The locals were already up. The smell of unleavened bread filled the back ways of Cuzco. He found a small bakery selling warm loaves and bought a flatbread, using currency Jenny had provided. He tore strips off it and ate as he walked, smiling and nodding to those who smiled and nodded at him.

And for a few minutes at least, it was as though the weight of the world wasn't resting on his shoulders.

Those few minutes would have to be enough.

He saw a small kiosk selling tobacco and news. He bought a paper that he assumed was their local version of the *National Enquirer*. The headline read 'El Chupacabra?' and there was a grainy black and white photograph of the 'black dog' beneath it. The image had obviously been doctored. Folding the paper under his arm, he headed back to the hotel.

SIX

They gathered in Cutter's room and locked the door.

"Right, we need to make plans," he said. "We can't just wander around playing tourists. Jenny, this morning you and Stark need to go and get Bairstow out of that hospital. We can't keep him here, not if we're being watched, but there's no way I am prepared to leave him in there like a sitting duck. Get onto Chaplin. He's got to have access to a safe house of some sort."

"Will do," she replied.

"Once we've got him out, we'll worry about babysitting. We're going to need to transport the gear, then set up a base camp in the forest. And there's something else we're going to need to worry about.

"Tell me what this says," Cutter said to Blaine, holding the newspaper out for him to read.

The SAS man skimmed through the article, and shrugged.

"Mostly wild superstition, by the looks of it." His eyes narrowed. "And yet..."

"Go on?"

"Someone seems to be claiming that there have been other deaths, elsewhere in the rainforest," he said, scanning the page. "One witness blames the greed of the scientists and the government for bringing the wrath of El Chupacabra down upon the heads of the natives. But the predominant opinion seems to be that Bairstow himself was responsible for the killings, including his brother's murder."

"What a nightmare," Cutter said, rubbing at his jaw. "This is exactly what we didn't want happening. Do you think Bairstow actually spoke to the press?"

"I doubt it."

"Almost certainly not," Jenny said. "This isn't good, Cutter. We need to talk to Chaplin. If this plays out the way I think it's going to, we've got some serious trouble on our hands."

"What are you thinking, Jenny?"

"You want the truth?" she asked rhetorically. She was sat perched on the corner of an intricately painted laundry chest beneath the room's only window. The sun on the side of her perfectly made-up face made her look like a vengeful goddess. "South American territories have always been a hotbed of lies and violence, Cutter. It's the way of the world down here. There's a reason the military parade about with their guns. If they want to keep anyone from investigating further, it would certainly explain the attempt on his life."

From the other side of the room Stark grunted in support of the notion. The soldier looked grim.

"My God, do you seriously think they'd murder him in cold blood?" The thought chilled Cutter to the bone.

"If he's being used as a fall guy, then it'll easier if he's not around to defend himself. And there's nothing to suggest he isn't already dead," Stark said bluntly.

"One thing in our favour is that the report appeared in a small-town paper, rather than the national press," Cutter noted. "It's not as likely to attract international attention, but it'll sure scare the hell out of the locals."

"If there were other killings, who's to say it wasn't the poachers themselves?" Jenny added. "We already know what big business it is. Chaplin was pretty clear about that. What's a little more death to preserve a multi-billion pound industry? It makes the job of trapping those endangered species and smuggling them out of the country that much easier, if no one dares enter the forest, don't you think?"

Connor, sat cross-legged on Stephen's bed, looked up with surprise at her words. There was a certain ruthlessness to that way of thinking that Connor had never imagined a woman — any woman — capable of showing.

"What the hell have we walked into the middle of?" Cutter said.

"But what about the, ah..." Connor glanced instinctively at the SAS men, his head spinning with all of the wild and frightening possibilities that had been put into it. Then he remembered that they had been fully briefed.

"Well, I mean, aren't we getting ahead of ourselves here? We know there's an anomaly out there, don't we? You said yourself that Cameron described seeing diamonds in the sky. What else could he have seen?"

"As much as I hate to admit it, Connor's right," Cutter said. "It's easy to let our paranoia run away with us, and get all wrapped up in politics and schemes. After all, it isn't every day we are shadowed, or have our rooms broken into, but we can't ignore the possibility that something really *did* come through. That's got to be our real concern. Anything else is just jumping at shadows."

"And if it came through, the odds are it's still here," Stephen said, giving voice to the one thought they were all sharing.

"Right, so let's stick with what we know, shall we?"

"There must be a million places out there in the rainforest a cunning predator could hide," Abby said. "It could be a paradise for an invasive species."

"That depends very much upon the creature," Cutter mused thoughtfully. "It's going to try to find something approximating its natural habitat, if it can. Let's work out what we're dealing with, and that'll narrow our search down. Meanwhile, where are the maps?"

Abby retrieved a detailed contour map of the region and spread it out across the bed. Cutter leaned over to study it, then took a red marker-pen and circled a particular spot.

"That's where Nando's based. He's reported strange behaviour in the animals under his care. That's our jumping-off point. Blaine, where's this village that's supposed to have been attacked?"

The soldier studied the map for a moment, looking at the contour lines and symbols. "Hard to say, Professor. The article doesn't really reference any local landmarks. If Bairstow was supposed to have passed through, though, it has to be somewhere between the outskirts of Madre de Dios and Cuzco, so it's probably somewhere along this path." He drew a line with his finger above the two points on the map.

"Good. Now, what other information do we have? Let's stop thinking like alarmists and start thinking like scientists. Thought, reasoning, extrapolation and evaluation, ladies and gentlemen. What else do we know?"

"Bairstow talked about a cat-like creature," Abby offered.

"Right," Cutter agreed. "That could also account for the repetition of the El Chupacabra myth at every turn. There's a grain of truth in every great lie, remember the saying? Myths are just lies we want to believe, so what's the grain of truth in El Chupacabra? Sheep and goat attacks are a matter of public record, the carcasses bearing puncture marks that are almost vampiric in nature. The bodies are bled through small incisions until they're empty. Hence the name, which translates as 'goat sucker.' He's your South American Dracula, basically.

"So, bite wounds, blood drinking, what non-cryptoid solution would account for that?"

"Prehistoric big cats?" Abby suggested.

Cutter nodded thoughtfully.

"That would be a reasonable assumption wouldn't it? Every culture has its devil dogs and black cats. Back home we have the Beast of Bodmin and the Baskerville hound, and, as the good detective was fond of saying, 'Once you eliminate the impossible, whatever remains, however improbable, must be the truth.'

"What if this creature has appeared elsewhere? Now that we've admitted to the possibility, it could explain a great deal. Anubis, the Egyptian guardian of the portal to the underworld, bears a striking resemblance to a big black predatory cat. The same iconography works its way into a dozen faiths across the world, and keeps on recurring throughout history and the collective consciousness. Now if we take science as a starting point for mythology, we're definitely talking about a predatory cat. The South American pampas were ruled by a unique group of marsupials during the Miocene."

"Borhyaenids?" Abby said, following his reasoning.

"Very possible, and certainly the introduction of such a predator would have a severe impact, wouldn't you say?"

"It would almost certainly drive the existing species into hiding."

"Exactly. And what do we know about the borhyaenids, Connor?"

"Those bad boys ruled the woodlands of the Amazon for close on 30 million years before becoming extinct. They have no known ancestors or descendants."

"Text book answer, Mr Temple, very good. We need to talk to Bairstow more than ever. He's seen this thing, whatever it is. He's the key."

"If he isn't dead already," Stark said ominously.

Cutter ignored him.

"Connor, can you pull some images of our black cats for Jenny to show Bairstow?"

"Will do."

"Great. Now this is what we're going to do today: I'm going to get in touch with Nando, I've got some questions I want to run by him. I'm assuming our watchers will return this morning, so the rest of you, I want you to play the perfect tourists for the morning. There are plenty of sights to see. Stephen, you've been itching to try out that new wing-suit of yours, I think this is the perfect time. You've got one job — make sure you are seen out and about.

"We'll rendezvous here for a siesta around one p.m., okay?"

SEVEN

Stephen collected a small backpack from the room, and went down to reception to see about organising transport up into the hills.

Truth to tell, he was excited about getting out and jumping. It was one thing to base jump from Brighton Cove and Beachy Head, out into the sea, and quite another to fly.

A lama stood in the hotel doorway, craning its neck to watch him as he crossed the foyer. It was by far the most peculiar moment of the trip so far. It tilted its head, as curious about him as he was about it.

The receptionist smiled one of those bland smiles offered by hoteliers the world over, and it said *I'm at your service, but I'm not actually listening to you.* As he stepped up to the counter, her eyes were focused over his shoulder at a flat-screen television that stood in the corner.

Sadly, he was going to have to interrupt her morning dose of soap opera.

"Hi, there," he said cheerfully. "Can you help me hire a driver for the morning?"

"You want a white taxi cab?" she asked, cocking her head slightly. The movement mirrored the lama's curiosity so perfectly that he almost laughed at the absurdity of it all. She was, he had to admit, considerably easier on the eye, though.

"I was rather hoping you might be able to put me in touch with some-one who would be interested in renting their car out for the entire morning," Stephen explained. "I want to go up into the hills to try out the thermals. It might be a bit pricey if a taxi has its meter running for five or six hours."

He could tell by the way her focus shifted that she hadn't really understood what he wanted.

"A white taxi will cost you maybe five soles for the ride to the mountains, the same to come back. It is a standard fair, two soles anywhere within the city, five soles to travel outside."

"That's great, but how much to wait?"

"You would have to negotiate with the driver. You should fix a price before you get into the taxi."

Ten or twenty soles was nothing, really, but the simple expedient of having his own driver for the morning made so much more sense.

The lama bumped its head on the glass door causing him to jump. He hadn't realised quite how skittish the whole being-followed-and-burgled episodes had got him. He quickly gathered his wits.

"Do you have a friend perhaps who has his own car, and would like to earn some extra money?"

She understood him well enough then, and after a moment of thought, she nodded.

"My brother Eloy owns a car."

"Perfect. How much do you think it would cost for me to hire him to drive me around for the morning?"

"Eloy has no permit to be a taxi driver, but I will check with him." She nodded toward the phone on the reception desk. Stephen nodded in return. She made the call, firing off a staccato string of words in a language that wasn't quite Spanish, nodded a lot even though the voice on the other end of the line obviously could not see her, and hung up.

"My brother says he will do it for twenty-five soles."

Stephen ran the calculation in his head; one sole was roughly ten pence, so that meant he would have to spend all of two pounds fifty for his own personal driver.

"Perfect. Um, stupid question, but does your brother speak English?"

"He grew up on MTV and James Dean films," she assured him.

A short while later brother Eloy blasted the horn to summon Stephen.

Wearing a baseball cap pulled down to shade his eyes from the glaring sunlight, Stephen grabbed both of his bags, opened the lobby door, and side-stepped the lama which was doing its best to graze on the stones of the pavement. The sheer intensity of the heat hit him hard. The sky above was crystal blue, like an Italian stream. There wasn't a cloud in sight, which meant no relief from the harsh caress of the sun as the day wore on.

A grinning face peered up at him through the rolled-down window of a battered red and white 1955 Ford Fairlane that looked like something out of just about every gangster movie ever made.

He wouldn't have marked the family resemblance if he hadn't been told the driver was the receptionist's brother. Though not exactly night and day, the pair were at least dawn and dusk to each other, variants on a genetic theme. Eloy sat hunched over the steering wheel, knuckles white where he gripped the leather. Stephen couldn't help but grin appreciatively at the Fairlane stripe that made the car look like a Liverpudlian Batmobile.

The engine purred like an asthmatic kitten as Eloy revved it.

"Mr Stephen?" he asked cheerfully.

Stephen nodded. "Eloy?"

"That is me," the driver said in his thickly accented English. "Hop in."

Stephen threw the bags into the back and clambered into the passenger seat. The leather burned uncomfortably against his back. Apart from the radio, it looked as though nothing in the car had been modernised or refurbished since it rolled off the production line. The leather was worn through to the foam in places, the dashboard trim shiny where the veneer had rubbed down to a thin patina of nothing. For all that, it was undoubtedly a classic — and so much more fun to ride in than one of those soulless new SUVs. The Fairlane was the epitome of a muscle car.

"Nice wheels," Stephen said appreciatively.

"I love my car like my sister," Eloy said, setting up a dozen inappropriate jokes for a punch line Stephen had no intention of delivering. "Where to, Mr Stephen?"

"Just Stephen, and I was hoping you would know somewhere. I want to go flying."

"You want I take you to the airport?"

"No, no," Stephen reached into the back for his bag, and pulled out his birthday present from Andy Mangels. The wingsuit had come along with a note saying, "If you insist on trying to kill yourself, at least look sharp when you're doing it." He tried to explain that he had a suit that would enable him to fly like Superman, and it wasn't the easiest conversation to have with a man who barely understood English. But Eloy kept nodding and saying, "Yes, yes," as though everything he heard made perfect sense. After Stephen was done, the driver sat in silent thought for a moment, then grinned broadly.

"We go to the hills, you fly like a condor!" Eloy said excitedly.

The car lurched as they pulled away from the curb, the gearbox grinding loudly as the Peruvian forced the stick into place without de-clutching first. As they left the lama in the rear-view mirror, Eloy turned on the radio and cranked up the volume. It took Stephen a moment to recognise the scratchy sound he was hearing. The speakers could barely contain Ry Cooder's bluesy guitar.

It was still early, so the streets were relatively quiet. Ry Cooder was replaced by Howlin' Wolf and then, rather incongruously, by Duran Duran's 'Save A Prayer', while Eloy spent the first fifteen minutes of the trip talking about the city.

"The old town was originally constructed to resemble a puma as it would appear when looked down on by the gods," Eloy said, though for the life of him Stephen couldn't imagine it visually. The streets and side-streets were a warren of squalor and false hope, moving toward a heart of spoiled tourism. There was nothing vaguely animalistic or noble about the place he had seen so far.

"Really?" Abby said, barely keeping the scepticism from her voice as Connor explained.

"Yep, they built the entire city in the shape of a puma."

"I can't see it."

"Well, I'm guessing that head lice rarely see toe nails, either."

"Ewwww..."

Connor scrolled down through the text on his PDA screen. He read through it as they walked, trying to take in everything at once. Mainly he was just trying to enjoy being alone with Abby.

"Pachacuti designed the old walls," he said, offering it like a nugget of purest gold.

"Pachacuti?"

"Yeah. The Incas called him Earthshaker. He was the father of the Inca nation."

"That's a lot of fathering," Abby said, grinning. He liked it when she smiled, even when it was because she was teasing him. *Especially* when it was because she was teasing him, if he told the truth. Encouraged, he continued.

"Well, I'm guessing it's hard to say what's true and what's just a good story. The Incas didn't record their histories in writing — it was word of mouth, stories passed down from generation to generation. Then the Spanish came and twisted them, like so much of the Inca culture and heritage." He paused to get his bearings. "Right, that building over there — " He pointed at the multi-coloured tiers, topped with an ornate dome, of what looked to be some sort of holy place. "That's the Santa Domingo church. It's built on top of what was once the Temple of the Sun. The wall around the base was the perimeter of the sacred enclosure where the Inca people would worship. The Spaniards came, bringing their god with them, and simply placed their holy church on top of the already sacred temple as though one might squash the other."

"It's like Christmas day all over again," Abby said.

"What?"

"Christmas day, yuletide, it was an old pagan festival and the Romans dumped their own holiday down on top of it."

"Oh, right. Get this, this is nuts. The sacred wall has withstood earthquakes, the lot, not a stone lost in nine hundred years. The Spaniards' church though, keeps falling down. I think someone up there's trying to make a point."

She could see the difference not only in the dark-stone foundation, but in the actual masonry of the two aspects of the building. The Incan foundation was made from some sort of slate-coloured igneous stone, while the church sat atop it was a patchwork of greys and browns that made it appear as though any and every stone to hand had been used to patch it up over the centuries.

"You've really been swotting up, haven't you?"

"It was a long flight," Connor said.

"Come on then, what other cool little factoids have you got locked away in that huge brain of yours?"

"How about this: once, they reckon, the labyrinth of walls around the city were sheathed in gold. They called it the sweat of the sun. Can you imagine a city of gold?"

"Only in the cartoon."

"Hey, I've got a joke for you, what do you call a judge with no thumbs?"

"Dunno?"

"Justice fingers!"

"Oh, that was just bad."

"Nooo, that was good. Okay, why did the pig cross the road?"

"Oh, I don't know, why *did* the pig cross the road?"

"To prove he wasn't a chicken!"

"That makes no sense at all," Abby said, shaking her head. She was smiling though, so he plunged on, dredging his memory for more terrible jokes.

"Two molecules are walking down the street and one starts looking around. The other asks, 'What's wrong?' 'I've lost my electron!' 'Are you sure?' 'I'm positive!'"

"Please shoot me now, I think I've lost the will to live."

"Why did the policeman climb the tree? To get to his Special Branch!"

She elbowed him in the ribs, shaking her head but laughing despite herself.

They wandered the streets, working their way down into the area known as Puma Chupan. The jokes got worse, the laughter louder. They linked arms, not caring for a minute that everyone they passed was giving them the most peculiar looks.

According to Connor, the Chupan was the puma's tail, made by the convergence of two man-made canals. The buildings in this part of the city were almost opulent in comparison to those nearer the great animal's head. It was hard to imagine that many of them were more than 800 years old.

Connor was still playing the proud tour guide, but Abby had stopped listening. A kid sat on the street corner, making a paper frog which he set down beside him. He had a small transistor radio that played a tinny version of Simon and Garfunkel's 'Mrs Robinson'.

"This was where the rich used to live, down in the puma's tail," Connor said.

"Things change, huh?"

"No kidding, I mean look at us." He almost wished he hadn't said it, but only almost.

"Yeah, you used to annoy the hell out of me all the time. Now you only annoy the hell out of me *some* of the time."

"It's part of my charm, I wear you down into submission."

"Right. I don't know about you, but one building's beginning to look very much like another to me." At that, Connor redoubled his efforts to keep her entertained.

"So if I've got this right, while the fortifications of the Sacsayhuamán temple formed the head of the puma, down here was the tail. So if you think about it, our hotel is somewhere around the great beast's —"

"Don't even say it," Abby threatened, a laugh bubbling up behind her lips.

"Belly! I was only going to say belly. You've got a filthy mind, Abby Maitland. Have to admit, I rather like that."

"Of course you do."

After the tail, they made their way back toward the ramparts of the old fortress on the outskirts of the city. Not once did Connor stop playing tour guide or telling terrible jokes. After a while Abby tuned it out, concentrating on the stunning landscape, the infinite shades of green and the too-blue sky. The hills were unlike anything she had ever seen; stone ruins sprouted from the hillside, and though the thatched roofs had long since rotted and disappeared, the *pirca* constructions of stone-and-mud mortar stood defiantly against the ravages of time.

What Abby saw went beyond a few desolate walls, there was a harmony between the man-made structures and the environment that modern architecture could not hope to replicate. It was breathtaking to behold, and all the more so to imagine these hillside palaces and storehouses being built without the sophisticated tools, cranes and winches of the modern day.

It made a mockery of skyscrapers and glass-domed cupolas.

"This was part of the Court of Pachacuti, the Inca ruler. He had a load of houses like this scattered throughout the hills around here. The idea was that his court wasn't tied to one building that might be attacked, which is pretty clever when you think about it."

"Connor, enough. I'm tired, I'm hungry, and my feet are killing me."

"Well, learn self defence."

She cuffed him across the side of the head.

"Enough with the bad jokes!"

Stephen was beginning to appreciate the godlike Incan ruler's reverence for the living rock. Everything he had fashioned came from the same building blocks of the world. It was omnipresent, like any spiritual entity.

The stark pinnacles of the Andes formed the axis of their known universe. In their more primitive theosophy they deemed the rock mystical, and believed it possessed powers of its own. It was not surprising to him that many of those long forgotten stonemasons crafted monuments that survived the Spanish depredations and the constant battering of the elements. Perhaps, of all the things that surrounded them, stone really was most worth their devotion. It did not fail, like flesh; it did not wither and fall, like the leaves.

It endured, holding within it the memories of the planet.

The realities of age were an occupational hazard. You couldn't live with your head stuck in the Permian or the Metazoic without some of your thoughts getting stuck there, too. Stephen had, after all, been seduced and abandoned by a woman who was technically hundreds of millions of years old. He hadn't thought about Helen in a while, or more accurately he hadn't thought about his own betrayal in a long time. There had been that freeze-frame moment with Cutter at the bowling alley, which seemed to condense it all down to a single look and a nod, and like typical guys, they buried it.

It wasn't that they were all right again, more that it had been banished out of sight, out of mind. That was centuries of evolution and the male psyche boiled down to its most essential components.

The trust had been eroded though — he knew that. He wasn't a fool. It would take a lot for him to earn it back. But he would.

As they rose higher into the hills Cutter's argument about the end of history was confirmed by the shrill crackle of Madonna's 'Like A Prayer'. Listening to it as he looked down upon a world seemingly untouched by time or progress, he could appreciate Cutter's point of view. Such banal Westernness really was vastly out of place amid the natural beauty of the Andes.

Mercifully, they lost the reception midway through the song. Straining with the steep incline, the battered car continued its ascent.

"This is a good spot," Eloy said a little while later. "You fly like a condor or fall like a rock now. Your destiny is controlled by the gods." The man seemed to enjoy the prospect a little too much for Stephen's liking. He had to admit, though, that it was a good place to launch himself. The grass fell away into a precipice that he could literally throw himself over, and surrender to the mercy of the winds.

He clambered out of the car. Most of the plateau was bald, with more of that grey igneous rock strewn across the surface. Two conical towers stood off to the left, a little removed from the scattered stones. They had crumbled now, their walls adding to the debris on the landscape.

"Those are Chullpas, grave towers for the powerful dead," Eloy explained, seeing him staring at the twin structures.

Nodding, Stephen proceeded to strip down and suited up quickly, bundling his clothes into the backpack. The suit was the most peculiar thing he had ever worn, the webbing between his legs and from his arms to his sides transforming him into something vaguely resembling a huge man-squirrel.

"I want you to meet me at the bottom," he said, pointing away into the middle distance. "Follow me along the road as best you can."

"You will not fall straight down, like Wile E. Coyote?" The Peruvian made an unnerving gesture with his hand, miming Stephen going over the precipice, plunging straight down and finishing with a cartoon-like *splat*.

"I certainly hope not," Stephen said. "The aerodynamics of the suit ought to allow me to glide up to twenty miles."

Eloy raised a disbelieving eyebrow at that.

"I will follow, but if you kill yourself, it will cost more than twenty-five soles."

"That sounds fair."

He took the second backpack out of the car, and removed a compact parachute from it. He strapped himself into the harness, cinching the buckles tightly. The last thing out of the bag was a small handheld digital video recorder. He turned it on, and filmed a quick three-sixty panorama of the peaks, and then walked slowly up to the edge.

"It's a long way down," he said. "Famous last words."

And with that he stepped out over the edge, and was falling.

The wind became a gale around his ears as it tore at the suit. It took a moment for him to catch his breath, and then he spread his arms and legs wide to arrest the speed of his descent. The nylon pockets stitched between his arms and torso filled with air. Almost immediately, instead of hugging the sheer stone face he was powering away from it, the wind beneath his wingsuit.

And then he was flying instead of falling. He let out a wild whoop of exhilaration as the ground swept away beneath him.

He was flying!

Blood pounded through his veins.

He twisted his body, arcing in toward the hills again. The air-filled pockets acted like wings. Stephen used the momentum to hug the contours of the trees as he hurtled across the top of them, then they were gone before he could focus. The ground flashed by beneath him. His heart raced, hammering against his chest as he swooped low across the stripe of the road, so close to the stones he could almost have reached down to pluck one of them up as he skimmed the surface, and then rose again.

The slightest error of judgement meant certain death. Unlike Wile E. Coyote, he couldn't very well dust himself off and stagger away from a man-shaped crater in the Earth.

Tears stung his eyes. The wind pulled at his flesh, drawing his lips apart with its ferocity and pinning his eyelids open in a mad stare. It was all he could do not to pull the chute and end the flight then and there. He had base-jumped a dozen times, but the vectors of the wind and the starkness of the earth were different here. They opened another dimension in his descent. The sensation of speed was incredible.

He fought to keep his head up and not let go of the camera. It was difficult to judge, but he must have been skimming the Earth at fifty or sixty miles an hour, if not more.

Stephen savoured the freedom now, knowing that too soon he would have to pull the chute and come crashing back down to Earth.

EIGHT

It seemed a lifetime ago since Nick Cutter had felt any sort of content-
ment. His world had become one of necessity and practicality, so
dwelling upon what was essentially the loss of 'self' was pointless.

From the window of his room, he watched Jenny leave for the hospital
with Stark and Chaplin. Even the way she moved was the same...

Jenny had arranged with Chaplin that the three of them would pick up
Cam, then rendezvous with the rest at the hotel. As a group they would
take him to the ambassador's summer house, which was the safest haven
they had been able to arrange. Once he was secure, they would proceed
into the rainforest.

At least that was the plan. Why, then, did he feel such misgivings?

The fan that functioned as the only air-conditioning was barely
capable of coping with the rising sun. Moving away from the window,
Cutter paced back and forth. He needed to focus on the job at hand, not
live his life somewhere in the past.

The irony of that idea had him snort a single bitter laugh.

He picked up the phone and dialled the number Nando had given
him. He listened for the tell-tale second click that would betray an
eavesdropper, but it never came. The phone rang through six, seven,
eight cycles before it was answered by a young woman.

"Hi, this is Professor Cutter calling for Nando Estevez. I believe he is
expecting my call."

"Of course, Professor Cutter," the woman said in flawless English.

There was no trace of an accent to her voice. That was another aspect to the end of history, he mused, the globalisation of language. With the prevalence of the Internet and English seeping into every culture and eroding the natural need to understand smaller languages like Quechua, it was hardly surprising that call centres in India and China serviced the industries of the UK, or that people could hardly tell the nationality of those who were answering the phones.

There were over six thousand languages in the world, and already thirty of them dominated global discussions. Soon enough, most of those thirty would be as useful as cuneiform in day-to-day life, as virulent strains of English spread.

It wasn't only species that were endangered.

I'm turning into a grumpy old man.

The line went quiet for a moment, then he was treated to more of that inane Muzak that phone companies considered soothing. Then he heard Nando's voice for the second time in ten years.

"Professor Nick! You are here?"

"Landed yesterday. We're heading out your way later today, just waiting for the two locals who are meant to be joining up with us. Look, I want to run something by you."

"Ask away."

"You said you've noticed peculiar migratory patterns in the species you observe, right?"

"Yes, most peculiar."

"Obviously I haven't seen anything, but what you've explained sounds as though a new predator may have entered the region and is asserting its dominance."

"That was my initial thought, but the wildlife in the reserve is all strictly monitored. We have not introduced any new species in over nine months. Any alien species would have had to find its own way into the reserve, which is highly unlikely. New species do not simply materialise from the ether."

"But it's not impossible, either. The presence of some new hunter would explain the dearth of animal life in certain regions. Have you looked for anomalies in the tracking patterns? Perhaps prints that do not belong."

"Honestly? No. We have thirty rangers in our team, covering several hundred square miles of territory. Looking for rogue tracks would be like hunting for that needle in the haystack. And we cannot change our priorities simply because I am curious."

On the face of it, Cutter couldn't argue with the logic, but the assumptions it was based upon were not absolutes. There was another way of attacking the problem.

"I'm not saying that you need to comb every square inch of ground, either. Let nature help you. Follow the lack of sound. Where did you last notice the behavioural peculiarities? Take a team of men there specifically with the intention of reading the land. Animals leave tracks, faecal matter — it's all out there waiting to tell its story, each unique, genetic fingerprint that will answer all of our questions."

"You have a theory?"

"I have a theory," Cutter admitted, not willing to go into it over the telephone, despite the fact that he was fairly sure there were no unwanted listeners on the line.

"Will you share it?"

"Not yet. I'd rather discuss it in person. Find me some tracks, Nando. Give me something to work with that either supports or destroys the theory. The truth is out there, it has to be."

"I shall take a team out today, and perhaps we will find something this time," Nando said, but he didn't sound overly optimistic.

"Excellent," Cutter said. And then, almost as an afterthought, he added, "One last thing. Have any of your rangers reported seeing a frost in the air?"

There was a silence for a moment as Nando pictured the image.

"No, not that I have heard. Does this have something to do with your theory?"

"No, it was just something I heard that the young Englishman who was attacked had said."

"Ah, well, no. Though something like that would not be uncommon in the rainforest; the mixture of the moisture and atmospherics can play havoc with perceptions. Coupled with the heat, jungle mirages are not out of the question."

"Really? Ah, well, I suppose there's always a prosaic explanation for even the most fanciful idea."

"Always, Professor. You taught me that much, at least."

"And you listened to me? Why didn't I have more students like you, Nando? Well, we should be with you this evening. Good luck with those tracks."

At that, Cutter hung up.

Just because they hadn't seen an anomaly didn't mean it wasn't out there. The breeziness with which Nando had dismissed the phenomenon as a jungle mirage suggested that they had been seen before though. That made sense.

More and more, he began to wonder if anomalies were opening up all over the world, most of them unseen. As far as they knew, there was nothing that bound them to the British Isles, or even Europe. The Sahara was vast, as were the Steppes and the Veldt. For all the billions of people on the Earth, there were massive expanses of land still remote and relatively untouched, places where anomalies could open and close unnoticed.

The notion sent a shiver through his soul.

NINE

Jenny Lewis and Alex Chaplin walked side by side through the antiseptic cleanliness of the hospital ward. They had left Stark out by the car.

Here, more than anywhere else she had been, it was painfully obvious that they were a million miles from home. The linoleum floors had seen better days, as had the paint flaking away from the walls. There was, at least, blessed relief from the stifling heat outside.

An ill-equipped crash-cart leaned against the wall. Where she expected to see defibrillators, adrenalin needles, and so much more, there were neatly folded white clothes, sealed hypodermics and other necessities — but a distinct lack of technology.

Their footsteps echoed down the corridor.

The wards opened up off the main corridor like ventricles off the main artery of the building. Linen curtains were drawn around steel-framed beds. Patients lay atop of the covers, their pyjamas stained with dark rings of sweat, despite the air conditioning.

She noticed Chaplin's hand stray to something at his waist. It took her a moment to realise it was a gun. All of a sudden she wished she hadn't left Stark back at the car.

They had spoken very little during the drive.

Jenny had taken Stark aside and confided her suspicion.

"It was Chaplin wasn't it? It had to be him that orchestrated the break in last night. He set the guards to watching the hotel, and had us followed. It all makes sense."

Stark agreed that it did. An ugly kind of sense.

Stark had confronted Chaplin in the hospital car park after they had arrived, but the man had protested vehemently. Yet there was something in the look he gave Stark that Jenny did not like or trust. It was as though his eyes were part reptilian. She had known plenty of men like Chaplin. He was hardly the last of the great liars.

"What were you looking for? What did you hope to achieve?" Stark rasped.

"It wasn't me, I swear," he repeated.

"No, it was just a random little slice of coincidence that had all of our rooms turned over while we were being stalked through the streets. What kind of an idiot do you take me for?"

"It wasn't me!"

"This is getting repetitive, Chaplin. No one but you knows why we are here, that we are anything other than a boring old scientific expedition. What did you do? Tip off the locals for a nice little cash reward? Playing both sides of the coin? Come on, you can't tell me it wasn't you who tipped off the newspaper,"

Chaplin didn't so much as squirm.

"Read my lips, man: I did not do it."

"I don't believe you."

"Then you are a fool."

"Have you heard of Occam's razor?" Jenny said. Then, "All other things being equal, the simplest solution is the best. In other words, when multiple competing theories are equal in other respects, the smart money is on selecting the most straightforward, because ninety-nine times out of 100 it'll be the winner.

"Our hypotheses are simple: either you are working for some mysterious paymaster and this is all your fault; you are working independently and this is all your fault; or you have nothing to do with any of this and some third party is playing us all. If it isn't you, then we've got some fairly serious security issues here, despite all those fancy call signs and secret frequencies. Assuming you aren't working against us, you've got a leak. Someone knew exactly who we were, where we were staying, and when we were out. That's one big set of assumptions that Occam's not too fond of."

Even as she said it, another worry — larger than all of the other concerns combined — entered her mind. *What if they know about the anomalies?*

Stark released his grip on Chaplin's throat and stepped away from the car, shaking his head.

"I suggest you start at the beginning," Chaplin said, his tone utterly reasonable and even conciliatory. That in itself disturbed her, that in the face of accusation and assault he was capable of dissembling so flawlessly. "Because you have me at something of a loss. Being that I don't have the slightest clue what you are talking about."

"I don't believe you," Jenny said.

"This is getting tedious, don't you think? I don't know what you are talking about, you don't believe what I am saying, I think we've established the baseline, so for the sake of our sanity let's just make like we don't think the other is a lying piece of shit, and go from there. Now please, what are you talking about? Was there a robbery?"

Jenny sighed.

"Okay, I'll play along for now. Our hotel was burgled last night. Nothing — so far as we can tell — was taken, but all of our rooms were ransacked."

"And you think they know who you are?" Chaplin asked.

"Why would they break in otherwise?"

If his troubled face was anything to go by, Chaplin's brain was working overtime.

"Could it have been a coincidence? I mean should we be jumping to all of these conclusions?"

"We were followed by at least three different observers last night. That's three that we know of. I think it's safe to say that it wasn't some random opportunist burglary. These people know full well that we aren't your average tourists."

"Shit. Shit. Shit." Chaplin said, staring at the pavement.

They walked in to the hospital together.

She saw herself in the glass, a small spot growing larger and taking on shape as she neared the entrance, until she was walking straight at herself. She hit the door and burst through it, five steps ahead of Chaplin.

He caught up with her at the lift.

Chaplin jabbed the buttons impatiently, but the lift came in its own sweet time. The doors wheezed open. They stepped into a pocket of peculiar aromas. She smelled sickness above, between and beneath all of the other fragrances; expensive perfumes, cheap aftershave, sweat, blood, ammonia, cabbage, pheromones and fear. It was a heady mélange. Individually each might have been pleasant, or at least not unpleasant, but together they made her nauseous.

The journey up to Cameron Bairstow's ward on the fifth floor was interminably slow. They shared the cramped lift with three green-scrubbed nurses who chittered and babbled incessantly in their own language. Sweat trickled slowly down the curve of her back.

Jenny's head spun. Her hair kept falling across her eyes. The sweat made it cling to her scalp. She remembered something her mother used to say: "Women don't sweat, dear, they glow." Well, all things considered, she was glowing like a pig.

Jenny counted off the numbers as the lift ascended until the doors opened and they stepped out.

Chaplin did not run. Everything about his demeanour changed as he emerged into the hospital corridor. He walked slowly, looking left and right, hyper-alert. Jenny saw in him the same predatory qualities Stark and the others possessed. He leaned against the wall, more paint flaking beneath his touch. For a moment he didn't move, he simply listened with his finger to his lips. Then he moved close enough that she could feel his breath against her ear as he whispered.

"My men have gone." The men he had ordered to watch over Cam were nowhere to be seen.

She nodded, immediately understanding the ramifications of their absence.

Jenny took a hair-tie out of her pocket and tied her hair up. She drew her fringe up out of her eyes.

Chaplin nodded and they moved on, the echo of their footsteps the only sound in the otherwise silent corridor. The quiet was unnerving. She expected to hear the bleeps and blips of machines preserving life, and the wheeze of ventilators and all of those other hospital sounds. Yet it was as though they had stepped into the Kingdom of Silence.

As they passed the crash-cart, Chaplin reached inside his linen jacket, behind his back and drew out a compact .45. He gripped it with both hands as he moved from door to door, checking each ward. A wheelchair was folded up against the wall beside the crash-cart.

His sudden change spooked her, not least because it served as a reminder of just how unstable the world around them truly was. For all the talk of civility and burgeoning democracy, eco-reserves and boosted tourism, this was still the kind of place where a boy in a hospital bed could be made to disappear, if deemed necessary.

Chaplin signalled her forward.

She followed him into a small ward. There were eight beds in the room, three of which were hidden behind curtains. There was a grizzle-faced old man with a Captain Birdseye beard who lay on his back with his leg up in traction. In the bed beside him an emphysemic wreck of a man was rigged up with oxygen and tubes. She saw the ashtray on the bedside table beside the big juice bottle and the wilted flowers, and shook her head. Three other beds were empty, though one of them had been slept in.

Chaplin pointed toward the furthest curtain.

He tensed, drew it back, and visibly relaxed as he saw the young man in the bed. Chaplin holstered his gun, and became very much business-as-usual as the mask of violence slipped from his face. Jenny joined him at the bedside.

Cameron Bairstow was asleep. His face must have been handsome once, but it was ruined now. Five deep scratches clawed from his left temple, down across his eye, cheek and nose to chin, each stitched with twenty or more sutures. The bruising around the eyes had left the entire left side of his face purple, though in places the flesh had already begun to heal, turning yellow. His throat and down across his bare chest bore the worst of the wounds. It was a miracle he hadn't bled out. His body had been opened up with a savagery that was shocking. She counted a dozen deep cuts. On each, the flaps of skin had been sewn together to leave lips of flesh gaping across his chest and stomach. *He looks like some abomination out of one of Connor's horror movies*, she thought, as she struggled to comprehend the severity of his wounds. Where he wasn't cut he was lacerated. The darker bruises and crusted puncture marks could only have been made by teeth.

No man had done this.

The precision of the long slices couldn't have been achieved by knife cuts. They mirrored the raking scratches of a hand — or paw — slashing down across Bairstow's face, though instead of nails they had almost certainly been caused by claws.

Tooth and claw.

Cameron stirred, as though sensing their eyes upon him.

"We've got to get him out of here," Jenny whispered.

"Are you sure? He's hardly in a state to go trekking through the jungle."

"He's not safe here. You know that."

"He won't be safe if we try to move him, and kill him instead. I don't see how we've got a lot of choice other than to leave him here."

"Can you have someone watch him?"

Chaplin grunted something approximating a laugh. "Who? The police? The military? Who, exactly, do you propose we should trust?"

"I hate this."

"I can't say I am particularly fond of it either."

"So we have to proceed as we planned, and get him to the safe house. If we get him out of here, at least we can have one of Stark's men babysit him until he's in a position to be flown home."

"All right, then we'll move him to the ambassadorial summer residence," Chaplin said. "That's the only place I could arrange where we could actually protect him, and it's on our soil, so to speak. I would have done so sooner, but after the attack he was in no condition to be moved. The doctors would not countenance it."

"Please don't talk about me as though I'm not here."

Jenny jumped with surprise. The young man on the bed spoke, his voice hoarse with disuse. He shifted, opening his eyes to look up at them. Despite the cocktail of drugs pumping into his body to ward off the pain, his eyes were bright, feverish even, with intelligence.

"And don't for a minute think I'm going home without my brother."

"Cameron," Jenny said, "My name is Jenny Lewis, I work for the British government. Your father sent me to help you. Jaime is dead, Cameron." Despite the tension of their situation, Jenny tried to keep her voice soft and sympathetic.

"I know that better than anyone else. I saw him die, after all." Then his voice became surprisingly firm. "I am *not* leaving his bones out there to rot. The animals might have got his flesh, but something of him has to go home. It has to. I am taking him home."

"I understand," Jenny said. Every word that came out of her mouth sounded like some soulless platitude. But this wasn't a fight worth having, not here and now. All she wanted to do was get him out of there, to somewhere safe.

They could argue about bones later.

"Cameron, I need to ask you something," Jenny continued. "Did you talk to anyone about what happened? About the attack, and the village? Anyone other than me, that is?"

"No, I didn't. Why?"

"Where are the guards, Cam?" Chaplin asked, looking over his shoulder, peering nervously toward the empty corridor.

It occurred to Jenny then that they had seen very few nurses or other medical staff since they had come onto the fifth floor. She picked up Cameron Bairstow's chart, skimming quickly over the scrawled Spanish. The only thing she was able to glean from it was the doctor's name: Mendoza. She asked Cameron if he had been visited by anyone.

"I haven't seen them since early this morning," he said, struggling to sit up in bed. The exertion brought beads of perspiration to his face, lending his already waxy complexion an almost ethereal quality. She thought he looked like death struggling to rise.

"I don't like this at all," Jenny said to Chaplin. It looked as if he was no happier about the situation. "We've got to get him out of here."

"I'll make some calls."

That struck Jenny as odd, since she thought it had all been arranged.

"Good," she replied. "I'll get him ready, and locate a hospital administrator."

Then Cam spoke up. "You're doing it again," he objected, but there was less strength to his protest now. "Talking over my head, like I'm not here. What's happening?"

"Can you walk, Cam?" Jenny asked him.

"I haven't walked in over a week. So I have no idea. I'm not paralysed, if that's what you mean."

"We're going to need to move you."

"I gathered that much, but why?"

Jenny looked back over her shoulder toward the empty corridor, not sure what she expected to see there. It was just a vague sensation, and the skin at the nape of her neck prickled, as though someone had walked over her grave.

"We think you are in danger here. There has already been one attempt on your life, and the threat is simply too great for you to stay here, when anyone can walk in from the street."

Cameron's eyes darted left and right. For a moment his fear looked furtive. He reached up to touch his face, but couldn't bring himself to let his fingers settle on the ruined flesh. He looked up helplessly at Jenny and Chaplin.

"I want this to be over."

"We know you do, Cam," Chaplin reassured him. "So do we. Believe me. So do we. You're in the wrong place at the wrong time, as the old saying goes. Don't worry, though, we won't let anything happen to you," he promised. It was one of those rash promises that was almost impossible to keep in the cold light of day, like a lover's promise never to leave or an adulterer's pledge of fidelity. The words themselves meant nothing, but they somehow lent strength to the person to whom the promise was made.

"I'm going down to the car to get it ready, and make a couple of calls," Chaplin continued. "Jenny will help you get dressed." He reached behind his back and drew the gun once more. He handed it to Jenny. "Just in case. I'll see you back at the car."

She didn't argue. She took the gun and slipped into it her pocket. It was heavier than she expected, but not as heavy as it truly ought to have been. It was a gun, it ended lives. It should have been every bit as heavy as the lives it ended, not just a few pounds of metal. Through the thin material, it felt cold against her skin.

"Trust no one," she said unnecessarily.

Chaplin nodded and left them to get ready.

That nagging doubt refused to go with him. He might not have been the mastermind behind the robbery, but he was most certainly wrapped up in this somehow.

What remained of Cameron's clothes were neatly folded and stowed in the cupboard beneath the bedside table: socks and shoes. There was nothing else. The bloody tatters he had arrived in had obviously been incinerated.

"Wait there," she said. As though he could go anywhere he chose, should the whim take him. Moving from bedside table to bedside table, she scavenged a pair of baggy shorts that looked like they would fit. Captain Birdseye watched her, then said something in Spanish, gesticulating toward his own cupboard. She took it to mean there was something in there he wanted her to see. Opening the door, Jenny found a bright yellow Hawaiian palm-print shirt.

"Thank you," she said, when he didn't start screaming *Thief!*

The entire time, she saw no sign of anyone who resembled a hospital official. Returning to Cam's bed, she helped him sit up, then dressed him one leg at a time.

The needle from the drip was still in his left arm.

"This might hurt a bit," she apologised. Before he could answer, Jenny withdrew the needle. Cam winced, but he did not cry out. A little blood bubbled out of the puncture; it was so little that it would scab over quickly, so she wasn't worried about it.

"I saw a wheelchair in the corridor. Finish getting dressed. I'll go and fetch it."

She stopped at the door, and peered around the corner, not knowing whether she was panicking unnecessarily — and uncharacteristically. It was difficult not to allow the feeling of isolation get to her, that sensation that came from being a stranger in a strange land. She needed to talk to Cutter, and for that matter, Lester, but without a working phone, she couldn't. It was one of the many things she took for granted back home. Out here, the lack of communication only served to add to the feeling of helplessness that had swollen all around her since they landed.

There was so much going on that she couldn't see. But things seldom remained hidden.

Jenny found the wheelchair, and pushed it back in the direction of the ward. As she did so, she passed a window, and her blood ran cold.

An SUV had pulled into a car park behind the hospital, and several men were getting out. They all wore dark glasses — nothing unusual about that. But she caught a glimpse of one of them examining a pistol. He put it away, then they moved calmly toward a back entrance, carefully avoiding anything that would attract attention.

I have to get Cam out of here. There'd be no time to sort it out with the authorities — that would have to wait until later.

As she entered the room, Cam was struggling with the buttons on the ugly yellow shirt, his fingers trembling as he tried to force them through the buttonholes. Jenny knelt at his feet and moved his hands aside so that she could button the shirt for him. In other circumstances it might have been a tender gesture, but everything about it now screamed necessity.

That done, she then helped him move from the bed to the chair. She tried not to look at his face as it contorted with pain.

When he sank into the wheelchair, Cam bit down on a scream. Still, a whimper escaped between his lips.

"Is there anything here you need?" Jenny asked, doing her best to stay calm and practical.

He shook his head.

"They deal the meds out three times a day. There's nothing else here worth having."

"Then let's get out of here before someone comes."

She checked the corridor again before wheeling him down to the elevator. Every step of the way she expected someone to challenge her. Mercifully, no one did. A nurse had returned to the station, but she didn't even look up from what she was doing. *No time to stop now.*

Jenny jabbed the call button and the lift doors opened. She pushed the chair in, and the doors closed behind her. She felt every revolution of the winch as they descended.

"There was a newspaper report, Cam. It claimed that you found a village on the outskirts of the rainforest, where everyone had been murdered. Is it true?"

He nodded.

"If you didn't talk to the press, then someone else did. It may be the same person or persons who want you dead."

"So who does?" Cam asked through his pain. "What would that accomplish?"

"That's what I'm trying to work out," Jenny said, honestly.

The lift doors opened, grinding on something that was stuck in the mechanism. She pushed the chair out, glanced left and right, and headed directly toward the glass-plated doors, moving quickly but in a way that wouldn't cause anyone to notice. Her footsteps sounded erratic, like an arrhythmic heart tripping over itself.

"There's a lot of money in this eco-reserve and the tourism it'll bring in. And the smuggling trade is worth millions of pounds. But I can't figure out what they stand to gain from your death, yet *someone* wants to keep you quiet."

The sensors above the entrance picked up their approach and the glass doors parted for them. The heat rushed in.

"We need to make you safe, then as soon as you're able to travel, we need to get you out of this country."

Jenny moved quickly across the car park, and saw Chaplin leaning against the SUV, his mobile phone pressed up against his ear. He had turned his back on them and was bent over slightly. She couldn't quite make out what he was saying, but it was clear that he was agitated.

Stark was nearby, sitting with his back against a tree, watching the hospital doors. As soon as he saw her, he was up on his feet and moving quickly in their direction.

Chaplin hung up, and was all smiles.

"Any trouble?" he asked.

"We've got to move quickly," Jenny said. "I saw some men entering the back of the hospital, and at least one of them was carrying a gun."

"Good God," he said. Then he turned. "Come on then, Cam. Let's get you somewhere safe." Chaplin popped the lock on the rear door. "You can call your old man later, and let him know you're all right."

As quickly as they could without injuring him further, they helped the young man into the car. Jenny watched the hospital the entire time, but to her relief, the men she had seen didn't reappear.

As they drove away, she knew she should have been relieved, yet she couldn't help but think that she was swimming with a shark. Chaplin said all the right things, *did* all the right things, but there was something about him that had every nerve in her body jangling.

Still, she had got into the car with him — but only because Stark was there, she realised.

She also realised that she had no idea where they were going. She was driving into the unknown, with one man who might betray her at a moment's notice, and another who had a death warrant on his head.

Stark would have to play her knight in shining armour.

TEN

She was late.

It was almost four in the afternoon. The others had returned at one.

It wasn't like Jenny to be late. She had that innate Civil Service punctuality gene. Cutter couldn't remember the last time it had happened. Something must have forced her to change her plans.

She had Stark with her, but that didn't make him feel much better, truth be told. The others were sitting around the hotel lobby, waiting for their local guide and translator to arrive before they set off for the eco-reserve. Connor played with a monkey on a stick, making it do summersault after summersault.

"This is so cool," he said, earning himself a withering glare from Abby. "Well it is," he said, defensively. "Can't I enjoy the local handicrafts?"

"It was made in China," Abby said, shaking her head. "You're such an idiot sometimes."

"I'm sure she's okay," Stephen said, coming over to stand beside Cutter.

"Of course she is," Cutter agreed, though his matter-of-fact reassurance wasn't particularly convincing.

Piped Muzak lulled around them. For once it wasn't some watered-down version of an Italian opera. It had a distinct South American flavour of pipes and the rhythmic slap of drum skins.

Lucas came down the stairs, a black rucksack hanging from his shoulder. He knelt, and delved into the sack, pulling out radio after radio, and tossing one to each of the team.

"Communication, ladies and gentlemen. We've finally got the gear unpacked, so now there's no way one of us should be going off alone without a way of getting in touch. It's suicide in a place like this. They're all tuned to channel 2112. If you need help, but can't speak, just give three sharp blasts of static." He demonstrated by thumbing down the transmitter on his own radio. The lobby filled with the crackles of life. They heard three distinct pulses. "Got it?"

They nodded.

"It's a bit like bolting the stable door," Cutter muttered, mangling the truism. He hadn't turned away from the hotel's entrance for the last ten minutes, and now he walked to the door and stuck his head outside.

The guards were back, and they stood to either side of the door, cigarillos hanging lazily between their lips, wraiths of smoke drifting up over their faces. They didn't acknowledge him. Beyond them, the broad plaza was its familiar hive of tourist activity. Cutter strained to see if the watchers had returned, but yesterday's vantage points were too far away for him to tell for certain.

Someone was sat beneath the fountain, but it could have been anyone. From this distance it was impossible to assign even a gender to the amorphous shape, let alone an identity.

"Professor?" Connor called behind him.

For a moment he didn't move, savouring the ripples of heat against his face. Its angry warmth reminded him that he was alive.

Chaplin's driver was parked against the curb; at least he assumed it was Chaplin's man. He was supposed to accompany them to the reserve. The tinted black windows of the SUV made it impossible to know who was actually driving. *He must have got the air conditioning working*, Cutter thought to himself. *Otherwise he's broiling in there.*

"In a minute, Connor," he said over his shoulder. He walked up to the car and rapped hard on the window with his knuckles. It rolled down and Fabrice leaned across the passenger seat to peer out at him.

"Yes, Professor?"

Cutter put his hands on the sill and stooped. "Do you have a way of contacting Chaplin?"

Fabrice nodded.

"Good. Call him. I want to talk to him. Now."

Chaplin's man opened the glove box and took out an oversized mobile phone. He hit redial and handed it through the window. Cutter took it, and listened to the dial tone cycle. Before the machine could kick in, Alex Chaplin answered:

"Fabrice? I thought I told you not —"

"It's Nick Cutter."

"Ah, Professor Cutter." There was a short pause. "This really isn't a good time."

"I don't care, Chaplin. I want to talk to Jenny. Put her on the phone."

A moment later Jenny's voice asked, "Cutter? What's wrong?"

"Where the hell are you? We're sitting here waiting for you guys."

"You were worried about me?" He couldn't tell if she was teasing, or relieved.

"Of course I was. What's going on, Jenny?"

"We've had a slight change of plan."

"I think you'd better explain. What happened with Bairstow?"

"He's with us. We're taking him directly to the safe house."

"You're what?"

He turned his back on the car and walked away a dozen paces. Lowering his voice he asked again, "What the hell's going on, Jenny?"

"We had to get him out of there, Nick. He wasn't safe. They were coming to get him — I saw them."

"Why didn't you bring him here?"

"There wasn't time," Jenny replied. "Besides, we don't know if there's anyone we can trust — even on the hospital staff. And if they know why we're here, they'll almost certainly be watching you, as well. We couldn't take that chance. This was the only way."

"Where are you taking him?"

"The ambassadorial summer house, just as we arranged. He should be safe there until we can get him out of the country."

"I don't like this, Jenny."

"Neither do I." There was something about her voice. She sounded strained.

"Are you okay?"

"I'm not sure," she said. And then for the benefit of Chaplin she added, "We need to get word to Sir Charles, he'll know what to do. We can't exactly put Cam on the next charter flight out."

"I'm coming to get you. Where are you?"

"I don't know," she admitted. "But it doesn't make sense for you to come here, anyhow. We've got Stark with us. More than ever we need to make it look like you're genuinely on a field trip. We can't change our plans. Get the gang together and head out as planned. I'll put you on to Chaplin, and you boys can work out the details."

"Jenny?" He heard the muffled sounds of the phone being handed over and Chaplin saying, "Professor?"

"I'm coming to join you."

"I'm not sure that would be wise."

"To hell with wise, I'm coming. Where are you taking them?"

"Take a look around you, Professor. Are you being watched now?"

Cutter squinted toward the rooftop across the plaza, and the bell-tower, but he couldn't see anyone. The guards beside the door tapped out ash from their skinny smokes, and said something to each other in Spanish. There were at least a hundred people in the plaza. He couldn't hope to know if one of them was there to watch them.

"I have no idea," he admitted.

"I could have Fabrice drive you to the safe house, but there's no guarantee you wouldn't be followed. It would hardly be a safe house then, would it? Your man Stark is here, surely that's enough?"

Cutter couldn't very well dispute the logic, but he wasn't happy with it. He certainly wasn't about to leave Jenny to the mercy of this creep while they went out into the wilderness. Forces were at work all around them, that much was obvious, and he still didn't know the role Chaplin was playing.

"There's got to be a way for me to reach you. I need to talk to Cameron, and that's one of my team you've got sat beside you. I'm not about to disappear into the rainforest without her."

"Oh, I quite understand, Professor. Cam's not fit to travel, that much is obvious, and I imagine it will be some time before he is. That means we need to hide him for a few weeks while he rests up. You can't very well sit in that hotel room of yours for a month, though. That doesn't work.

"You need to be seen doing what you came here to do. Otherwise the people who want to assassinate Cam will almost certainly find him, and the easiest way for them to do that is to follow you or another member of your team. I'm not naive enough to think that there were no security cameras at the hospital, either. One of them has to have captured Miss Lewis' face. Two and two isn't very difficult to put together from there."

Cutter let the implications of Chaplin's words sink in.

The guards appeared to be paying rather more attention to him now than they had been. Connor stood in the hotel doorway. Cutter covered the phone's mouthpiece.

"Go back inside, Connor."

The young man did as he was told. Cutter turned his attention back to the phone.

"This is a mess, Chaplin. If Jenny's face is on one of those films, and they can trace her back to the Home Office, we're talking a major political stink. This is exactly what we were instructed to avoid. So what do you suggest?"

"We need to destroy any evidence they might have from their surveillance cameras, and make Cam disappear for a while. That's *my* job. You need to be seen to be doing yours."

"Fine. I still need to talk to Cam."

There was a protracted silence on the other end of the line as Chaplin obviously thought about it.

"I'll need to talk to Fabrice. We can try and pull a switch. But it's on your head if this goes wrong, Professor. Am I making myself plain?"

"I'll bring Blaine."

"I'm not sure that's necessary. Double the chance of something going wrong."

"If Jenny's at risk, I want my men there to look after her."

And if things get ugly, I'll make certain I am not on my own, Cutter thought.

Cutter and Blaine clambered into the back of the SUV.

Fabrice was wearing shades that hid his eyes.

"We are going to drive around the town for a while, then I am going to let you out and Mr Chaplin is going to pick you up in a second car. Two of our men will take your place, and we shall continue to drive for a while, then I shall return your replacements to the hotel."

"Hopefully no one will look too closely," Andy Blaine said. He was packing a snub-nosed pistol strapped to his ankle, and a long-bladed knife in a sheath beneath his shirt. His most dangerous weapons by far were not concealed, though. He cracked his knuckles and sank back into the soft leather, turning the air-conditioning up in the back of the car. He had a small black rucksack between his feet.

"They can look as closely as they like. They will only see what we want to show them," the driver said with a broad grin.

The bait and switch was an old espionage manoeuvre. Cutter had seen it pulled off in a dozen poorly made spy-thrillers. That didn't make it any less efficient. As long as the switch was done subtly, the eye had a way of seeing what it wanted to see. It was the same principle a stage magician worked by. It was all about being seen.

They had lingered outside the lobby, making a show of climbing into Fabrice's car. They had chosen to wear the brightest, gaudiest clothing that could be found in the hotel gift shop: luridly patterned Hawaiian shirts. Beneath them they wore plain white t-shirts. Once in the car, they took the Hawaiian shirts off, leaving them behind for their body doubles.

Cutter and Blaine each had a baseball cap stuffed into their pockets, along with a pair of utterly unremarkable sunglasses. They'd be out of the car and across the street in five seconds, looking like different men. That was all it would take, five seconds out of prying eyes, and in that time Fabrice would pick up their replacements, then continue the bogus tour.

Fabrice drove slowly around the plaza, going with the flow of traffic, then turned off beside the cathedral. He drove at a steady thirty, not wishing to draw any unwanted attention. Thirty was an anonymous speed; people saw a car pass them, but did not register it — it didn't stand out in their minds, since it was just a car like any other.

Cutter peered out through the rear window. At first it was difficult to be sure that they were being followed. But after a dozen leisurely turns that took them onto side streets and further and further from the main drag, it became clear. Fabrice didn't accelerate. Doing so would have made it obvious. He took his mobile phone from the glove compartment and made a brief call, warning the body doubles to be ready to move.

"It's all an illusion," Blaine said, beside him. He already had his fingers wrapped around the door handle.

Cutter saw Fabrice nodding.

"A bloody great trick," the driver said, turning onto a narrow street. Their tail was less than fifty feet back now. Counting stopping time, opening the doors, and reaching the side of the road, that was nowhere near far enough away.

"Don't worry," Fabrice said, no doubt reading the doubt in Cutter's face. "The next turn will bring us onto a main road. There are five sets of traffic lights along it. We will catch one but drive through it. The manoeuvre will buy us all the time we need to make the exchange."

They had no choice but to trust him.

The SUV hit the third set of lights, driving through just as they changed to red. There was no way that the car behind could follow without causing a collision at the intersection.

Again without the slightest acceleration, Fabrice indicated and turned off the main road onto a smaller side street. As soon as they were out of the line of sight, he pulled over.

Cutter and Blaine scrambled out. They were outside a small café whose seats and tables had tumbled out onto the street. Beside it was a florist. The scent of the flowers, mixed with the caffeinated rush of the café's own aromas, was intoxicating. Two men got up from their table, drinks untouched, and without a word climbed quickly into the back of the SUV. The doors slammed and the car was on its way again in less than ten seconds.

Cutter pulled on his hat and sat down in one of the recently vacated chairs. Blaine sat down beside him. The coffee was still hot and his pastry had a single bite taken out of it. Cutter drank the warm liquid and waited, counting out the time silently in his head. In less than a minute their tail came around the corner. He did not recognise the driver, nor the passenger, though both appeared to be European. He filed that away in his memory.

The car didn't slow as it passed. Fabrice would lead them on a merry little chase, giving Cutter and Blaine ample time to walk back through the streets to the arranged meeting place where Alex Chaplin was waiting.

The safe house was anything but safe, in Stark's eyes.

He came to meet Blaine and Cutter at the gate. He had been laying down precautions, should the worst come to the worst.

The soldier's gaze swept across the compound, taking in all of its vulnerabilities in a matter of seconds. The art-deco building was removed from the main thoroughfares by a long and winding road that curved up through thick foliage. It looked picturesque, even palatial, but all of those beautiful trees were just more places an intruder could hide.

The chain-link fence was the same kind of fence they used to keep kids in school, which meant it could be tugged up from the ground far enough for a slim man to wriggle beneath without too much effort. He saw a number of motion detectors, and tried to overlay their parabolic arcs across the terrain, looking for blind spots. There were three he could see, though depending upon the angle of a fourth sensor there might well have been another.

Moving from one blind spot to the next would prove difficult, but it wasn't impossible.

"This is the ambassador's summer residence," Chaplin explained. "One of the safest buildings in all of Cuzco."

"And if you believe that, we're going to get along just fine," Stark finished for him. Blaine chuckled.

The building was built on two storeys. There were three balconies, one grand one that ran thirty feet along the front of the façade, the other two smaller day balconies aimed at catching the sun as it moved across the sky.

"How many rooms?" Blaine asked.

The question seemed to puzzle Chaplin.

"Eight bedrooms, several day rooms, utilities, study, kitchen and dining room, perhaps fifteen in total, plus a triple garage. Why?"

"The bigger the building, the more difficult it is to keep a determined someone out."

"Ah, I see."

"Alarm system?"

"Of course. A dual system. One silent alarm that goes directly to the police house, another that sounds in the British Embassy."

"Good. Response times?"

"I couldn't possibly —"

"Pretend you could," Stark interrupted. "Best guess?"

"Seven minutes, I suppose."

"That's a remarkably specific best guess. Good. Points of egress and ingress?"

"The main doors, of course. There's a door through the servants' quarters. The patio doors, and there's a side door through the garage, as well as cellar access."

"Five points of entry, not counting every window, or any of the second-storey access points." Blaine turned to Cutter. "The place is a sieve."

"How many people know you've brought the lad here?"

"A few trusted members of my staff," Chaplin said.

"A few being?"

"Mark Nolan, head of the Embassy Security, ex-SAS; Ed Schubert, the ambassador's personal secretary; and Niall Maybury, my number two here. I'd trust all of them with my life."

"Good, because you are," Stark said. He counted off fifteen paces to the left, turned on his heel like a duellist and measured off twice as many back. "There's only the one road in and out, right?" Chaplin nodded. "So we can assume that anyone looking to infiltrate without being seen won't come down the road. The most logical thing for them to do would be to leave their vehicle back before the turn off, which is what, two miles down the road?" Again Chaplin nodded. "As the crow flies, where's the turn off? Point it out for me."

Chaplin took a moment to get his bearings, then pointed down the hill into the trees.

"Are you sure?" Stark pressed.

Chaplin seemed to hesitate a moment then shifted his feet a couple of inches, moving the direction his hand pointed by nearly ten degrees.

"Good. Now take Cutter into the house. We'll sort out a distant early warning system."

"What do you intend?"

"Nothing too explosive," he promised, patting the rucksack. "Just a little something to tilt the balance of surprise back in our favour."

Cutter followed Chaplin into the safe house. Being out of the oppressive heat was a blessed relief. His white t-shirt clung wetly to every contour of his torso. As soon as they'd entered, Chaplin excused himself.

"A call of nature," he explained, and he directed Cutter through to the kitchen.

The house was almost cold, so extreme was the shift in temperature. The air-conditioning hummed audibly. There could never be silence in this country. It was either the constant chitter and thrum of cicadas and tree frogs, or the rumble of air-conditioning units battling the heat. In the absence of city noises — cars and the constant yammer of people — Cutter had expected silence, but remoteness brought its own sounds.

He stepped into the kitchen and closed the door behind him.

Jenny sat there nursing a glass of iced water. She looked up at him. He tried to read her eyes, but all he could think was that he was glad she was all right.

Glad.

That was such a *vanilla* word. It didn't convey an ounce of feeling to it.

"Are you okay?" he asked.

She nodded. "It's a mess, Nick."

"What were you thinking? You can't just kidnap a suspect from a hospital. It doesn't matter whether you think he is innocent or not. You just can't do it, Jenny. Lester's going to explode. And as much as I like the image, an exploding Lester isn't what we want.

"It's not like we can even claim plausible deniability. In the morning your face is going to be all over the news. Hospitals have surveillance cameras you know. An employee of the British government, kidnapping a murder suspect. How the *hell* are we going to explain that one away?"

"There's something going on here, Nick. Something bigger than us." She wasn't apologetic. She was frightened. That realisation quelled the anger he felt.

"There always is, Jenny."

"I think we were brought here to cover for something else." She looked over her shoulder to be sure they were alone.

"I'm sure we were, but we're here now, and we have to stop playing into their hands — whoever *they* are." Cutter reached across the table and took her hand, and for a minute he wasn't looking at two women, he was looking at one. Jenny Lewis. For all that she looked like Claudia Brown, she wasn't. She was a completely different woman with different strengths and different vulnerabilities.

"It will be all right," he promised. "I'm not going to let anything happen to you."

"I think they know," she said, the words barely a whisper. "I think they know about the anomalies."

Chaplin coughed politely as he entered the room behind them. Cutter didn't remove his hand from hers. He had no idea how long Chaplin had been standing there, or whether he had heard. He had to hope not.

"Where is he?" Cutter asked, doing his best not to appear startled or suspicious. "Where's Bairstow?"

"Upstairs, sleeping."

"I need to talk to him."

"That can wait, surely. Moving him has put quite a strain on young Cam."

"I don't think it can," Cutter said. "We need to be seen heading out to Madre de Dios tonight, and we have no idea how many pairs of eyes will be looking. Something happened to Cam out there, and I need to know what it was."

"We know what happened, Cutter. His brother was murdered, and he barely escaped with his life. My sole priority is sending him back to London alive. That's what Sir Charles has entrusted me to do."

"I understand, but I really need to talk to him."

"You need a lot for a scientist, Professor."

"I'm not the enemy here, Chaplin," Cutter said, doing his best to sound reasonable. Something about the man irked him. Hell, something was off about the entire situation. He wouldn't have put it beyond Chaplin to have engineered the whole thing, manipulating Jenny into this impossible corner.

He was glad he had had the presence of mind to send Jack Stark along.

"We're on the same team," he said firmly, "And we both need to remember it."

"Yes, yes, of course we are. The boy deserves to rest, that's all. You can talk to him later and ask him questions to your heart's delight. Right now, I don't know about you, but I'm hungry. Let's eat."

Cutter let it drop for the moment.

Chaplin had the cook, Marta, prepare a meal for all of them, setting a table for five in the dining room. While the preparations were being made, Cutter took the opportunity to explore.

The house itself was quite old. He wasn't sure how he would have described the décor — colonial chic perhaps? The wealth on display was positively vulgar. In the main foyer he found a huge Incan stone, fourteen feet in diameter.

Every inch of it was carved with gods, rivers, rituals, and impossible animals beautifully rendered by the mason all those hundreds of years ago. Each image in the stone was haunting and stylistic. The stone itself was almost certainly a unique relic, a priceless part of the nation's heritage. That it was hidden away in an official residence, like some piece of stolen treasure, was criminal.

Cutter traced the lines with his fingertips, wondering what memories were locked away within the ancient object. Had the Incas prayed to it? Had they pledged themselves in its shadow, becoming man and wife? Had it been used to mark off the seasons, recording the triumphs and tragedies of a people who had no words of their own for history? It could easily have been all of these things, or none of them.

Marble stairs led up to the first floor, worn down by the shuffling of the household's feet over the decades since the house was built. Earthenware vases sat in sconces measured out evenly along the rise, each filled with bright flowers that must have been changed daily, regardless of whether or not the ambassador was present.

The rooms were all similarly opulent, hiding away their own unique treasures. Cutter found himself admiring pottery and figurines, and reading along the spines of books lined up regimentally on shelves. The tapestries hanging from the walls were thicker and the colours more vibrant than the replicas hanging on the walls of their hotel in Cuzco.

He moved from room to room. The ambassador obviously had a taste for the written word. The library was filled with first editions of M.R. James and, under glass, faded copies of the Penny Dreadfuls that had first printed Dickens. There was a separate smoking room, with neatly folded newspapers and a rack of magazines from across the world. Surprisingly, the dominant language appeared to be German, with *Das Spiegel* taking pride of place on the table.

The study was unlike any other room in the house — a small slice of Regency England transported to the Americas. The room was dominated by dark wood. The central desk looked like something out of a Dickensian drama, the green-glass shade of a banker's lamp angling the light down onto a leather blotter. The books in this room were decidedly less fictitious in nature, consisting mainly of biographies of the rich and famous, from the diaries of Pepys to more modern recollections of David Niven and the various actors who had played James Bond.

He found a small box radio on the windowsill, and out of curiosity tuned it in to 87.6 on the FM dial. There was none of the tell tale interference that would have suggested an anomaly in the vicinity. Of course, that didn't mean the anomaly had closed, only that it was out of range of the receiver.

The desk diary listed a number of appointments for the coming week, including the Israeli cultural attaché and a representative from the World Bank. There was only one name Cutter didn't recognise: Mannfred Eberhardt. It was ringed in red, a few pages back. The entry pre-dated Nando's e-mail to him by almost a full week, which would place it right around the time Cam and Jaime were attacked.

He closed the book and headed back down stairs.

The SAS men had returned, and were sitting with Chaplin and Jenny. Cutter looked at his watch. By rights, the others ought to be on their way to the eco-resort now, but they would almost certainly still be waiting in the hotel for their return.

"I need to make a phone call," he told Chaplin.

"By all means." Chaplin indicated the handset on the wall, beside the huge industrial refrigerators.

Cutter took the receptionist's card from his pocket and dialled the hotel. She answered on the first ring.

"Hotel Del Prado. How may I help you?"

"This is Nick Cutter. I am staying at the hotel with the scientific expedition."

"Ah, yes, Professor. How may I help you?"

"I need to talk to one of my colleagues, Stephen Hart, if you can locate him."

"One moment please."

Her voice was replaced by more of that interminable Muzak meant to soothe the savage beast. Mercifully, Stephen answered quickly.

"Hello?"

"Stephen? It's me."

"Where are you?"

"Something's come up. I need you to make sure everyone gets out to the Madre de Dios reserve. Nando's expecting us this evening, and I don't want to raise any more alarm bells than we already have. We'll take a car out later tonight."

"Is everything okay?"

"Far from it, but we've got to make the best out of a bad job. I'm trusting you, Stephen." Then he remembered a loose end. "Have the guide and translator shown up?"

"No sign of them, but don't worry about it. I'll keep things together at this end. All this cloak and dagger makes you long for the old Permian era reptile, though, doesn't it?"

Cutter chuckled. "Yes, it does. How could you tell? On second thoughts, don't tell me."

"All right, I won't."

"Stephen, have Connor dig up everything he can find on black dogs. Use those gadgets of his for something useful."

"Will do. Are we still thinking borhyaenid?"

"Until it's proved otherwise. I'm going to talk to Bairstow. I'll fill you in when we get to the reserve tonight."

"Great. Travel safe."

"You too, Stephen."

He hung up. The others were looking at him expectantly.

"We'll meet up with them later. If we're going to keep up the pretence of being a scientific expedition, we'd better keep to our schedule."

"Makes sense," Chaplin agreed.

A little while later Marta the cook came through to tell them that the food was ready. To everyone's surprise, Cam came down to join them in the dining room. He was accompanied by a small man who introduced himself as Pilo, the ambassador's physician. Cutter couldn't help but wince at the extent of the young man's injuries. Pilo helped Cameron sit, then left them.

"Do you mind if we talk while we eat?" Cutter asked.

"Not at all," Cameron said. He moved uncomfortably in his seat, no doubt trying to find a position where one set of stitches or another wasn't been pulled apart. Half of his face was purple with bruises. In the candlelight it almost looked like the umbra of shadow, but it didn't shift even as the small flames flickered. "But who are you?"

"Sorry, sometimes I get too wrapped up in things. Cutter. Professor Nick Cutter."

"Do you work for my father?"

"Not really. I work for a branch of the Home Office. But I'm here on his behalf."

"Really? You're a long way from home, Professor."

"Likewise, Cam. Now, I understand that this might be painful, but I need to hear exactly what happened out there, in your own words," Cutter said.

Cam's bruised face twisted, at least until the pain made him stop. The memory was obviously one he would rather suppress. Where it sat on the table, his hand — Cutter saw — was clenched so fiercely that the knuckles had blanched bone white.

"Take your time," he said soothingly.

"I've told Alex everything already," Cameron said hoarsely, and clearly he hoped that would put an end to the questions.

"I know, and I am sorry, but sometimes just the simple act of repetition can bring back a detail that you thought you'd forgotten."

"A detail that would help a government scientist?"

"I'm sorry, Cam," Cutter said, genuinely. "But you'll just have to trust me."

"Fine," the young man said. He paused for a moment, breathing heavily, then continued, "We had made camp beside a ruined temple; we'd found it that morning but hadn't had time to explore it properly. It was so much bigger than any of the other temples we'd encountered. The earthworks beneath it had been excavated into a number of passageways and chambers. It was huge, so we thought it might be one of the main places of worship for the Incas, yet it had been so utterly reclaimed by the forest that it was hard to imagine anyone had set foot in it in a hundred years, at least."

"That must have been quite something to see," Cutter said, surprised at how genuinely excited he was becoming at the young man's words.

"It was incredible. It was why we came out here. Jaime was always into the buildings. He used to tease me because I was always more captivated by the social archaeology, reconstructing the lives of the people and the time, than I was in the old stones. This one might have been dedicated to Supay, judging by the pictorial representations carved into the crumbling walls. The rainforest is filled with these unexplored ruins that have been swallowed by the vines, the huge trees, and simply lost. So, we hadn't explored more than a quarter of it, if that, when our lights started to fail. We had other supplies back with the tents so we decided to make a few days of it, really explore the temple."

"I can understand that," Cutter said, and he could. It was precisely the same sort of curiosity that motivated so much of his life.

"We went back to the camp, cooked some food, joked about, you know, and then I had to go for a piss; curse of the small bladder. It was weird, though. I noticed how quiet the forest had become. I can't explain it — the rainforest is never truly quiet, there are always a dozen sounds out there, but suddenly there was nothing.

"No, that's not true, there was the sound of the rain, and something prowling in the underbrush. And then Jaime was screaming.

"I was too far away. I couldn't help him. By the time I got back to the fire he was dead."

Cam closed his eyes. For a full minute he didn't say another word. He was reliving his brother's last moments, Cutter knew. He had no choice but to leave the boy there, hoping that something would come back to him.

Something that would help them.

"Can you describe the creature that attacked you?" He had to resist the urge to feed the description to Cam. He needed him to remember, not to have a memory fashioned for him, then made real by the trauma.

"I don't... It all happened so quickly. I came back into the clearing. I remember seeing the fire scattered. It was very dark. I heard it before I saw it, turned and then it hit me."

"Can you describe it?" Cutter pressed.

"It was big. Powerful. A big cat or a dog. A jaguar or a panther maybe. I don't know. I only saw it for a moment, these huge teeth bared, snapping down toward my throat."

"That's good, Cam. That's good. Do you remember what the teeth were like? Were they small? Sharp? Long?"

Cam's eyes flared wide at the memory.

"They were too big for its mouth," he said, "more like tusks than teeth."

"And what colour was it, Cam? Can you remember?"

The young man shrugged, then winced against the flare of pain the careless gesture earned him.

"Like I said, it was dark. The fire was out. Black? Dark brown? I don't know. It wasn't the same, if that makes sense?"

"You mean it was mottled, or that there was some kind of pattern to it, like a leopard or a tiger?"

"Yeah, maybe," Cam said awkwardly, obviously unsure. Cutter decided to let it go for the moment.

"Thank you, Cam. That's great. You've done really well." But the young man continued.

"Its jaw was weird." The intonation of his voice shifted with the nature of his remembering. His eyes focused on something far away.

"Weird? How so?" Cutter asked.

"It was droopy, like it had a huge handlebar moustache."

Cutter nodded. He had what he needed — he was certain of it. The rather clumsy description had more in common with a Thylacosmilus, or pouch blade, than any jaguar or panther the pampas had seen in the last couple of million years. The creature was akin to the more common sabre-tooth cat, but not truly its kin, more an example of convergent evolution. Thylacosmilus was neither a cat, nor of the feline genus. It was actually a pouched marsupial. Indeed, it was more closely related to the opossum or kangaroo than it was any placental mammal.

And tellingly, the Thylacosmilus had left no known progeny. If it had indeed been a Thylacosmilus that had attacked Cam and his brother, it could only have come through an anomaly. There were no other explanations.

Cutter pushed his chair back and made to leave the table, then paused, mid-movement, and asked, "Just one last thing, Cam. You described seeing diamonds in the sky. What did you mean by that?"

"I don't know how else to describe it. It was as though the sky was filled with shimmering crystals, like it was a sheet of mirror that had just been shattered, and the shards hadn't fallen. They just spun lazily in the air, round and round, catching the light. It was the most beautiful thing I have ever seen. I wanted Jaime to see it, but when I took him back there, it was gone, as if it had never existed. That was what he was teasing me about before I left him to go for a piss. You know what the last thing he ever said to me was? He teased me about being a coward because I didn't dare touch it, and made some crack about me gearing up for a career in politics instead of archaeology. It just feels like... after everything, he didn't know me."

"Or perhaps he knew you too well, Cam," Cutter said, gently. "None of us are our fathers. We might share some genetic traits, but we're not clones. You're not necessarily genetically predisposed to be a pompous arse."

"You know father, then?"

Cutter chuckled despite himself.

"I know his type, and I know your type, Cam. You aren't your father's son, not in the way you fear. Your brother knew that, too. He knew you better than you know yourself. He was just teasing you. It's what brothers do. They prod the sensitive spots on our psyche because they get a laugh out of it."

He sat back down and finished his meal.

After a while, Chaplin and Pilo gently saw Cam back up to his room. Cutter drew Jenny, Stark and Blaine aside and spoke to them in an urgent whisper, "He saw an anomaly. There's no other explanation for it. Best guess, the creature is a Thylacosmilus, a Plio-Pleistocene predator. Nasty. Similar in many ways to Smilodon, the sabre-toothed great cat. It's not a cat though, there's no shared ancestry at all. Thylacosmilus was a marsupial. Still absolutely lethal. It was lord of the pampas for two million years."

"Which means we need to find that temple," Jenny said.

"Cameron's not fit enough to travel, so Stark, I want you to stay here and keep an eye on him. I trust this Chaplin character about as far as I can throw him."

"Okay, Professor."

"Jenny, Blaine, we're leaving tonight. With a bit of luck we'll not be too far behind the others."

"It's not exactly God's own country out there on the roads, Professor. It can get pretty hairy in the more remote territories, especially after sundown."

"I didn't think it was Surrey, Stark."

"Just drive safe, okay? You get lost and it's me who's got to sort out the search and rescue, when I should be wrapped up warm at home in bed, if you catch my drift."

"Consider it caught, but you do realise that it's not us who's shacking up with a suspected murderer?"

ELEVEN

Jenny excused herself and left the boys to it.

She went out into the garden with the handset from the cordless phone and dialled through the international router back to a number in England. She listened to the dial tone and the chirrup of the nocturnal insects out in the long grass beyond the patio, each vying for her attention.

"Lester," that faraway voice said.

"It's me," Jenny said.

"Do you have any idea what time it is? No, of course you don't — you're off gallivanting with Indiana Cutter, so why would you possibly worry yourself with the niceties of time zones?"

"We've got a problem here."

"Well, there's a surprise. What has the good Professor gone and done now?"

"It's not Cutter. It's Bairstow."

"Tell me, though I am quite sure I don't want to hear this."

"There's no doubt it was an anomaly he saw. Cutter thinks he might have been attacked by a Thylacosmilus, which, the best I can tell is a —"

"I'm well aware what a Thylacosmilus is, Jenny. Spend enough time with the geeks and some of their geekiness can't help but rub off on you. So we have a prehistoric big cat on the loose." She suppressed the urge to correct him. "We're talking needle in the proverbial haystack. One animal in thousands of square miles of trees. I fail to see the problem."

"Well, it's not quite as straightforward as that," Jenny said, wondering how to broach the subject. In the end she could see no alternative but to wade in. "There was a newspaper this morning, with the story of a village not far from where Cameron was attacked. The entire village had been wiped out. The locals are blaming El Chupacabra, but the local press is blaming Cameron. It was almost certainly a creature attack."

Silence, then Lester sighed down the long-distance line.

"It gets worse," Jenny said.

"Don't sugar-coat it for me, will you?"

"We couldn't leave Cameron in the hospital, Lester. After the attempt on his life, it just wasn't safe for him there. But we didn't have time to clear it properly."

"Hold on, Jenny. When I sent you with Cutter, what was the *one thing* I asked you to do?"

She knew full well what he had said. It was what he always said: *Keep it low key, keep it out of the press, hide the truth. Obfuscate.*

"Keep it low key," she said.

"Keep it low key. Exactly. What part of that order makes you think that kidnapping a suspected murderer from a hospital would be a good idea?"

"He didn't do it," Jenny objected.

"I don't care if he shot their Queen Mum, assuming they have one out in that heathen wilderness. Guilt has nothing to do with it. Just tell me they don't know you are responsible."

"Sir Charles' man on the ground claims he is taking care of it."

"Meaning they might know," Lester intuited, reading very much between the lines she was trying to blur.

"It's possible," she admitted.

Another silence.

"You disappoint me, Jenny. I expect this kind of thud and blunder from the Nutty Professor, but not from you."

"Sorry."

"Where are you now?"

"We are at the ambassador's summer house. We're heading out to the reserve tonight. Cutter's got the bit between his teeth now."

"I should call you home immediately," Lester said, and his voice was cold.

"There's an anomaly out there, Lester. No question. And there's at least one murderous creature out of time. Cutter's not about to pack up and come home now. And frankly, nothing screams diplomatic incident like turning tail and running. We're here as part of a zoological exploration. There is nothing to link it to Bairstow's disappearance. To come home now though, well, that not only leaves the anomaly wide open, it points the finger of blame squarely at us."

Lester sighed audibly. Clearly he was far from impressed with the options she had laid out for him. "Well, I suppose there's no real alternative, but for God's sake, low key, Jenny. Understand? Low bloody key."

Lester hung up. She did the same.

TWELVE

Chaplin wormed his way into the driver's seat.

When the guide and translator hadn't shown up, he had apologetically offered his own services, and found a dozen other reasons they needed him, right down to the fact that it was *his* car and they couldn't get out to the reserve without him.

"How very noble of you," Cutter had said, his Scottish accent laced with cynicism. More than ever he didn't trust the man, and he was certain Chaplin's motives included little or no thought of actually helping. "We're good though. We've got all the maps we could need, and Blaine's a dab hand with Spanish, it seems. So there's really no need for you to worry yourself."

But Chaplin wouldn't have it.

"Ah, well, I'm sure I can help in a dozen other ways," he said stubbornly. "Procedure and all that. I have irreplaceable experience using my silver tongue to get around the local authorities, should we encounter them." And as the discussion dragged on, they were losing valuable time. So Chaplin turned the key, and they departed through the gates.

It was almost eleven. Away from the compound, the night was absolute, the sky around them so very different to London, where it never truly seemed to be dark. Not like this, at least. Jenny gazed out of the window in the back seat. Blaine was propped up next to her, his eyes closed. Like all soldiers, the man seemed capable of falling asleep if ever there were five minutes of downtime. Cutter envied him that. He still had that hung-over-haven't-slept muzziness in his head.

Chaplin adjusted the rear-view mirror against the glare of the headlights of a car that had appeared behind them. Though there were still occasional dwellings alongside the road, proving that they hadn't left civilisation entirely, there were no streetlights, no cat's eyes in the middle of the road, nothing indeed to say where the road ended and the grassy ditch began. The further they travelled from Cuzco and the main commuter routes that led to the ruins and Lake Titicaca, the more inhospitable the terrain became.

They drove with the windows down. It made a pleasant change to have the night winds on their faces after the constant battering of daytime heat. It was a strange heat, quite unlike a hot day in London because of the humidity, which was up around 100 per cent at times, the air thick enough with moisture that Cutter could simply reach out to touch nothing, and bring his hand up to his face peppered with moisture.

After that, the night was blessed relief.

The quality of the roads changed, too. Fifty miles outside of Cuzco they were jouncing and juddering along dirt tracks that had no right to be called roads. These were strips of hard-packed dirt with the skeletal limbs of trees dragging down across them to form tunnels in the gathering forest, or narrow winding lama paths cut into the side of towering hills. Every few miles the track climbed, curving up the side of a slope to reveal the stunning vista below. With the sun down, the pale glow of the low moon — nearly full — bathed the tree tops with its silver, holding back the true dark of the night as long as it could. Occasionally clouds scudded across it, and the world around them disappeared. The black then was complete and utter.

The headlights barely penetrated twenty feet ahead. The car behind them fell further back, but still followed, and turnoffs became fewer and fewer.

The terrain edged beyond remote.

Stark's earlier wisecrack about God's own country couldn't have been further away from the reality; if there was anywhere on the planet that humbled a man more with its majesty and beauty, Cutter had never seen it, at least not in this epoch. It was untouched. Unspoiled. In some ways it was exactly like stepping back through time to a place before cars and skyscrapers, trains and roads and factories and pollution. It was a glimpse of something pure.

He could only imagine what it would be like in the full glory of the day. The scale of it was daunting, the huge expanse of trees spread out like another world beneath them.

Cutter leaned forward and turned on the radio, turning the dial through the frequencies. He let it linger a moment on 87.6 FM, then turned it off. He didn't need to hear anything more, the vague, haunting pulse of static was there. Somewhere out in that vast wilderness there was at least one anomaly.

"You'll get no reception out here," Chaplin said, adjusting his mirror again. The car had been with them for ten miles or more, occasionally annoying them with its full-beams lighting the inside of the SUV. All side roads seemed to have disappeared, though, so they were going to be travelling together for a while yet.

"I've got a few CDs in the glove compartment. Nothing stellar, some Creedence, Springsteen's *The River* for when I am feeling suicidal, Buena Vista Social Club, not sure what else is in there. Feel free to have a rummage if you want something to listen to."

"No, it's fine," Cutter said, content with the sounds around them already: the wheels on the makeshift road and the rush of the wind through the open window.

After a few more miles, the headlights disappeared from the side-view mirror. Nevertheless, Cutter refused to be reassured, and kept watch as best he could.

All of the paranoia that surrounded Cam Bairstow's current predicament had begun to distract him from the root cause of it. He had heard a story once about a woman standing in a river when a dead fish floats downstream. She takes it up onto the riverbank because she doesn't want it poisoning the water. A few minutes later a dead sheep floats by. She drags its carcass out of the water for the same reason. A little while later it's a cow, and the cow is followed by a dead horse. All day dead animals come floating by, and she's frantically dragging them out of the water, struggling to keep pace with the rotten corpses. A man comes by and asks her what she's doing and she tells him she's trying to keep the water pure so people in the villages downstream can drink it without getting sick. She asks him if he will help and he says yes, but instead of getting into the stream beside her and dragging all of the rotten carcasses out of the now red water, he walks off. She shouts after him, demanding to know where he's going, and he tells her he's off to find out who is throwing the animals in the river, and stop them.

It was a simple story, and so fitting of the way Nick Cutter lived his life. He wasn't interested in the corpses in the river; he was interested in how they got there. That was what mattered — the cause, not the effect.

Everything that was happening to Cam now was because of what had already happened — finding the anomaly and being attacked by the creatures that had come through it. Without that instigating event, he would never have been in the hospital, there would never have been the attempt on his life, and they would never have had to kidnap him for his own safety.

It all came down to the anomaly. If it had never opened, none of this would have happened. The rest of it was distraction.

The boy would always have to live with what he had seen. Cutter couldn't change that. Likewise, he couldn't resurrect the dead. All he could do was try to protect the living and stop any more corpses from being thrown into the river. That was where he needed to focus his attention, not on silly games of espionage. He was a zoologist, not a spy or special ops. He wasn't the kind of man who stood in the centre of the river, fishing out bodies.

"Come on Cutter, get a grip," he mumbled to himself. He knew what he had to do. That steeled his resolve.

From time to time, he thought he saw a gleam in the right-side mirror, but never enough to indicate that their travelling companions had reappeared.

The road eventually curved down through enough twists and turns to level out on the valley floor. In the glare of the headlights Cutter saw a signpost pointing the way to the Madre de Dios Reserve. Jenny was asleep in the back seat, now, her head lolling occasionally with the rhythm of the road. He watched her through the rear-view mirror. She had her arm across her stomach as though hiding the most intimate of treasures. Watching her felt wrong on so many levels, but he couldn't stop himself — and he didn't want to.

She was living proof of just how fragile "reality" could be, how every action they took had ripples and consequences. Only he understood that fully, yet he couldn't allow it to deter him from his path. *That way lies madness*, he knew.

Beside her, Blaine snored slightly.

Chaplin yawned, but kept his eyes on the road.

An hour passed without any conversation, each preferring the solitude of his own thoughts.

He saw lights up ahead, and the silhouettes of a number of cars parked between the dark shadows of fabricated huts and supply sheds. The dirt road doubled back, opening out into a driveway that led up to the main office building — though it was nothing like the modern offices of London. Quite the opposite, he realised, as it was caught fully in the glare of their headlights. Unlike the outbuildings, it appeared to have been reclaimed from the forest itself. With ample wood everywhere it was obvious that they had built the reserve's offices from the most abundant building material to hand.

There were six smaller Terrapins, four to the left of the main block, two to the right, though beyond those two lay the dark line of a large storage facility. From the brief glimpse he saw of it, Cutter assumed it was fashioned from sheets of corrugated iron, like an old World War Two aircraft hanger.

The lights were on in the main block, transforming its façade into a jack-o'-lantern face with a wide leering mouth and little beady eyes.

"Wakey wakey, sleepy heads," Cutter said to Jenny and Blaine as they swept around the driveway and pulled up beside the other SUV. The rest of the vehicles were a mixture of ancient Land Rovers and Range Rovers held together by duct tape and a prayer.

Nando stood in the doorway, an idiot grin on his backlit face.

Abby and Connor stood silhouetted behind him, both easily recognisable, Connor for his slight slouch and Abby for her waifish form. Lucas and Stephen, he assumed, were inside.

Chaplin killed the idling engine and the lights went out.

Cutter opened the car door.

As the dome light came on and he placed one foot on the gravel, he saw that Nando and the others had moved and were standing a few feet away from the car, their poses identical. It was almost as though he had blinked and — like some game of standing statues — they had rushed to their new positions.

He smiled. His bones were tired, deep through the tissue and into the marrow. It wasn't just that he hadn't slept in days, or that he had travelled six thousand miles from home. Cam's recollections of the ruined temple haunted him. The static hum on the car radio was just one more spectre to the army of ghosts that kept him awake.

He swung his other leg around and clambered out of the car.

The humidity here was worse by far than back in the city. The air was so thick as he breathed that he could have choked on it.

Nando stepped forward and clasped Cutter's hand, pumping it hard.

"It is good to see you, Professor." There was genuine gratitude in his voice, and relief and excitement and worry, all tumbling together. Cutter thought he sensed a note of desperation, as well, but couldn't put his finger on it.

"You too, Nando." The rear door of the car opened, and he turned. "This is Jenny Lewis, she's part of my team; Alex Chaplin, who works with the British ambassador in Cuzco; and Andy Blaine, a soldier alongside Lucas. So," Cutter said, brushing all niceties aside, "did you find something for me?"

"You better come inside, Professor. There's something I'd like your opinion on."

THIRTEEN

The 'something' was a single plaster cast of a print taken from the region where Nando had last noticed the peculiar silence.

It was no bigger than the bottom of the whisky tumbler Nando handed him, but it was far more potent a thing. Cutter took it and ran his fingers over the contours of the cast, lovingly feeling out the raised areas which corresponded with the pads of the Thylacosmilus' paw. A slow smile stole across his face. He looked up at Nando, who hovered over him.

"Talk me through it."

"It was out on an area we call Kon Ridge, after the god of the wind and rain because it is so exposed; the elements are all heightened there. The wind bellows and the rain lashes down. It is not an area for moderation in weather, or in anything. We were tracking the area, looking for anything out of the ordinary, like you asked, when Xavier, one of the more experienced rangers, found a carcass in the undergrowth. It wasn't the animal that interested us; it was the tracks that circled its body. As you can see by looking at the cast we made, it isn't a jaguar, though it appears to be some species of big cat."

Cutter peered at his old student trying to superimpose the boy he had been ten years ago over the face of the man he had become. It was difficult, but it wasn't impossible. That was one of the things about being a teacher, especially fitting when it came to dealing with the past; the brain had a way of fixing the lives of those you came into contact with into a single space and time, and didn't allow for the notion of ageing. In his head Cutter still saw the nineteen year-old Fernando Estevez, not the man nearing the end of his third decade. Salt-and-pepper grey had crept into his temples and his stubble, and there was a darkness around his eyes that hadn't been there before, but it was easy to see how the boy had become the man.

The work area in which they stood was compact, and segregated by mosquito nets from the steel-tube framed bunks in which the rangers slept. The nets hung like curtains around the individual carrels. There were six bunks, but only three desks, which made sense as most of the day the rangers would be out patrolling the territories, not cooped up behind a desk marking inventory or recording their observations on the migratory habits of the animals under their supervision.

The lazy ceiling fans revolved like something out of an Edgar Rice Burroughs novel, while a beetle scuttled across the hardwood floor. There was a mobile air-conditioning unit cranked up to full power, pumping out its BTUs, and a small portable radio beside a pile of mouldering paperbacks. Beneath the window there was a long distance radio-set and a solitary computer. The machine must have been ten years old and working on an obsolete operating system, yet it was a window into the world via a satellite uplink and a web-browser, which was more than most jungle outposts could boast, he suspected.

There was a large topographical map pinned up on the shortest wall, marked out with various coloured tacks and lengths of string. Cutter assumed they demarcated the individual territories and duty regions of the rangers. A territorial division made sense. A fly crawled across the heart of the rainforest, then took flight, drawn to the light bulb that was dangling on a raw cord in the middle of the ceiling.

"Jenny," Cutter said, "I think perhaps Mr Chaplin should be 'debriefed' while we get on with the boring science stuff. Outside."

She nodded. "Of course — come on Alex, come with me." Jenny held out an arm for him to link his with hers, and steered him outside, away from the conversation they had no wish for him to hear. She closed the door behind them. Cutter had no idea what kind of debriefing she would provide, but it would *not* involve anomalies and creatures that crawled out of the Plio-Pleistocene. That was good enough for him.

Connor lay on the nearest bed, still wearing his shoes, thumbing through one of the ratty paperbacks. Abby sat cross-legged on another of the beds, her back pressed against the logs of the wall. She looked dead on her feet as she listened to Nando describe the peculiarities of the place he called Kon Ridge. She crossed her hands and arms behind her head and leaned back, cracking the vertebrae in her spine one bone at a time.

"Sorry," she said, sheepishly, when all heads turned her way.

Blaine and Lucas lay top and tail on a thin mattress with their eyes closed, and Stephen leaned against a wall nearby.

"So, Nando," Cutter said, "why do you think this is what I needed to see?"

"Because in all my years monitoring the various endangered species in the region, this is the first time I have seen this particular set of tracks. I've encountered hundreds, probably thousands of different tracks out there, and yes, I have seen similar, but nothing the same as the ones we've cast."

"How can you be sure?" Cutter asked, laying the plaster cast aside.

"I do this day-in and day-out, Professor. I head a team of thirty rangers that are solely responsible for the monitoring of all of the species that live within our territories. We track their movements, even keep count of their number as a lot of these truly are on the verge of extinction. I know all of our animals, and these tracks do not belong to any of them. Trust me."

"I do," Cutter said, smiling. "Stephen," Cutter picked up the cast and tossed it under-arm to his assistant, "what do you make of it?"

"I'm not sure," Stephen said, but there was excitement in his voice. He turned the cast over and over again in his hands. "In terms of track pattern, it's not dissimilar from the jaguar, though these are more lozenge-like, as opposed to the pads of the ball-like phalanxes of the jaguar's paws. It's amazing stuff."

"Exactly," Cutter agreed. "So what does that mean in terms of our predator?"

"Same approximate size and build as a jaguar, but not a jaguar."

"Not a jaguar," Cutter concluded. "Would you concur, Abby?" Stephen handed her the cast. She took it, turning it over and over in her small hands.

"It's not a bobcat or a coyote, definitely not a panther, though actually it does bear a striking resemblance to the track of the so-called black panther. Taken in isolation, it's difficult to be sure. The track patterns give an idea of the animal's gait, size and weight."

"But your first impressions?"

"Not a jaguar," Abby said.

"Which is all well and good," Nando said, sounding somewhat confused, "but I don't see how knowing what something *isn't* actually helps us?"

"That's science for you," Cutter said, without the slightest hint of irony in his voice. "You can't prove anything, you can only disprove things. I'd be curious to match these tracks to the ones of the animal that attacked Cameron Bairstow."

"You think it is the same predator?"

"On the surface, there's a good chance," Cutter said, peering at the floor. "Cam reported the same sort of erratic behavioural patterns you noticed from the wildlife. I certainly wouldn't rule out a link just yet." He turned back to Nando. "We need to take a look at the scene of the attack, and at some of these places where you've noticed this eerie silence."

"Of course, we shall head out at first light."

"Great. One question before we all turn in: you know this area well, tell me, is there much in the way of Inca ruins around here?"

"Oh, yes. The Incas were a great building nation, and unlike the conquistadors that followed, what they built has lasted. Within thirty miles of here there are a number of burial sites. There is much yet to be discovered, too. That is the nature of Peru. So many of her treasures still lie hidden beneath the jungle. Only ten minutes walk to the south there are a series of anthropomorphic mummy cases lined up along a cleft in the hillside. They were only found last year, during the foundation of the reserve."

"Really?" Abby said. "I'd love to see them."

"They are quite impressive, especially when you consider they are made from vegetable fibre and mud. Amazing how they've lasted 600 years."

"They don't make 'em like they used to," Connor chipped in.

"It is amazing that so much is yet to be discovered," Stephen said. "Whenever I think about our world, I tend to imagine we've seen it all and done it all."

"That is the temptation," Nando agreed, "but the jungle is loathe to surrender her secrets. For a while at least there is still stuff out there waiting to be found for the first time. Can you believe we found an entire limestone city with, honestly, thousands of structures, just last month? Some of them are over forty-feet tall, and are built into a hillside to the east of here. We call it *La Ciudad de los Muertos,* the City of the Dead, because of the cliffs beneath it, where we discovered more than four hundred burial chambers. It is our hope that we might invite archaeologists to help us preserve the ruin. I do not know how much you know of the ways of my people, but our settlements often had very different purposes, and having explored these ruins myself, I believe we have discovered a holy city."

"How can you differentiate between a city of war and one of worship?" Stephen asked.

"It is in the cut of the stones and the geometry of the settlement," Nando explained. "Many of the stones used in Muertos possess what we call huaca, or a holy aspect. It is that aspect that leads us to believe it was a place of worship all those centuries ago. A city of warriors would be constructed in a very different manner. The geometry of war is different to the geometry of worship. War requires organisation and straight lines and conformity, worship is a celebration of the sun and the earth."

Stephen nodded.

Abby handed the cast of the Thylacosmilus print back to Cutter.

"How about a temple?" Cutter asked. "At least some part of it would be subterranean."

"There are many such temples in the jungle, Professor. My brother Esteban was close to one when he... disappeared," Nando said. At that, he glanced down, and his voice cracked. Cutter was surprised at the sudden change.

"I didn't know... When did it happen?"

"Soon after I contacted you for help," Nando explained, scratching at his eyebrow. His ever-present grin had disappeared. "He radioed in to base to say he was going to investigate a settlement. He had seen panicked villagers fleeing through the jungle. We lost radio contact. When I went to investigate, the settlement was abandoned. Esteban has not returned. Neither have the rangers who were with him."

"It doesn't have to mean..."

"I was in the settlement, Professor. I saw the animal tracks there again. Esteban had reported the peculiar cone of silence around him. I warned him to be careful. Now..." he shrugged and fell silent.

Being the one left behind was always the hardest. Cutter was struck by the similarity between young Bairstow and Nando, the resonances between their two very different lives.

He moved across to the window, indicating to Jenny that it was safe for her to return. A moment later she and Chaplin came back into the office.

"Tell me about the ruins," Cutter said, for want of something to say.

"Our ancestors were devout, if nothing else. Where they did not build up to celebrate the gods of the sky, they built down to celebrate the gods of the Earth. Thus there are tunnels beneath many of the structures."

"Ah, this might help," Chaplin offered. He took a crumpled piece of paper from his pocket and handed it to Cutter.

"What is it?" He smoothed out the wrinkles and read what appeared to be a series of co-ordinates.

"Cam and his brother were not completely hopeless," Chaplin told the others. "Before they set off into the rainforest, they recorded their intended location with the embassy, in case they got into trouble. It's fairly standard practice. Of course this isn't definitive, but it would give us a place to start looking. And Jaime is out there somewhere. I promised Sir Charles we would bring both of his sons home."

"I could kiss you," Cutter said, grinning. But in the back of his mind he was thinking, *It might have been nice if you had shared this information sooner.*

"I think that would involve a rather substantial lifestyle choice I'm not ready to embrace just yet," Chaplin told him, smiling wryly.

Cutter pushed himself to his feet and went across to the map to check out the grid-reference. Reading off the co-ordinates, he jabbed a red pin into the board.

They had a point-zero.

It might not have been precisely where the anomaly opened, but it was close.

"Any ruined temples in the vicinity?" He asked Nando, who came to stand beside him.

The diminutive Peruvian nodded. "It has many names. It used to be known as The Temple of the Broken Land, then it was renamed The Temple of the Four Winds. Today we call it the Temple of the Dead Earth, because it was buried in a landslide nearly a century ago. It was dedicated to the death god, Supay."

"Then we know where we are going tomorrow," Cutter said.

FOURTEEN

Cutter woke before dawn, to the chorus of the jungle.

The small cabin they shared was like a sauna. He lay in bed listening to the insects and the birds and the haunting elegiac whisper of the morning wind through the high trees. Despite the fact that he didn't move for twenty minutes, his skin was still bathed in a sheen of sweat. Finally he turned his head.

Stephen was asleep on his back, the sheets tangled around his legs. Connor lay like a dead man minus the chalk outline, arms and legs in a whorish sprawl. Abby was curled in a foetal ball, her knees up by her chin. Blaine and Lucas were already up. He listened to them goading each other on through a series of reps, crunches, curls and press-ups, after which they moved to the veranda, where they sat talking about nothing, their voices muted by the thin walls.

He had no idea where Chaplin was, nor Jenny for that matter.

They had a busy day ahead of them. He wanted to check out the tracks and the temple if at all possible. The answers were there, rather like so many of the Inca ruins Nando had described, hidden in plain sight, just waiting to be found.

He got out of bed and stretched, working the kinks out of his muscles. The mattress was old and thin and his lower back ached viciously. Still, a bed was a bed, and given the circumstances, any mattress was better than sleeping on a strip of carry-mat.

He dressed quickly, doing his best not to wake the others. He had no idea what the time was; the sun rose around four-thirty in the morning, and it had been up since before he had opened his eyes, so he guessed that it could have been anywhere between five and seven-thirty a.m.

In other words, time to make tracks.

He took a water flask from his backpack and swallowed a few mouthfuls of almost-hot liquid. Opening the cabin door, he took another mouthful, gargled and spat.

"Morning, Prof.," Sean Lucas said, without turning. Cutter had been about to ask him how the hell he knew who it was, when he saw his own reflection in the silver of the soldier's broad-bladed knife.

"Morning, Lucas. Have you seen our Mr Chaplin?"

"About twenty minutes ago. Said he was going to get some grub."

"Sleep well?" Andy Blaine asked. Blaine, he saw, was stripped to the waist and sheathed in sweat. The man was all tightly coiled muscle. His back was heavily tattooed with Celtic imagery, crosses within one huge endless knot that spanned his shoulder blades and went all the way down to the hollow of his coccyx.

"About as well as can be expected," Cutter replied.

Behind him, Connor yawned theatrically, rubbing the sleep out of his eyes as he stood and wandered out into the daylight. He took one look around him, muttered, "I feel like I've woken up in an episode of *Lost*." Then he wandered back into the more subdued semi-dark of the cabin.

Cutter stuck his head back inside and half-shouted: "Rise and sunshine, my lovelies."

The noise earned him a lot of groans, a few moans, and a disgruntled roll-over and sigh.

"We're leaving in twenty minutes," he continued mercilessly. "It's up to you whether you choose to sleep them away, or get something to eat, but if you pass out from dehydration, I'll not be carrying you."

More groans, a bit more theatrical this time.

Stephen sat up, his hair plastered flat to his scalp. His stubble had grown through thickly and was almost wild enough to be called a beard. Cutter rubbed his own chin. There was no 'almost' in it in his case.

"Nineteen minutes," he said ominously. Then he left them to it, and went in search of food.

Nando had set the table. It was nothing fancy — some cut meat, hard bread and butter, with fruit juice — but they had eaten a lot worse. Jenny, looking fresh and alert despite a hot uncomfortable night's sleep, was already there, along with a dishevelled-looking Chaplin, who was wearing the same sweat-stained shirt as the day before. Black rings circled his eyes. The embassy man — he didn't really know what Chaplin was. Not a bureaucrat per se, ex-military almost certainly. Perhaps special forces or MI6. Regardless, he hadn't slept, and he had taken on the aspect of a haunted man.

Cutter had wanted to send him back to whatever hole he had crawled out of, but Chaplin had remained insistent that he wasn't going home until they had recovered Jaime's bones. He had his orders, he maintained. Cutter didn't like the man, but he also didn't have a great deal of choice in the matter. Sir Charles had tied his hands, so he reluctantly agreed that Chaplin would remain with the expedition.

They would just have to be very careful what they said around him.

"Do you think we can find the remains?" Chaplin asked anxiously as Cutter sat.

What did he want him to reply? To lie blithely and say, "Yes, of course," or to tell the truth and say, "Not a prayer." Cutter took a slice of the hard bread and smeared butter across it. One advantage of the ridiculous heat and humidity was that it spread like melted margarine.

"We'll try," he said. It was the best he could offer without making a liar of himself.

Lucas and Blaine joined them. The stragglers came through while they ate, and for a while at least there was an air of normality about the table, as though they had managed to forget where they were, and why.

"This place really is in the middle of nowhere," Connor said, scratching at his scalp.

"My people have a saying," Nando told him, planting his elbows on the table, "with one little step after another we find we have travelled far." He looked every inch the superstitious tribesman with his shirtsleeves rolled up his forearms to reveal intricate tattoos. The black ink formed the face of a movie star on his left arm, caught in her familiar ooh-boo-be-do pose, and on the right arm there appeared to be some sort of sun or super nova, surrounded by mystical symbols that looked as if they had been culled from the Cabala and other ancient texts.

"We're talking about a lot of little steps here, Nando," Connor said.

"One or two," the Peruvian agreed.

"So, Nando," Cutter said, "how are we going to do this today?"

"Genaro Valdez, one of my rangers here, will travel with us out to the site so that you and your team can examine the tracks for yourselves. I have made arrangements for a local guide to join us later at the site of the temple, so that he can fill you all in on the legends and history of the place. He is a well-known and respected historian from the university at Trujillo, an expert in the Inca culture and the significance of their holy sites."

"Thank you," Cutter said. "That should be most enlightening." Inwardly he worried what might happen, should so many civilians witness an anomaly, but he decided to cross that bridge when they came to it.

"It will involve a lot of walking today, I am afraid," Nando apologised, "since the temple is very much off the beaten track. We cannot get a car any closer than about ten miles. Little steps."

"Ten miles?" Connor echoed plaintively, the exhaustion of every one of those little steps wrought in his voice. "Are you trying to kill me? A gun would be easier, you know? Less painful."

"It could be much worse, friend Connor. Many of our ruins are so remote that a visitor must walk for a day or two just to reach them. In comparison, a few miles is no hardship at all."

Cutter enjoyed Connor's expression as just the thought of walking for two days in the smothering heat of the Amazon drained all the energy from the young man's body.

"Chin up, Connor," he said, smirking. "Think of it as good exercise. Ask yourself, what would Luke Skywalker do?"

"Probably smack you around the head with a lightsaber," Connor grumbled.

Cutter chuckled.

They finished their breakfast and packed up what they anticipated needing; with a ten-mile hike on the cards, it was all about travelling light, taking plenty of water, energy bars and so forth, along with some essential equipment and emergency supplies.

It was ironic that their cover had demanded that they bring so much gear. After all, an expedition with no equipment was going to raise every curious eyebrow in Peru. But now that they were out here in the wild, everything needed to be light and easily transportable. And they didn't need to maintain the sham when there was no one to see them. Connor took his PDAs, as well as the handheld anomaly detector — a small receiver locked to the 87.6 FM frequency with a GPS screen display built in. It had enough battery power to last around three hours, so he took a single spare. If they needed to listen to the thrum of static for more than six hours, the odds were that they were going to be in trouble, and another battery wouldn't help all that much.

Cutter insisted that they each carry at least four litres of water. Given the extreme heat, they were going to shed all of that on the long walk.

Stephen was quiet, subdued even for his normal brooding self. Cutter watched him around Abby and Connor. He seemed ill at ease — *uncomfortable in his own skin* was the phrase Cutter would have chosen. It was a little sad to see how much of the old Stephen had been stolen by Helen when she left through that anomaly. He wasn't the arrogant young man he had been; the world had hurt him. It hadn't lessened him, though. Rather it had reshaped him.

The notion that a man was the sum of his experiences struck him again. Stephen was different because the world had treated him differently. He had loved and lost, and that old cliché didn't offer much in the way of comfort. He didn't talk about it, but who could he talk to, really?

Cutter? Hardly.

Connor?

Abby?

None of them were the kind of friends Stephen could turn to when he needed to share his burden, so instead he bore it alone. Cutter wanted to feel sympathy for him, but the very basis of their friendship had been impacted by the affair. No, Cutter couldn't bring himself to feel sorry for the man. He had brought it upon himself.

The SAS men, Lucas and Blaine, set about their own preparations with astonishing efficiency. They had been fully briefed back in the UK about the danger posed by any anomaly and what could conceivably come through. There would be no surprises for them. They stripped their kit down to a bare minimum, though both — Cutter noticed — remained armed. They weren't about to underestimate the hostility of the environment or romanticise the trek, as the others might have. They moved with the same kind of economy of gesture that marked them as men of war.

He wondered what passed through their minds as they stripped their pistol mechanisms down and cleaned out the barrels. Did they think of killing, or protecting, or nothing at all? How did they sleep, under such circumstances? How did they lie down? How were they not jumping at every sound and shadow? He couldn't begin to imagine their lives. He most certainly would not have wanted to share them.

"Have either of you checked in with Stark?" he asked, sitting down on his own bunk, unpacking and repacking his gear.

"Earlier this morning," Lucas said. "All quiet on the Western Front."

"That's good to know. One less thing to worry about."

"Bet he's chuffed to bits at having pulled babysitting duty," Blaine said, tugging the drawstrings on his backpack to cinch the top closed. He hiked it up onto his shoulders and effortlessly shrugged it into place.

"Least he's not walking ten bloody miles," Connor moaned. "Give me a hand would you?" He struggled to balance the pack and the bottles of water he had secured to it, while tying off the cord and trying to smooth down the canvas he had laid over the electrical gadgets to fend off the moisture in the air.

Cutter got up to help. "Multitasking at its most primitive, eh?"

"Something like that. Ten flippin' miles, Cutter. No one mentioned marathons when I signed up for this job."

"Connor, you do realise that a marathon is more than twice the distance?"

"Yeah, but it's only half as hot."

Cutter couldn't quite make the connection, but let it slide; he was sure it made perfect sense in Connor's head. Lots of things did that made little sense to the rest of the world.

"Let's get this show on the road, shall we?" he said.

To call it a road was an optimistic use of the word — it was more like a bridle path wending its way through ever-encroaching trees. Every dozen or so yards it was rutted or cratered and filled with sucking mud and overflowing puddles left over from the last downpour.

He didn't know the genus of ninety per cent of the trees, only that they were towering old sentinels. The group slowed to negotiate a fallen tree that had come down across the road. Cutter saw that it had more rings to its growth than most of the monuments in London could have claimed if stone had similarly marked the passing of time. That one dead tree put things into perspective for him.

At Nando's insistence, they had divided themselves into three of the battered old Land Rovers. The SUVs were fine for the mountain trails, but they weren't suited to the realities of the jungle tracks. Neither Cutter nor Chaplin were about to argue with him, no matter how much they might have liked the air-conditioned interiors. The SUVs looked the part and promised so much, but weren't truly all-terrain vehicles. The picture Nando had painted involved broken axles, ruptured sumps, tracks too narrow for the wider loads of the SUVs — what it all came down to was a series of long, bone-weary walks back to the reserve without adequate food or water, their transport abandoned.

The Land Rovers, on the other hand, were workhorses more than capable of handling the extreme terrain the Amazon had to offer.

Cutter rode with Jenny and Blaine, with Nando in the driver's seat. Chaplin drove with Abby and Connor, while Lucas and Stephen travelled with Nando's ranger, Genaro Valdez. They kept in constant radio contact.

"So tell me, Professor, why are you here?" Nando asked.

"Because you asked me to come," Cutter said.

"No, really?" His voice said that he wasn't going to be satisfied by anything short of the truth.

"Something in your email caught the interest of my boss." This time Cutter didn't look at him as he offered the explanation. He stared out of the window at the thick-boled trees and at the lichen that grew in their shade.

"But still, that is not enough to bring in the embassy and the army. I am not stupid, something is going on here."

"You're right. But I'm not sure I can tell you what."

"Secrets and lies," Nando said, as though he understood perfectly, and it disgusted him. "This is my life now. I work more with the government than I do with the animals, it seems. There are so many stupid regulations put on my job, even down to sectors of the rainforest that fall outside of our jurisdiction, where we are not allowed to go. What do they think they are hiding from us? The fabled cities of gold?" He laughed bitterly at that. "I live with secrets, fear not."

"Well, if I am right, before the end of today I might be able to show you something you have never seen before."

"That is something at least."

"I ought to warn you, though, that the next twenty-four hours are pretty much guaranteed to shake the foundations of everything you believe in as a scientist."

"You make it sound... intriguing," Nando said, and the disgust had been replaced by genuine curiosity. He decelerated suddenly to negotiate a deep puddle that had turned half of the track into mud. The Land Rover lurched away beneath them, throwing Cutter up hard against the restraint of the seat belt. In the back, Jenny and Blaine had no such security and were thrown about violently. Nando apologised profusely even as he hit another deep pot-hole in the track and had them grasping at the back of the seats to stop them from sprawling all over each other.

It took the best part of an hour, driving through the stifling heat and the cloying air, to reach the clearing where the rangers had found the curious tracks. Before they got out of the car, Nando cracked open a flask of water and passed it around. They each drank deeply, wiping their hands across their lips before they passed it on to the next to drink. Rarely had warm water tasted so good. He handed out small sesame seed and honey cakes, as well.

"Good for the blood sugar in the heat," he promised. They tasted a little like Baklava, sweet and chewy.

When they got out of the Land Rover, Stephen pulled Cutter aside. "We should warn them," he said under his breath. "They deserve to know what they might be going up against."

"And how do you propose to convince them that a Plio-Pleistocene relic might be stalking their jungle, Stephen?" Cutter responded. "How do you explain the entire ARC, in a nutshell?"

"I don't know. Just tell them," he pressed, but even as he did his expression said that it was a pointless exercise. They needed Nando to see for himself. The evidence of his own eyes would be difficult to refute. But still, they knew, there was something inherently wrong with not warning him about what they were likely to find out there in the trees.

"We can't," Cutter said. "We just need to do what we can to protect them, until the proper moment arrives."

"Ready?" Nando asked, joining them and placing a hand on his Professor's shoulder.

Cutter nodded.

He walked around and opened the Land Rover's trunk, then lifted out a sheathed machete. He fastened the belt around his waist, so that it hung like a sword, and then secured the bottom of the sheath with its leather ties around his thigh. He drew the blade with a flourish then re-sheathed it.

"Ready."

The sweat peppered his temples and cheeks as he trudged behind the rangers. Mercifully, the trees were not silent. The fauna was making itself heard with a vengeance. It was easy to see why they called the Amazonia the lungs of the planet. The sheer number of leaves from the canopy all the way down to the forest floor was incredible. So many shades of green and so many other colours, as well. Truly the jungle was alive.

He knelt, reaching out to touch a bright yellow orchid-like plant.

"I wouldn't if I were you," the guide, Genaro, said quickly, when Cutter's fingers were only an inch or so away from the thick velvet petals. "That one secretes an hallucinogenic residue through its stamen and leaves. The natives have been known to dry it out and smoke it to aid communion with the earth goddess."

"Ah, thanks," Cutter said, putting his hands in his pockets. Now that he was aware of it, he could just make out a fine dusting of powder that lay across the yellow petals. Without Genaro's warning, he would have taken it for nothing more dangerous or exotic than pollen. The others gathered round to take a closer look, and then they walked on in single-file. No one else reached out to touch any of the beautifully pattern-ed flora.

"The ecology of this region is an entirely different world, Professor," explained Genaro, walking ahead of him and pointing out a number of different plants. "That one there —" it appeared to be a clam-like plant, an oversized Venus flytrap "— is a flesh eater."

"No way," Connor said enthusiastically. "A flesh-eating plant? Like Audrey Two? That's *wild*. What does it eat?"

"People," Genaro said flatly, then seeing the look of horror on Connor's face, he burst out laughing.

"You're so gullible sometimes, Connor," Abby said, coming up behind them. "This isn't *Little Shop of Horrors* with its purple people eater from outer space."

Connor ignored her teasing, and resisted the temptation to correct her mistake.

"So what do they eat?" he pressed.

"Birds, mainly," Genaro explained, his chuckling slowly subsiding. "The plant secretes enzymes that break down the flesh, and allow it to dissolve into the leaves."

"Crikey. That's strangely cool." Connor peered at the plant with fascinated respect.

"Yes, it is," Cutter said. "But let's not test it out. Let's keep our fingers to ourselves, shall we?"

"Too right," Connor said, following his boss's example and stuffing his hands into the pockets of his shorts. "Are there a lot of dangerous plants around here?"

"Everything is dangerous, if you don't know how to handle it," Genaro replied. "You *are* aware of the food chain, no?" Connor nodded. "Everything subsists on something else. To protect themselves from extinction, species develop defence mechanisms. It is about survival. No species willingly becomes extinct. They scatter more and more pollens, lure creatures in with their bright colours, and snap their traps shut. It is how they survive."

"Sounds just like the West End on a Saturday night," Connor said. "Only without the prostitutes."

"Connor!" Abby cuffed him across the back of the head.

"All right boys and girls," Cutter said, "we'll have none of that."

"This way, Professor," Genaro said, leading them through the trees. He described the ecology and the history of the place as they walked. "The canopy of Amazonia is less studied than the ocean floor, did you know that? It's thought that it may contain half of the world's species. Over 500 mammals, 175 lizards and more than 300 other reptile species. As incredible as it may seem, one third of the world's birds live in Amazonia. And 30 million insect types."

"That's a lot of bugs," Connor said.

"More than one or two," Cutter agreed. "It really is a hell of a place."

"And it would all fall apart without the ants," Genaro said. "Leafcutter ants, that is. They prune away about a sixth of all the leaves, stimulating new growth in the process. The dead leaves break down and feed the soil. It's all amazingly self-sufficient."

They followed the ranger as he stepped over a thick tangle around the trunk of a tree. Most of the roots stayed very close to the surface, rather than burrowing down deep in search of nutrients. The loam on the top layers of soil was fed by the decaying vegetation, yet there was very little goodness to be found beneath it.

"It's hard to believe that more than half of it has been destroyed in the last fifty years," Cutter said, looking up the length of the almost leafless trunks at the thick canopy above.

"Criminal, is what it is," Nando said vehemently, joining him. "Across the world 200,000 acres of trees are burned every single day. That's 150 acres every minute, or two-and-a-half acres a second being stripped from the earth."

"Jesus."

"He has very little to do with it — they only made one cross to nail him up to," Nando said solemnly.

"Not when you think about it," Connor disagreed. "I mean, how many Catholics are there with crucifixes on their walls and —"

"I don't think we can blame religion for the deforestation of the Amazon, Connor," Cutter interjected, mildly amused. "It's got more to do with charcoal burning for industrial power plants, and deforestation to create space for cattle farming, just to meet the hunger pangs brought on by the sight of the Big Yellow M. Logging, mining, and other demands from our so-called civilised society."

"Yeah, but I was just saying. When you think about it, with all those icons, that's a lot of wood just to crucify one man."

"I'll give you that," Cutter said.

"Well, you better enjoy it now, because it'll all be gone by the time you retire," Nando told Connor. "At the current rate of deforestation, we're looking at no more forest by 2050. Sounds a long way off, but it's only forty years. We're losing around 150 species of plants, animals, and insects a day."

"Holy shit, but that's —"

"Genocide," Genaro interrupted. "For want of a better word."

"Oh, no, I think that word is just fine," Cutter agreed.

"In the time of my ancestors, ten million people lived in this forest," Nando explained. "Now, across the millions of acres, we have less than 200,000 making their homes here. The tribes are dying out just like the insects and the plants. It is the brave new world. That is why I came back here, rather than taking a job in a zoo in England. I wanted to do something. I felt the call in my heart."

"I can understand that," Connor said.

"People do not seem to understand that the plants are our salvation, far more than merely the providers of air. New drugs for AIDS, cancer, diabetes, arthritis and Alzheimer's come from plant-derived sources. Fully twenty-five per cent of all drugs are derived from rainforest ingredients, but scientists have barely tested one per cent of the plants our industries are destroying. The cures are all here, all around us — my people have always believed this. I am sorry, this was not the kind of tour I intended to give you. It just depresses me to think of all that we are losing every day of our lives."

"No need to apologise, Nando. We owe a debt to these trees, and we are not repaying it with kindness."

They trekked on silently, each of them wrapped in his or her own thoughts. Within a few minutes, however, they were gathered around looking down at a series of Thylacosmilus tracks. The ground was covered with them, as though the creature had circled and circled before finally dragging down whatever had drawn it to the clearing.

"There's more than one," Stephen said, crouching down and pointing out the subtle size difference between some of the depressions in the soft mud. Cutter leaned forward to inspect the indentations, feeling out the marks with his index finger. Stephen was right, they were substantially different depths, though that could have been accounted for by a shift in weight distribution; perhaps the predator had entered the clearing at a run, and then slowed. *Prowling*, he wondered.

"How many more do you think there are?" he asked.

"Hard to say, at least one more, look." Stephen scraped away the mulch of fallen leaves from around a single set of tracks. "Judging by the distribution, I'd have to assume this one was moving at a pace — look at the grouping of them. But over here, not only are the prints themselves slightly larger, they sink deeper, as well."

"Couldn't that just be because the creature stopped running?" Abby asked, echoing Cutter's initial thought.

"Possibly, but I am inclined to say no."

"Why?" Cutter pressed. He followed the line of tracks, trying his best to separate one set from the other.

"See, here, the weight distribution is different. Let's assume no two creatures walk exactly the same, this one is putting more of its weight on the rear of its paws than the other."

"But again, couldn't that just be down to the fact that it's running?"

Stephen shook his head.

"No, not really. That's not how it works. You see, you have a stride pattern, a natural way of moving. Fast or slow, it doesn't matter, you'll inevitably distribute your weight in the same manner."

"Really?" Connor asked. "What about if I'm walking on tip-toes?"

"Then you'd look like an idiot," Stephen said. "Abby running will leave a different indentation to Connor tip-toeing like an idiot, to Cutter, to me. I'm taller, but more muscular, so there's more weight distributed across a smaller surface area."

"Excellent," Cutter said. "Then, I'd say there were at least two sets of tracks here. One male, one most likely female."

"How can you possibly tell the sex?" Chaplin asked, moving away from the soldiers and Jenny to question the scientists.

"I take it you weren't listening to Stephen, Mr Chaplin. Weight distribution, size, it all reflects in the indentation left behind by the animal's track."

"Impressive," Chaplin conceded.

"Here," Stephen said, "once it slows from the run —" He pointed to a place where four prints appeared remarkably closely together, and then again, some distance away where the same grouping of four occurred, then beyond that, where four became two matching pairs. "— the stride breaks into a more even gait."

"And that tells you it's a male? Or a female?" Chaplin asked, still puzzled.

Stephen laughed.

"Not at all. That tells me it stopped running and started walking. Prowling the clearing most likely. Whatever it was hunting stood pretty much exactly where we are."

"Well, isn't that a comforting thought," Chaplin said with a visible shudder. "So how do you tell the sex?"

"The males and females of most species have slightly different tracks, it's quite easy to see the differences when you know what to look for. Especially when the prints are so well defined."

"Ahh," Chaplin said, still obviously none the wiser.

"Hey, guys, this is interesting," Abby said, standing up suddenly and stalking across the open ground. She pushed through the press of branches and tangle of vines. "There's something here," she called back as the undergrowth closed up around her to swallow her from view.

Cutter was the first to follow. She slowed, making less noise.

"Can you hear that?" She whispered over her shoulder as he neared. He had to listen hard, but he could. It took him a moment to isolate the sound, and work out what it was he was hearing.

Flies.

He nodded and unsheathed the machete. Knowing what they were going to find long before they found it, Cutter hacked away at the trailing vines that tangled to block their way. The razor-sharp blade whistled as it sliced through the air, hammering home hard into the thick meat of the vines. It took three or four hacks to cut through the thicker tangle, one or two to sheer through the individual vines. He pushed his way forward, deeper into the belly of the underbrush, until he stood over the carcass of a sloth. The animal was most assuredly not resting, nor conserving energy. Its skull was intact but its eyes were glazed over in the blank stare of death. More horrifying was the way the skin had been ripped to shreds so its killer could feast on its warm wet insides.

Flies swarmed around the dead animal. Its carcass was alive with writhing movement where white maggots squirmed.

Abby backed away from the dead animal, her hand over her mouth as she spun and dry-heaved. Cutter stood over the carcass for a moment longer, then knelt, ignoring the pustular maggots to examine the damage that had killed it. The manner with which the animal's insides had been ravaged coincided with the attack mode of a jaguar or a panther or similar big cat.

But equally, it matched perfectly what he would have expected from a Thylacosmilus attack.

FIFTEEN

Stephen knelt, examining the tracks again. He hadn't followed the others into the underbrush.

That made six unique imprints by his reckoning, which meant they weren't following a single predator, but rather a pack. The thought sent a shiver of dread through his body.

He licked his lips. His tongue rasped like leather across the chapped skin. His throat was parched. He could taste the moisture in the air, but couldn't seem to get any of it into his body. Grunting, he shucked off his pack and pulled out a bottle of water. He uncapped it and swallowed gulp after gulp, breaking all the rules of hydration by surrendering to his fearful thirst. With more than half of the litre downed in a matter of seconds, he wiped off his lips, recapped the bottle and stuffed what little water remained back into his pack.

"Bad news," he said, as he saw Cutter emerge from the smothering press of vines.

"Tell me?" Cutter said.

"We're not looking for one critter here."

"How many?"

"Six by my count," Stephen said.

"Six? Oh, God."

"Yeah. What did you find back there?"

"Nothing good. The carcass of a sloth. Its insides had been ripped out."

"Which is consistent with what we know about the hunting behaviour of the borhyaenids."

Cutter nodded.

"I'm all for going home any time you guys want," Connor offered. "Just so you know."

"That doesn't feel like such a bad idea right now," Stephen said.

"Nando, are there any settlements around here?" Cutter asked. The notion hadn't even occurred to Stephen, but now that it had been voiced, he felt that shiver of dread seep into his blood and freeze it in his veins. He looked at the Peruvian, willing him to shake his head.

"The nearest is maybe fifteen minutes away as the crow flies."

"Fifteen minutes is far too close for comfort," Cutter said.

Stephen ran the numbers in his head; a big cat could travel anywhere between thirty and sixty miles an hour, in short bursts. A pack of hungry predators catching the scent of fresh meat could stalk their game patiently for hours. No settlement so close was entirely safe.

Blaine asked the question that was on all of their minds.

"Is it in the same general direction as the temple you're taking us to?"

"Very much so," Nando confirmed.

"That's not the best news I've heard today." Cutter wiped the sweat from beneath his eyes. He looked slightly manic, with the machete hanging loosely in his grip.

"Thank God the trees cut out most of the wind. Keeps the scent from carrying too far." Stephen offered.

"Let's hope it's enough."

Following a warning look from Jenny, Cutter drew Connor to one side, away from Nando, Genaro and Chaplin. "Check the anomaly detector."

The burst of static pulsing told them all they needed to know.

The sweat clung to Connor. His shirt was saturated with it. The dark stains from under his armpits reached all the way down to the waistband of his shorts. He shrugged. The cloth didn't move with the gesture. Sweat trickled down his calves. Even his socks were soaked through. It felt as though he were walking on water.

He knew what he must look like — a rebel without a clue, dressed up in his big brother's cast-offs.

He trudged along behind the others, trying to take everything in; all of the colours and scents and sounds. He put the small detector in the side pocket of his cargo shorts. Nervous energy tingled through his skin, prickling with life.

According to Nando, the village was just over fifteen minutes walk away, down a steep decline. As they peered in that direction, they could see that a mist covered the valley.

The anomaly detector had fallen silent long before they reached the settlement, which meant one of two things. Either the original anomaly had closed, or they had moved out of range of it. He knew which one he would have put his money on. Given that the maximum radius for the detectors seemed to be somewhere shy of a mile, it was likely they had just moved out of range. Without consulting a map, he couldn't be sure, but he suspected all of the readings he had taken lay along the same vector. He tried to picture it in his mind, using the map he had seen on Nando's wall to frame his reference.

He had been toying with an idea about the anomalies for a while, but didn't dare broach it with Cutter, at least not while he was in the mood he was in. It was one thing to detect and play storm chaser with the anomalies, but shouldn't they be looking for ways to control them? To hold them open, or more importantly snap them closed? It was only a step away from being able to open them themselves, removing the risk that an anomaly would open, a creature come through — from the past *or* the future — and become stranded out of time.

It was all very sci-fi, but it made sense to him that they should at least be exploring the possibility. He knew exactly what Cutter would say though: it wasn't their job to play God. Scientists didn't make things happen, they observed, they recorded, they discovered, but they didn't make things happen! And that was the crux. If they gained control over the anomalies and learned how to open and close them at will, what price would be paid for their discovery? What politico or military genius wouldn't want to tear a hole in the fabric of space and time, to put right what once went wrong?

He shuddered at the thought.

Connor wanted to believe that for once — just once — they could do something good that wouldn't be turned into something awful.

He was brought up short from his mental rant by the sudden curious absence of noise. He hadn't noticed it at first, with the others blundering through the undergrowth, but as he had fallen behind he had become more and more distant from their clumsy feet and hushed chatter.

He stood there for a moment, eyes wide, knowing exactly what the silence meant. He held his breath, listening desperately for any out of place sound, any noise that would tell him he was panicking over nothing.

But in the thirty seconds he stood stock still, there was nothing.

He started to run, shouting "*Cutter!*" as he blundered through the undergrowth, chasing the others. "Wait for me!" He slapped aside trailing branches and thick leaves, looking about frantically for the predator that had driven the wildlife away.

Breathing hard, he ran blindly into the back of Stephen, who grabbed him.

"What is it? What happened?"

"No noise!" Connor gasped, trembling as the adrenalin pumped through his system. "Listen!"

Everyone fell silent, caught suddenly in the preternatural silence of the empty trees.

For a full minute they were shrouded in complete and utter stillness, not even the whisper of the wind through the high canopy to conjure a rustle and break the silence. Then a deep-throated growl rumbled through the press of trees.

They weren't alone.

Connor heard the hunger in the growl, and wanted desperately to pretend he had imagined it.

The growl was echoed on the other side of them a moment later. The sound resonated chillingly inside Connor's heart. He felt his pulse trip alarmingly and his vision sway with the shimmer of heat. He closed his eyes. The growl became a roar and was followed by a scream that sounded too human to be anything else. It was a blood-curdling sound, drenched with fear and hopelessness.

He fumbled the anomaly detector out of his pocket and turned it on; there was no blat of static, no tell-tale pulse of an anomaly.

"Cutter?"

"What is it, Connor?"

"I really want to go home now."

"We're not its prey, Connor," Cutter said, sounding almost calm.

A second scream sounded, closer, but with the trees effectively reducing their visibility down to a few yards, it was impossible to say how far away it really was. All Connor could think was that it wasn't far enough away. And then the reality of the screams hit him and he knew, and felt sick with the knowing.

Without thinking, Connor started running again — this time toward the screams.

"They're at the village!" he yelled over his shoulder. "Come on!"

He didn't wait to see if the others were following him; he knew that they would.

The creatures came out of the jungle, shrouded in death and darkness as they bounded into the narrow paths that lay between the adobe huts. At first they could not be seen, only heard, like ghosts emerging from the mist, and then they solidified into the stuff of nightmares. These great powerful beasts, bounding on all fours out of the thick white fog, huge jaws tearing into the soft flesh of the frightened villagers.

There were screams.

There was blood.

There was death. Over and over, there was death.

The beasts roared, herding the living toward the well in the centre of settlement.

They ran, but there was nowhere to run to.

Instead, they died as the beasts fell upon them, rending flesh and bone in vicious and bloody mouthfuls.

The sound carried strangely up the hill. It wasn't only that it made the cries sound closer than they were; nor that the weird acoustics seemed to amplify every sound, folding in on itself as it rose. With the high mist beginning to settle around the peaks above, and swell across the bowl of the valley below, robbing them of dimensions and points of visual reference, sound became their only guide.

And sound lied in ways that Cutter could never have imagined.

The path from the Land Rovers had led them through felled trees and storm-torn deadfall, through thick gorse and clogging weeds, always on a steady decline, before suddenly dropping away beneath their feet. Connor stood on the edge looking out over forever. Cutter moved up beside him.

The world fell away beneath them, hundreds of feet down to the valley floor of treetops and the ice-blue meander of a river. It was a spectacular hidden piece of the geography of the world, but he couldn't begin to savour it. The cries of the dying clawed up the hillside from the area below, and there was no quick way to get there that didn't involve plunging hundreds of feet straight down.

Across the great divide the hills became true mountains, their stone faces harsh and jagged as they stabbed up into the firmament of sky. The landscape was raw. Elemental. They were like children's drawings of mountains. They rose and fell sharply, jagged teeth in a gap-toothed smile.

The group took off along the edge, no longer running. The rarefied air burned in Cutter's lungs. There had to be a way down, he knew, but the question was, how far away was it? Too far, and their weapons would be useless to the screaming tribesmen.

Suddenly the screaming stopped.

Cutter wanted desperately to believe it was because of the peculiar acoustics of the mountainside, but he knew in his heart it meant that the dying was done. He wasn't a fool.

The edge crumbled beneath his foot, forcing him to back away.

"Connor, come on," he yelled, grabbing the younger man by the arm and dragging him away from the drop. "It's too dangerous."

"There's got to be a way, Cutter," Connor said, pulling away so forcefully his momentum almost carried him out over the edge. Cutter refused to let go. He dragged Connor back toward the safety of the trees. The fear in the young man's eyes broke his heart. He knew what they were going to find, and still he was desperate to get down there and help people who were already dead. The size of his heart and its ability to suffer for others spoke volumes about the usually flippant research student. Cutter grabbed him and held him.

"There's nothing we can do," he said, hating himself for saying it even though he knew it was the truth. "You are a good man, Connor Temple. You've got a good heart. But this, this goes beyond heart and courage into a world of injustice that even the biggest heart can't conquer. I'm sorry. I'm so very, very sorry."

Connor said nothing.

He didn't need to.

There were times when words could never be enough. He held on tight to Cutter.

Nando and Genaro found the way down.

It was all wrong.

The oppressive silence remained, the forest holding its breath.

Everything was off-kilter, from the absence of the bird calls to the bubble and splash of the river. They knew they were walking into a graveyard. And, Cutter felt sure, the creatures were still there. It had only taken them five or six minutes to scramble down the hill. The Thylacosmilus would still be feeding, gathered around the dead in a pack, savouring the meal. He trod softly through the undergrowth, placing his feet carefully on each narrow ledge and strip of stone that had been carved into the slope. Beyond the ladder of stone there was dirt and weeds and long grasses that rolled down toward the basin below. The wind whistled all around as he skidded and slipped and stumbled down the steep slope. It sounded like the Devil singing.

He could see smoke from the low huts where cooking fires still burned, then the dry reeds of the roofs came into sight and the mud and vegetable fibre walls themselves. And finally, the bodies.

Cutter stopped dead in his tracks as he reached the first.

The hanging mist shredded to reveal a crystalline sky. The light streamed down like something holy, bathing the slaughter in a radiance that was almost perverse for its beauty. Cutter stood in a field of gold looking down on one of the most shocking and brutal images he had ever witnessed. The juxtaposition of ugliness and beauty made him feel sick to the bone.

He could not tell whether the body was male or female, so extreme was the damage.

He knelt beside it.

Like the sloth, the body had been split from stem to sternum, guts spilled like some vile lesson in the secrets of anatomy. There were no eyes left to close.

Cutter saw Connor on his knees, head down, heaving into the long grasses. Stephen stood beside him, and a step behind. Abby knelt beside him, drawing him into a comforting embrace. She rocked him slightly, whispering soft words to soothe him.

Neither Blaine nor Lucas stopped. Instinct took over. They drew their weapons. There was a brutal economy to the sign-language that passed between them. Lucas gestured right, then left, then brought his finger around in a small arc — *you go left, I'll go right, sweep the village and meet back at the centre.* Blaine nodded, and together they broke rank and ran into the spectral heart of the village.

Nando and Genaro drew their own weapons, but did not follow. Strange expressions played across Nando's face. *He's probably wondering if this is what happened to his brother Esteban*, Cutter guessed. Unfortunately, it probably was.

"There's no need. They're gone," He said, meaning the Thylacosmilus or whatever predator had slipped through the anomaly, though he might as easily have been condemning the villagers.

Nando unclipped the radio from his belt and spoke into it rapidly. His voice was greeted by a burst of static, and then a voice barking what might have been commands or questions, it was impossible to tell.

Cutter caught wind of a peculiar scent on the air; something out of place and quite unlike anything else he had smelled since they entered the forest. It was a potent and intoxicating fragrance that seemed to somehow inhabit his lungs as he inhaled it. Yes, that was the word for it, *inhabit*. He didn't merely breathe it in, it in turn breathed him in. It took him a moment to realise what it reminded him of. Burnt cookie dough. It wasn't a fragrance he expected to encounter in the middle of the Amazon.

He continued down the short slope to the settlement proper. There were no trees now. Ahead of him he saw a hand-pumped water well, the body of a woman hunched over it. Her legs had been severed by powerful jaws. It was a mess. Blood pooled around the foot of the well. Cutter stared at the tableau. It seemed almost artfully arranged, as if to strike fear into the hearts of those who stumbled upon it. It was more than a killing, it was a promise that so much more death waited beyond it.

And there were more bodies.

Twenty.

Thirty.

The exact number didn't matter. There were too many of them for Cutter to make sense of.

The smell of burnt biscuits was almost overpowering now.

He had seen death before, of course. From the intimate grief of Ryan and Tom, to the more abstract loss of strangers unlucky enough to be in the wrong place at the very wrong time. He had visited desecrated tombs, crept through the crypts beneath Vienna, and seen the thousands upon thousands of bones piled one on top of another. It wasn't like the kids' nursery rhyme. There the thigh bone connected with somebody else's skull bone and the ankle bone connected with a wrist bone and back bone and so many other bones that the notion of identity lost all meaning.

This was different. This was new death. This was fresh, and on a scale that beggared understanding. He had heard them screaming. He knew he would never forget that sound.

Cutter stumbled into the centre of what had been a thriving community only an hour before. Now it was a ghost town in the most horrible and tragic sense of the word. The men hadn't had time to defend themselves from the sudden ferocity of the creatures' attack. They had run out of their homesteads wielding whatever they could lay their hands on, to meet the predators so intent on their doom.

Still, it was all wrong.

He wrestled with the things he saw, trying to make sense of them against what he knew, or *thought* he knew.

Everything about this slaughter was wrong. Cutter could read incredible organisation in the scuffed tracks. There were signs aplenty of blood frenzy, but there was also evidence of awesome restraint. It was hard to stand in the middle of so much blood and think of the word restraint when looking at the slaughter, but it was evidenced everywhere. The creatures hadn't given over to a wild mêlée; they hadn't revelled in the corpses, feasting on the flesh. They had killed and moved on, killed and moved on. It was ruthless and efficient and utterly wrong.

This death did not fit the pattern he understood. It was more like the killing spree of a mass-murderer. Beyond the blood and the gore it was disturbing on a psychological level. He had pegged the predator as a relatively predictable hunter-killer. The scene around him shifted that perception alarmingly.

And then there was the smell, the burnt cookie dough. It didn't fit with the primitive surroundings, the tribesmen or the predators. The fragrance nagged away at him, sickly sweet as he breathed it in.

There were survivors. Somehow that was the worst of it. Seeing them cradling the bodies of the dead, weeping uncontrollably, their simple world in tatters. Walking between them as he moved from house to house, Cutter could not help but share their grief.

He saw Jenny walking toward him, tears staining her cheeks. She looked like a little girl as she held out her arms for him, sobbing. Cutter took her in and held her close, sharing her emotions instinctively. *Normal people were not equipped to face such mindless tragedy.* She shuddered against him. For a moment her natural musk masked the burnt biscuits.

She sobbed into his shoulder, then pushed him away, wiping at her eyes and — as quickly and as completely as that — the vulnerability was replaced by practicality and efficiency.

"We should bury them," she said.

He didn't know what to say to that. It made sense, in the most pragmatic of ways. They did not need thirty bodies coming back to haunt them. Bodies seldom stayed hidden, it was one of the immutable laws of the universe; corpses bobbed to the surface of the river or were dug up by dogs in copses of trees. But out here it was different. The entire village, houses, bodies, dreams, lives, loves and hopes, angers and vendettas, could simply disappear if enough dirt was thrown over them.

They had seen the alternative on the front page of the newspaper the day before. Nothing would be served by more sensationalism, save the budding El Chupacabra industry. Low-key it most certainly was not.

And Cutter could imagine Lester picking up the memo, reading through the recitation of events, and the paroxysms of apoplexy. Lots of ranting and raving and tight gestures as he wanted to lash out but refused to lose even that much control of himself.

Burying them made sense, not least because it was the right thing to do.

"We should," he agreed, "but it's not our place. They will mourn the village and bury their dead."

Blaine came back. He had talked to one of the women, as best he could. She told him the story of the attack. The animals had swept down out of the trees and through the village, killing occasionally and herding them with ruthless efficiency toward the well, where the slaughter began in earnest. He shared the story with the others. There was blood on his hands from where he had handled the bodies. Lucas joined them from the other direction. Similarly, he shook his head. Then something caught his eye and he went down on one knee to examine the dirt.

The air was thick with the tang of blood and the filthier smells of death. The bodies would turn quickly in the heat, and stink like rancid meat.

Cutter tried to think it through: the predators had come not as primitive hunters but as a force as elemental as the death they brought with them, surging out of the trees. Between Blaine's story and his reading of the tracks, they had hit the village from left and right, driving the frightened tribesmen like sheep. He could visualise it clearly, the powerful creatures descending upon their frightened prey, the panic.

But as his mind began to picture the frenzied attacks of a jaguar or panther, the rending teeth of a sabre-toothed tiger or the crushing power of a Thylacosmilus' claws, he had to stop. Not because it was too bloody or vile, but because the attack hadn't been like that. It had been dispassionate, almost humanly calculated. It seemed instinctive, like any predator attack, but something about the nature of the violence, the heightened aggression, made it appear certainly not animalistic in nature.

What could have caused a primitive predator to function in such an uncharacteristic manner?

He wiped the sweat from his face.

The peculiar aroma of cookie dough was fading; dispersing on the air.

He turned his back on the dead, but he could feel the tribal spirits fleeing toward what they thought was safety, the bitter residual energy of their fears playing out their slaughter over and over. The very air was tainted by their visceral deaths.

The hairs across his body prickled.

The day wore on, the digging reaching deeper into the earth. The rangers had found primitive shovels in the village huts, enough for everyone, and conveyed to the remaining villagers their willingness to share their sad labour.

The mist thickened around the peaks and again filled the valley with fog. They could no longer see the sky or the river, or even many of the adobe huts.

By the time they had helped the survivors bury the dead, the sun was low, and the shadows were becoming long. Soon, it would be dark.

Lucas didn't relish the thought of making camp in the village, but it made sense. There were buildings and beds. There was no need to freeze in the night. Their emergency bags and tents were back in the Land Rovers, so the choice was a dead man's bed or a very hard, very cold mattress of leaves beneath a misty blanket of sky. That was one of the peculiarities of the Amazon — the temperature change between day and night was more extreme than the shift between winter and summer.

The last thing any of them needed to be doing was blundering about in the dark trying to find their way back to the Land Rovers.

Lucas pulled Cutter aside. What he had seen by the well had been nagging him for a while, and he had finally worked it out.

"Prof., I reckon there's something left to see here."

He led Cutter back to the side of the well, then knelt. He gestured for Cutter to kneel beside him, and pointed out the blood spatter.

The answers were always in the blood.

Cutter followed the direction of his fingers, squinting at the dirt in the failing light. Darkness was closing in quickly.

"What am I supposed to be seeing?"

"This," Lucas said, pointing at the at-first seemingly random splatter darkening the earth.

"And this." He pushed himself to his feet and walked four steps forward, pointing down at the cluster of animal tracks, and a second dark stain.

"And this," he walked six places this time, before tapping the earth.

The tracks — and the blood — disappeared toward the line of trees. There were other tracks that didn't make sense in terms of what they knew, but these bloody prints were far more compelling in terms of what they had just been through.

"The villagers wounded one of them," Cutter said breathlessly.

"Looks that way," Lucas agreed.

"Well now," Cutter muttered. He pushed himself to his feet and walked in the footsteps of blood, following them back toward the trees.

Lucas walked behind him.

"You want to be careful, Prof. I wouldn't want to come face to face with something capable of doing all this," he gestured over his shoulder, "in a hurry."

He saw Cutter slide the machete from the sheath at his hip. It wasn't exactly what he'd had in mind. He couldn't help but smile, though. For a man of science, Cutter was willing to get his hands dirty, and wasn't frightened of getting physical. He liked that in a man.

Lucas put his fingers to his lips and whistled long, high and sharp, causing the others to look his way instinctively. "Come on boys and girls, the Professor's found something."

Blaine was the first to reach him. Together they took off after Cutter, both moving hard, fast and low, their guns clasped in sweaty palms as they plunged into the trees. The others followed.

Ahead of them, they could hear Cutter's laboured breathing as he slashed and cut a swath through the thickening tangle of vegetation. There was a crack, then a branch whipped back from Cutter's blade, slashing toward Lucas' face. The soldier reacted instinctively, ducking under it before a stray thorn could take his eye out. He hit the dirt hard, his knees grinding over fragments of stone and twisted root. Pain rose up from one of his knees in a dark black surge. Through it all, though, he could see that the trail of blood had thickened in front of him. Lucas stayed on his knees, examining the low lying leaves that were smeared redly with the stuff where the wounded creature had plunged through the undergrowth.

It was difficult to tell how badly it was hurt, but if the blood trail was anything to go by, it wasn't in a good way.

Lucas stood, straining to separate the sounds of Cutter's hacking from the tell-tale rustle of leaves that would betray the creature as it lumbered away through the claustrophobic press of trees. The air was colder now, the sweat chilled as it prickled his skin. The team was making such a racket as they charged recklessly through the tangle of twisted thorns and choking weeds that it was impossible to hear anything else.

Then Cutter pulled up short, and Lucas saw the dark shape of the animal at his feet.

SIXTEEN

Almost two hours from the charnel house of a village, the windows in the reading room of the ambassador's summer residence rattled, bowing inwards from the shockwave that followed Jack Stark's not-so-silent alarm.

A heartbeat later the sound of the detonation caught up with the physical wave.

Stark slipped the catch off the holster on his Browning and drew the gun. He crossed the room silently, careful to stay out of sight of the window. He didn't want any stray glance to catch his movement and betray him. Someone was out there in the black, beyond the floodlights of the patio and the neat lawn spotlights. Whether they were still alive was another matter. An incendiary device blowing up in your face wasn't exactly conducive to longevity.

He chuckled bleakly at the thought, then moved silently up the stairs, knowing he had perhaps two or three minutes until the house was breached. They'd be a little more cautious now, unsure of what was and what wasn't booby trapped. A little insecurity was good for the soul.

He knocked once, sharply, on Cam Bairstow's door and entered the room. The young man was sitting upright in bed, wild eyed and vulnerable.

"We knew they were going to come," Stark said. He drew a second pistol from his ankle strap, and made sure the safety was off before he handed it across to Cam. "Six shots. It's not much more than a pea-shooter, so make sure they're really close before you let rip."

Cam cradled the pistol in his lap as though it were a snake that might just as soon turn on him.

'Let's hope it doesn't come to that," he said timidly.

"I don't traffic in hope, lad. It's all about eventualities. I'm going out there now. If you hear shooting, get yourself hidden as best you can. If they can't find you, they can't kill you."

"I'm frightened, Stark," Cam admitted.

"Good, you should be. If you weren't, I'd be worried. I do this for a living. I'm not going to bullshit you, I've got no idea how many of them there are out there, but if I were running the show I'd be using two teams of two, with a fifth in reserve to co-ordinate things. Assuming that hand grenade just upset one of them, that would leave four unaccounted for. Four against one seems hardly fair to me."

"They haven't got a chance," Cam said, smiling weakly.

"Something like that, lad," Stark said. "Just remember, wait until you see the whites of the bastards' eyes."

Cam nodded again. "Whites of the eyes," he repeated, focusing on the detail to help push aside all of the other fears pressing in on his mind.

"Good lad."

Stark closed the door behind him, the game of hide and seek starting in earnest as he slipped quietly down the stairs to the kitchen, then through to the utility area. He had scoped the place out early, locating the junction boxes and the fuse housings. He pulled the switch, plunging the huge house into absolute darkness. Pulling a second switch he disabled the floodlights, which were on a different circuit. A third switch turned off the lawn spotlights.

And all around him, there wasn't a sound.

Until he heard the faint scratching of a cutter on the glass of the patio doors.

Stark's smile was cold. What they couldn't know was that he had been waiting for them. That first little tripwire was hardly the most inventive surprise he had lined up. They wouldn't know what hit them. To quote Bruce Willis: he was the fly in the ointment, the monkey in the wrench, the pain in the ass.

This was the kind of thing he lived for.

"Yippee ki-yay," Jack Stark muttered, clicking off the Browning's safety.

* * *

The darkness was his friend.

Stark crouched low, watching them come. He had ordered the residence's staff to hide in the cellar, since he couldn't worry about them and become distracted.

He could see the enemy, three darker outlines against the black glass of the doors. The diamond bit of the glass cutter did its job, opening a small circular hole in the door wide enough for the intruder to reach through and fiddle with the lock mechanism. It happened in a single swift motion; these were professionals.

Stark counted to five, then went for it. He stayed low, and moved fast, running from his hiding place beside an exquisite nineteenth-century Carrara marble statue of a voluptuous nymph. The piece was life-sized, which made it the perfect lure for what he had in mind. There was a small speaker wedged into the clamshell clutched by the stone maiden. He held the receiver in his hand.

Six more miniature speakers were placed strategically around the room at head height.

He waited, counting the seconds.

The patio door whispered back on its runners and the three men came in from the cold. Two were slim, average; the other was bulky, out of shape and breathing hard as the adrenalin pumped through his system. *He would be the first to break*, Stark reasoned. He was of a type, shot full of steroids to enhance the iron-pumping, overly bulky around the shoulders and neck, narrow around the waist, and small in one crucial area: the brain.

These guys strutted and acted the big man, taking risks that should never be taken. Couple their inferiority complex with a pea brain, and it was a recipe for disaster.

Each of the three had small Maglites and played the beams quickly across the surfaces.

The world outside had suffered a temperature inversion. The air on the ground had grown colder and colder, effectively trapping itself beneath the warm thermals above, meaning that without a wind to disperse it, and unable to rise, it was forming an almost marshmallow-like fog. With the torch beams and the trapped mists, they looked like something out of a bad science-fiction movie.

Stark waited until the big man was level with the marble statue. After four deep and slow inhalations and exhalations he whispered, "Fe Fi Fo Fum, I smell the blood of some rotten scum."

His voice echoed in seven different parts of the room.

The big guy reacted with surprising alacrity, ratcheting off three shots into the stone nymph's torso and one into her neck. The Carrara marble splintered and powdered. The clamshell fell and shattered on the floor.

"Missed," Stark whispered, his voice coming from the floor by the steroid warrior's feet. Incensed, the gunman fired off three more shots at the silhouette but still the stone maiden refused to fall.

"Not too smart are you?" Stark hissed, then he backed away, deeper into the shadows of the next room.

He counted off eleven silent beats in his head, then pressed down on a small metal plate. It would take nine seconds to rise again and break the contacts. Nine seconds.

"Over here," he called, still on the move.

Eight.

Seven.

Six.

He saw the bulk of the big guy loom darkly in the doorway.

Five.

Stark heard the soft click of the plate rising beyond the point of no return.

Four.

One of the others moved up behind the big guy, whispering something in his ear. Stark couldn't have planned it better.

Three.

"Your move," he said then, loudly.

Two. They turned to stare straight at him. The little guy hit the light switch. Nothing happened.

One.

Stark launched himself to the left, behind the cover of a partition wall as the two wires within the metal plate came into contact, completing the circuit that blew the top off, and took away the lower half of the big guy's legs in the detonation.

And then there was pandemonium in the small room, as smoke and flame and screams were met by crumbling walls and groans as the joists in the ceiling above buckled and caved, bringing a ton of plaster and timber down on their heads.

Stark stood, his ears ringing with the tinnitus of the explosion.

Flames licked around the ruined legs of the steroid warrior, but he was in no state to care. A second corpse lay on its back, arms and legs akimbo where the violence of the detonation had hurled him from his feet. With the fire rising, Stark could see that most of the dead man's face had been burned away by the heat of the explosion.

He could not see a third body.

That didn't mean it couldn't have been buried under the rubble when the ceiling came down. Still, he wasn't prepared to risk his life on it, and that was what it came down to. Best case, one more man inside the house and one left outside for him to deal with.

Worst case, well, he didn't want to think about it.

Three dead, and he hadn't fired his gun. That was the kind of return he liked.

He had stood stock-still for a full thirty seconds, listening to the snap and crackle of the smouldering fire as it ate away at the plaster and the timber beams of the ambassador's ruined home. Stark had been careful when he'd planted the charge, judging the actual construction of the floor above so that the detonation would cause maximum structural damage without leaving Cam Bairstow stranded, or worse, consumed by the explosion.

The plaster wept from the raw wound in the ceiling like Solomon's tears.

Stark felt the thrill of anticipation as he picked a path through the debris.

"Who sent you?" he called out, not really expecting an answer, and not knowing if they'd understand the question, anyway.

"You're a dead man," a thickly accented Germanic voice growled behind his left shoulder. Stark didn't hesitate, and threw himself forward in a tightly controlled roll, then came up in a crouch, gun-hand braced on his knee. He fired off a single shot into the smoke. It was greeted by a grunt and the sound of a body stumbling back into the wall.

"You were saying?" Stark replied, a sudden calm settling over him. He had hit the third man; he had no way of knowing how badly. If the bloke didn't answer, then the odds were he'd put him out of commission. He waited, listening for a second tell-tale sound to guide his gun. When it came, he squeezed off a second shot, the muzzle of his Browning flaring as he held back the recoil. There was no grunt this time, only the soft sound of meat offering the least line of resistance.

"Come on, who sent you?"

Why was there a German mixed up in this?

It made no sense. Then, as he thought about it, it *did* make sense, in a peculiar sort of way. Cutter had said it himself: Peru was big money for the wrong kind of people. If it wasn't drugs it was animals that was the toxicology of this once proud nation. Pizarro's legacy of exploitation and death lingered on. Who stood to gain the most by preventing the truth from coming out? At first he had thought it was the government itself, but then he'd forced himself to think beyond what he was being shown, and to ask no, who *really* stood to gain?

Private money.

It was always about private money. And often foreign 'investors'.

So a German lying on the floor, bleeding out, wasn't so improbable after all. With its central location and the wall down, it made perfect sense for business to pass through from the East to West, and vice versa, and from North and South. Germany was a nexus. A pivot in world trade — at least of the illegal variety.

Drugs or animals?

He knew where he'd bet his money.

Animals; they were a multi-billion-dollar business after all.

He shook his head. The heat from the dwindling flames warmed his face. And because of its crackle, he didn't hear the soft crunch of footsteps behind him.

"Say goodnight," the German whispered into his ear.

Stark didn't so much as flinch. As the German's knife arm wrapped around his throat looking to slice into the carotid artery, he caught it and yanked down on it, hard, slammed his head back at the same time as he pulled the German forward. Stark's vision blurred as the back of his skull ruptured the German's nose.

He yanked on his attacker's arm again, twisting it savagely, then breaking it across his knee. The German reeled, but Stark wouldn't let him fall. Not yet. He turned to look the man in the eye. The face he found there was a mess of blood and cartilage. The red stuff pooled thickly around his eyes, making it almost impossible for the man to see.

Stark didn't feel sorry for him.

"You talk too much," he said, driving his fist into the man's throat. The single punch caved in his hyoid bone and left the German choking slowly to death on the floor.

And still, Stark did not feel sorry for him.

The man had come here intending to kill him; where was it written that he should feel pity just because the assassin had failed?

He stepped over the soon-to-be-dead man and went in search of the last of them. It would be over in a minute or so — of that he was certain.

And then he would go looking for Chaplin. This place had never been a safe house. It had been an invitation to come finish whatever sordid business he had got himself mixed up in, nicely isolated with plenty of backyard to bury a couple of bodies. The whole thing reeked of a set-up.

He needed to get this done. And as much as he wanted to get out there to the reserve, to find them, he knew he couldn't. He needed to make certain Cam was safe, and to do that, he had to stay here. He had to find someone he could trust.

Right now, though, it was Cutter who was in the greatest danger, out there in the darkness, trusting the snake as it coiled slowly through the long grass and, unseen, around his legs.

The last man died an inglorious death.

Stark crawled forward on elbows and knees, his belly pressed low against the dirt. The stench of burning flesh had begun to waft out into the foggy darkness. The shallow low-lying layer of white mist was almost perfectly inert. There wasn't so much as the slightest sigh of a breeze in the cold night.

He kept his shoulders and head beneath the white. It allowed him to creep slowly across the lawn and into the trees. Only then did he stand, amid the remains of his handiwork. A dozen trunks stood lopsidedly, their bark shredded with shrapnel, the pulp exposed to the night. He had been right.

The first man lay with his back pressed up against one of the ruined trees, his hands clutching his guts. His face was as colourless as the mist, utterly drained of blood. Killing him would have been a mercy, but keeping him alive was more expedient. He couldn't just go blundering off into the Amazon looking for Cutter and his crew — he needed to use his head; numbers, co-ordinates, anything and everything that might tilt the balance in his favour as he waged a one-man war against the poachers and their mercenary army.

Beyond the dying man he found the last of them, panicking, walking in circles, muttering desperately to himself and casting fretful glances up at the dark windows of the house.

"Boo," he whispered, enjoying it as the man's bones tried to lurch out of his skin.

"Stay back! Get away! Don't come any closer!" The man shrieked, spinning around frantically, slashing the air with his torch as though it were a knife. The light cut across Stark's throat, but he did not bleed. He stepped forward, his grin slow and malicious and all the more haunting for the roving torch light.

"Who are you?"

"Banquo," he said, naming the uninvited guest. Recognising that he was cornered, the man launched himself.

A moment later, a shot rang out across the Cuzco night sky, and it was over.

Stark went back to get what he needed from the dying man.

SEVENTEEN

Alex Chaplin hadn't run into the forest with the others.

Instead, he sank down against the well. His back was so thoroughly soaked with sweat that he had to check twice to be sure he hadn't leaned against stones still slick with the dead woman's blood.

He put his head in his hands. He wanted to weep.

All he could think — over and over — was, *What have I done?*

For a full minute he couldn't move. Every muscle in his body tightened, constricting and conspiring to undo him. If it had been possible, he was sure his lungs would have seized up, clogged with the humid air, and his heart would have tripped a final beat, such was the grief that wracked his mind.

The mist thickened around him, conjuring wraiths that danced around the empty square.

It had been an angle, nothing more than twisting a story to meet a need. He'd taken the money from Eberhardt without a second thought, and sold the kid's words to the first journalist who'd bite. He tried to tell himself that he hadn't had a choice. Eberhardt was that kind of bastard. You did what he said, or you ended up floating in the muddy waters of the Amazon.

He licked his lips.

How was he supposed to have known?

That was the great defence? Ignorance?

He was a businessman. It had been a simple proposition. Eberhardt's man had turned up on his doorstep the day after Cameron Bairstow stumbled out of the jungle, and offered him the proverbial thirty pieces of silver to take advantage of this unique opportunity. All he had to do was kick up some dust to keep the locals in line, and scare the tourists away from the jungle for another year or two. Keep them limited to the beaten tracks of Titicaca and Machu Picchu, Lima and Trujillo.

That way Eberhardt's crew could continue to farm the ripest assets of the rainforest.

The man was vile, but that didn't make him any less powerful. He was more than just a smuggler. That was such an outmoded term. He didn't row some tiny skiff into a cove in the dead of night. To the outside world, Eberhardt was legitimate. He dined with the ambassador, played polo with big wigs, and ran one of the most successful import-export companies in all of the Americas, North or South. He owned people; such was his power in this backwater world Chaplin had found himself in.

It was like something out of a Fitzgerald novel, full of the underclass bowing and scraping to the rich white man.

And God help him, Chaplin had enjoyed it.

Playing both sides against the middle was hardly new, and his thirty pieces of silver had been a very bankable half a million dollars for himself, and one hundred thousand apiece for the men he had brought in to do the job.

But this... this wasn't his doing.

This was real.

And wrong.

And frightening.

It was as though by conjuring up the illusion of their precious El Chupacabra, he'd given life to the demon. It was one thing to lay out your needs in some detached, almost academic manner, but it was quite another to see the evidence of your lies brought to life like some bloody curse.

At first he had thought that it would be simple. One boy was already dead, and the other already had one foot in the grave.

Then Sir Charles had called, said he was sending people to bring his son home, and it had all become so very, very complicated.

And it appeared as if the fates had a wicked sense of humour, he thought now, huddled up against the side of the stone well, shivering, his hands stained with more than merely metaphorical blood.

Could lies conjure demons?

Alone with the dead, surrounded by the criss-cross of animal tracks and empty huts that once had been homes, no matter how primitive, it seemed all too believable that the gods could damn him so completely.

Chaplin shivered, and not because of the creeping chill.

He wept for himself and for the dead — but mostly for himself.

And because he hadn't run, he saw the shadow-shape move across the tree line.

It most certainly was not a jaguar or panther.

It was El Chupacabra, brought to life.

"Oh, God," he breathed, fingers clawing down into the blood-stained earth.

Of all things, he smelled the sickly sweet aroma of burnt cookies.

And then the creature came bounding out of the undergrowth.

He struggled to his feet and turned to run, managing perhaps a dozen terrified paces before the sudden shocking weight knocked him down. He screamed, but the sound was strangled as the beast pinned him down and tore into him with its teeth. Blood bubbled in his throat, spilling out across the dirt to mingle with the blood of the tribesmen.

He struggled to lift his head, the weight of the animal crushing down on his spine. The world around him reeked of burnt biscuits, and something else. Vanilla? The smells made no sense to the dying man. He clawed at the dirt, trying to drag himself another inch away from the teeth that tore at his hide. The grass stained his teeth and his face as the weight drove him down, forcing him to eat it as he gasped for air.

After the first bite, there was no pain.

His body was protecting itself, shutting down one organ at a time in a rapid flood of endorphins. He was delirious, smelling things that weren't there. The biscuits and the vanilla were blood and faeces, they had to be. His body was playing tricks on his mind, to protect him.

That had to be what was happening: one last sensory deception from the body of a liar and a cheat, just to make his own passing less traumatic.

He managed to bring his head up, and he gazed upon the hook beaked face of Pacha Kamaq, the Earth-Maker of Inca mythology. It had to be a statue, yet it looked so alive.

And it *moved*.

He knew then that he had lost his mind to the pain. The gods did not walk the earth. They never had, and they never would.

A heartbeat later, he lost what was left of his life.

EIGHTEEN

Nick Cutter crouched down beside the dead pouch-blade.

The creature's wounds went beyond severe. He had expected to see a deep cut from one of the tribesmen's blades, but what he found instead was a ripped and torn carcass. The marsupial was almost as long as Cutter was tall, though so thickly muscled it was twice as wide. One of its two great teeth had broken off, leaving a jagged edge.

"Isn't she amazing," he breathed, almost reverentially as he reached out to touch the broken tooth. The damage was recent enough that the tooth was still incredibly sharp. *It had most likely broken off during whatever life-and-death struggle had killed it,* Cutter reasoned. Even in death, the creature retained much of its almost mythic prowess. The definition of the musculature was incredible, and the claws huge. It was easy to see how one crushing blow could cave in a victim's skull.

"'Amazing' isn't the word I would have chosen," Lucas said. The SAS man crouched down beside him, more interested in the mess of tracks around the dead Thylacosmilus than in the beast itself. They evidenced a ferocious struggle, the earth churned up by claws scuffing at it. Long gouges in the dirt suggested that the pouch-blade hadn't gone down without a fight.

Cutter pushed himself up to his feet and sheathed the machete.

"Well, something had it in for her, by the looks of it," Blaine said, stating the obvious. The perfect predator had been humbled by something considerably more lethal. Cutter poked and prodded the tears; some were ragged, others clinically smooth. There were clusters of puncture wounds where the animal's hide had been pierced, over and over.

But the most disturbing — even bizarre — of all of the Thylacosmilus' wounds was over its heart. The thick fur was discoloured, and appeared to have been twisted to the point of ripping, almost as though a pincer had grasped and ratcheted round, again and again, until the hide had ruptured, exposing the still-beating organ. There was no way a tribesman's blade had caused the creature's wounds. Some, perhaps, but not all, and not the worst of them.

The first flies had already begun to gather around the open wounds, drawn by the turning meat. In a few short hours death would make way for so much more life, as the bloated white maggots fed themselves into a frenzy.

"Poachers?" Lucas asked, though he obviously didn't believe it himself.

"Not a prayer," Cutter said, ending that line of speculation before it had begun. A man would never have been able to get in close enough to inflict those clustered puncture wounds, not without the Thylacosmilus' fangs piercing his body in the process. Whatever had killed the animal was faster, and deadlier than the beast itself — and that left them with a short list of hunter-killers in any epoch.

Before he could dwell too much on the nature of the beast, the distant sound of a scream shredded his nerves. Cutter's first thought was: *But that's impossible, we buried everyone! Who's left to die?* Which was just wrong on so many levels. He turned, scanning the faces of his team. No one was missing. He felt a huge tidal surge of relief wash over him then, only for it to evaporate in the vacuum where his heart ought to have been beating.

"Chaplin," he said, the name a death knell as it stained his lips.

Lucas and Blaine reacted first. The two men turned and charged back toward the settlement, leading the way with gunmetal and testosterone as they burst from the trees. Cutter and the others chased after them, sweeping Nando and Genaro, who were just joining them, along with them, fighting through the tangled undergrowth, as it tried to trap them in its smothering embrace.

They left the flies behind, but the buzzing showed no sign of abating.

Mosquitoes, Cutter realised. They hadn't been in evidence while they had dug the grave, but now that the sun was going down, they had risen in a new cycle of life. He felt the first one against his face. Beside him, Connor slapped at his own forehead, smearing the insect across his hairline.

Chaplin's body lay sprawled at an impossible angle beyond the stones of the well, legs and arms twisted as though he had tried to burrow into the earth to escape his attacker.

"Oh, God," Jenny uttered, her hand pressed to her mouth as she stared down at the ruined corpse. Then she peered at Cutter, fear dominating her features. "We can't stay here," she said pleadingly. "They'll pick us off one by one."

"Ten Little Indians," Connor said, his arm curling around Abby's shoulder protectively. Abby just stared mutely down at the man who had brought them out into the wilderness.

Cutter turned to the soldiers. "Let's get out of here."

"What about him?"

"I don't think we've got time for the niceties, do you?"

Lucas shook his head.

"But we can't just leave him there like that," Jenny objected. She looked horrified at the notion of simply leaving Chaplin as food for the birds and the worms.

"At least he's biodegradable," Cutter said, and immediately wished he hadn't.

"No man gets left behind, isn't that the motto?" she protested. "Would you leave *me* there if that was my body?"

Cutter stared at her, but this time he wasn't seeing Jenny. He was seeing Claudia Brown, staring at him through her eyes, accusing him of doing just that: leaving her behind to rot in his memory. He felt his heart shiver, a tiny crack opening in it.

"I didn't... I couldn't..." But he had no words, not to convey the hundreds of emotions that suddenly crowded his mind. It all came crashing back down over him.

"Oh God, Claudia. I'm sorry."

"Don't call me that," Jenny said, but for once there was no harshness in her voice as she did. He saw himself haunted in her eyes. He had tried so hard to put it behind him, to move on — to do just what she had accused him of, to leave her behind in a different forest, in a different history. And the realisation of his betrayal threatened to crush him.

Cutter stumbled forward. It was Stephen who stopped him from falling.

"There's just so much senseless death," Cutter said, so quietly that only Stephen could hear him. "Their world should never have been this way."

"Neither should ours," Stephen said, "but it is."

For a moment it was as though his angst might paralyse him, but that moment did not last long. Something inside of him pulled itself together, and Cutter followed suit physically by straightening, drawing himself up, becoming what he needed to be for them.

"I'll bury him," Connor said. Cutter saw that he had one of the makeshift shovels in his hand already. He nodded.

"Good man."

"We don't have time," Blaine told him. "The sun's almost down. It'll take forty minutes or so to get back to the Land Rovers — longer, if we can't see where we're going. The last thing we want is to be blundering about in the dark with whatever it is out there stalking us."

Connor drove the shovel into the dirt, not listening.

"I'll help," Abby said.

Jenny nodded. The two women went back to the larger grave and picked up the tools.

"If we do it together we'll have it done in just a few minutes," she said, tossing what looked like a hybrid shovel-pick to Blaine. The soldier didn't argue, and instead joined the effort.

This time they broke the earth with something approaching frenzy, each of them scooping up as much of the rich black soil as they could, and shovelling it aside, over and over again. In a few minutes they were standing around a shallow grave. Blaine and Lucas rolled the corpse into the hole, took his wallet, identification, and keys, and then unceremoniously filled it back over him.

It took less then ten minutes to remove all physical traces of Alexander Chaplin. *Barely enough time to boil an egg and eat it*, Cutter thought. Was it the sum of the man's worth? Ten minutes to dig a hole and fill it again? It was a chilling notion. He wanted to believe in all of the other things — the minutiae of life that made it whole — but right then and there, standing over another shallow grave, he couldn't.

Life came down to its most basic elements: carbon and decay.

Perhaps there was nothing left to believe in.

"We need to go," he said.

This time they did.

NINETEEN

They could feel the eyes on them.

They moved slowly but steadily, hand on the shoulder of the person in front of them, forming a snake in the darkness. The encroaching night was a far cry from the lethargic heat of the day. There was a chill to it that defied all the memories of even an hour before. The cold had closed in that quickly, and that absolutely.

Cutter cursed himself for a fool. He had gone off running stupidly, and now Chaplin was dead. There had been too much carnage today, and too much stupidity. He needed to clear his head and think. At the moment everything they were doing was reactive. He needed to change the nature of the game, go on the offensive.

But first he needed to get everyone to safety.

They were four miles away from the Land Rovers in what would soon be pitch black forest. The camping gear was all back in the cars. They had to continue to move, even just to stay warm, but movement brought with it its own dangers. The darkness crept and crawled with unseen hunters, drawn to them by the rich pulse of fear that throbbed beneath their skin.

The whisper of the trees was a chilling promise of what lay just out of sight, behind the leaves and dragging vines. Every so often the deep-throated rumble — it couldn't be called a purr no matter how cat-like the pouch-blades were — would remind them that they were not alone.

But the creatures didn't attack, which only served to make it worse. Instead of confrontation, the pumping adrenalin of survival or failure, there was this constant nagging uncertainty, the doubt that promised demons and devils lurking out in the darkness.

None of them spoke.

They had nothing to say.

The clammy press of Stephen's hand against his skin sent a shiver through Cutter's exhausted body. Nights without proper sleep, jet-lag, and the spiritual crucifixion of the last few hours left him feeling like a shell of himself. *How appropriate*, he mused. *It was all a shell game*, he thought, his mind too tired to really focus. He was a shell, Jenny was a shell, Chaplin was a shell, and none of them were the shells they had been a day, a week, or a month before.

What made the man or the woman? The soul? The flesh? The...

He stumbled. The hand on his shoulder was the only thing that stopped him from falling. He came back to the moment, and he was determined to stay there. He wouldn't allow his brain to fool him into hiding elsewhere. He needed to be clear-headed for a while longer, at least. He could sleep tomorrow.

Tonight he needed to stay alive.

"Stop for a minute," he said, fumbling to get his pack off his back even as he stopped walking. He uncapped the last of his water bottles and drained it dry in three long chugs. He wiped the back of his hand over his lips.

They were out there.

He could feel them. It didn't matter that he couldn't see them. He was a scientist; he lived in a world full of things he couldn't see, that he still knew to be irrefutably true.

"What are we doing?" he asked.

It was Genaro who answered, the young ranger pragmatic as ever.

"Going back to the vehicles."

That was true, but it was only *part* of what was going on. They were also running away from what they had seen back at the village; they were blundering about in the dark, so close to being lost; they were reacting to the predatory growls of the creatures that lurked out there. They were moving instinctively away from the sounds of their hunters — and that was what ate away at his subconscious. He knew how these creatures worked. He knew how they hunted. And now they were breaking all of the rules.

Cutter and his group were being steered slowly away from their path, away from the Land Rovers and toward the Thylacosmilus' chosen hunting ground.

"Check our compass reading, because I don't think we are," he said.

Genaro fumbled in his pocket for the small device, and read it by the glow of his Maglite. The ranger scratched at his scalp then looked at Cutter.

"Eighteen degrees off," he said, sounding as if he didn't quite believe it.

"They're steering us *away* from where we want to go." It was time to take charge again. *Here we go...* "We need to start thinking. I'm tired; you're tired. After what we've been through today, my soul is bloody empty. But that's no excuse for stupidity. Not thinking is going to get us killed."

"What do you propose, Professor?" Connor asked — at least he *thought* it was Connor. The speaker was no more than ten feet away from him, but he was completely swallowed by the darkness.

He swung his own torch around. The beam roved across the leaves, distorting the world around them as it settled on Connor.

"We need to go back to basics. What do animals fear?"

"Fire," Connor said.

"Fire," Cutter agreed. "Not torches. We need burning brands. Something we can use to tilt the balance back in our favour."

"Only problem is I don't think my Zippo will do much against the Ravenous Bugblatter Beast of Traal out there."

"No, but it's a start." Cutter reached back into his pack, rummaging around for something burnable. There was nothing that fitted what he had in mind, so he pulled his shirt off and tore away the sleeves. He shone the beam of his torch across the ground, looking for suitable deadfall. It took a few passes of the torch, but he found two fairly straight branches. He wrapped and tied the material around the ends. "Lighter?" he said to Connor, holding out both brands.

"Burn, baby, burn," Connor said, igniting the Zippo. He touched the small blue and yellow flame to the cloth and watched it blacken, smoulder, and finally ignite.

Cutter tossed one of the flaming brands to Genaro and the other to Nando. "You know this place, get us back to the vehicles. We are not staying out here all night."

"He who turns and runs away lives to fight another day," Connor joked.

"Precisely. Now, come on."

Cutter gathered up his things and shouldered his pack. The natural light of the burning torches was very different to the channelled beam of the battery-powered ones. The brands crackled and spat, throwing shadows and phantom shapes all across the wall of vegetation. The brands brought warmth with them, too. They found themselves clustering around the two rangers. Still, beyond the ever-shifting shadows they could feel the darkness rise.

Cutter caught the scent of a peculiarly out-of-place aroma, not cookie dough this time, but strong, and unmistakably coffee. The fragrance intensified as he walked deep into the darkness, peering forward. It was enough to raise the hackles on his neck.

Someone was out there, watching.

It all happened in an instant, that frozen moment between seconds.

The Thylacosmilus came roaring out of the darkness, feral lips curled back on those enormous teeth.

It was on them, then, so much worse for the fire that turned the scene nightmarish with the erratic light. The great black-shadow beast pounced, and huge claws raked toward Abby's face.

Only Blaine's instincts saved her. The SAS man caught the flicker of movement out of the corner of his eye and reacted without a second thought. As the barbed claws slashed out, Blaine threw himself at her, hitting Abby so hard the impact hurled her from her feet and left her sprawling on her stomach in the dirt. The claws sliced through the thin material of his shirt, gouging out huge bloody runnels along his forearm and into his bicep. He came down on top of Abby, driving the air from her lungs.

A sudden and blisteringly painful heat seared across the length of his spine. He gritted his teeth through the agony, only for a second vicious cut on his shoulder blade to tear the sounds of agony from his throat.

Screaming himself hoarse, Blaine rolled off Abby as the great pouch-blade delivered another scything blow aimed at cleaving into his brain-pan. He felt the sizzle of claws that raked across the back of his scalp as he barely avoided them.

All around him the world exploded into light and angry sound as the rangers came charging toward him. One of them — he couldn't see who — lunged, the flaming tip of his firebrand scorching the side of the Thylacosmilus' head. The beast howled in pain but didn't flee. Enraged, it threw itself at him with renewed purpose.

The beast's jaws snapped at Blaine's face savagely, so close that he tasted its foul breath in the back of his throat.

He brought up his wounded arm to ward off any bites, and reached down for the long blade he had sheathed at his side. Before he could draw the knife, however, the beast's incisors clamped down on the soft meat of his already bloody forearm, piercing through to the bone. The pouch-blade seemed incensed by the heady tang of blood in the air, and the promise of flesh.

Blaine's cries went beyond screams into an agony of silence. As the pain threatened to overwhelm him, turning the world to black, he lashed out wildly, hammering his free hand into the side of the creature's face brutally once, twice, three times, until its head snapped back.

The blackness receded momentarily.

The pain did not.

Blaine wrenched his arm free, the sharp teeth taking lumps of muscle and tendon with them as he tore himself out of its grip.

And then three sharp cracks drove the beast off; the gunshots resonating throughout the heart of the darkness.

Blaine rolled over onto his back and looked up at the black canopy of the trees and the ghostly flickers of the torchlight. His heart lurched wildly in his chest. He could feel the creeping loss of feeling moving down from his fingers. He tried to turn his head, but it hurt too much. Sweat and blood chilled his skin.

"Well," he said, grunting through the pain, "that kitty's got some nasty claws."

"Shhh, lie still," one of the women said.

He could see them. The fog was rising. At least he thought it was the fog. White tendrils crept across his chest. Lung-shaped plumes leaked between his lips, forming wraiths above him.

He saw Lucas standing over him.

The rising mist made it look as though coils of gun smoke were drifting from the muzzle of his SIG-Sauer P226.

PRIMEVAL

He had never been so pleased to see a still-smoking gun.
He tried to move — and then the pain took him.

TWENTY

There was no air.

"We've got to get him to a hospital," Abby said. She crouched down beside the wounded SAS man, unravelling the gauze and bandages from the small first-aid kit she carried. Lucas stood over her with a Maglite, shining down so that she had illumination to work by.

Her heart still hammered unevenly against her breastbone, as it had ever since the attack. She bunched up the gauze to make a compress, wadding it against the worst of his cuts. The white cloth turned red too quickly.

"Press it down hard," she instructed, taking Blaine's cold hand in hers and pressing it down against the cut to try and staunch the bleeding.

It made precious little difference. His hand went limp.

Beside her, Jenny was doing the same.

"How is he?" Cutter asked.

"How does he look?" Abby said brusquely, without looking up at him. She didn't want to think about what had just happened. But for a wrinkle in time, a split-second reaction from the man on the floor of the forest, they would have traded places, and the team would have been looking down at her, knowing she was going to die, and asking: "How is she?"

A cough wracked Blaine's body. A bubble of bloody phlegm dribbled out of his mouth. His eyes were clouding over.

"No one else is going to die today," Abby said to him, even though he was in no fit state to listen. And to Cutter, and Jenny, and all of the others.

She meant it, too. *Lives weren't meant to be snuffed out like cigarettes.* She pressed down harder against the wound.

"Lucas?"

"What do you need?"

"A needle and thread from the kit, a naked flame, and more luck than any one girl ought to have," she said, through gritted teeth.

"How does two out of three sound?" The soldier took his pack off and opened one of the side-pouches to retrieve a small sewing kit. "Physician heal thyself, and all that," he said.

"You're such a boy scout," she said. "I love it. Thread it and heat it. It's not exactly going to be sterile, but anything we can do to lessen the chance of infection the better. Stephen? Cutter? We're going to need something to carry him out of here."

"Got it," Stephen said. She didn't look to see where he went or ask what he had in mind. She trusted him.

Abby leaned in close to Blaine, talking slowly and clearly. "This is going to hurt, Andy. I'm sorry, but we are going to get you out of here. I promise you that."

He nodded. Or at least she thought he did.

Jenny held his hand as Abby lanced the blackened tip of the hot metal through the flap of skin. Blaine didn't so much as wince as the needle penetrated.

"Come on, come on," Abby breathed, the words becoming a mantra. There was nothing holy to her prayer; it was totally selfish. She didn't want him dying for her. "I'm going to need some water," she said to no one in particular. Blood continued to leak from the worst of his wounds, the cuts so deep they showed no sign of clotting — and they wouldn't, unless she could close them up.

Jenny took the last of their water bottles and spilled a thick dribble of water down over the cut to cleanse it. This time Blaine did cry out, against the sting. It was a weak and pitiful sound.

"I'm not waiting here," Lucas said, handing the light to Connor. "How far away are the vehicles?"

"A mile or more at least," Genaro told him.

"Fine, how about you two come with me. We'll cut a path through the trees and see if we can't bring the cars a little bit closer?"

"Better than standing around doing nothing," Nando said. Something in his voice smacked of betrayal and bitterness, and seemed to say, *How could you bring us out into this, knowing what was happening, and not warn us?*

Abby didn't look up. She continued to thread the needle through the soldier's skin, drawing the flesh closer together with each stitch.

Her hand shook as she threaded stitch after stitch, closing up the worst of the wounds.

All the while, she felt the grim sensation of hungry eyes on her.

Cutter stripped the leaves from four long, straight branches, and a single short one. He used vines to lash them together, placing two perpendicular and the other two on the diagonal, forming a cross-brace. The shorter one he laid down across the middle to stabilise the frame. As stretchers went, it was barely worthy of the name, but it would do the job.

It had to.

With Stephen's help he finished binding the wood tight.

"It'll have to do," he said.

He caught it again, that faint whiff of an out of place fragrance.

"Can you smell that?"

Stephen cocked his head slightly, inhaling deeply and slowly. He closed his eyes, as though to minimise sensory input so that his world might be reduced to an olfactory one.

"Apples?" He said.

"Apples," Cutter agreed, thinking about it. That made vanilla, baking biscuits, coffee and now apples. Not one of them was an aroma that he would have expected to encounter in the middle of the wilderness. "There's something going on here with these smells, something that I don't understand. It's there, like some finger puzzle, and the more I worry away at it the further away the answer to the riddle gets."

"I've never heard of a hunting theory that involved scents like this," Stephen admitted. "Not for a borhyaenid, or any other species, for that matter. That's what you're thinking, isn't it?"

"I don't know," Cutter said. "It just doesn't make sense. My first instinct is that they're using the aromas to mark us. Like the smells are sensory tags. That would make sense if we were smelling the same things, like back at the village where the scent of baking biscuits was so strong. If that smell was somehow involved in inciting the creatures to attack, surely it would have to be the same aroma we'd be smelling now, after the Thylacosmilus attacked Blaine.

"That's what doesn't make sense to me. What if it's some kind of glandular thing? Perhaps they secrete certain fragrances in their sweat?"

"It's not out of the question," Stephen mused, drying his hands off on the legs of his shorts. "After all, in the most basic of ways, that's pretty much how deer hunters work. They lay out scents, knowing that the adult buck will invariably try to get downwind of the source. Then the hunters wear charcoal suits to mask their own scent, and lay in wait, downwind of the false trails they've laid out. What you're talking about is an extrapolation of that, surely."

"Now take it a step further," Cutter said, his mind racing with the possibilities. "Queen bees use scent as a form of mind control, to keep the youngest bees in the hive well-behaved. By controlling their aversive memories, she's able to keep some of them around to help groom her."

"So what you're saying is that maybe it isn't the borhyaenids using the scents at all. That it's something else entirely that's using the scents to control them," Stephen said. "As impossible as it sounds, that would explain the different scents, each for a different use."

Cutter stared at him for a moment, then smiled grimly in the darkness. Had they not shared their experiences with the anomalies, such a thing would have seemed like madness. Now it seemed like something else altogether.

"Stephen, you're a bloody genius. Of course it's something else! That makes perfect sense. Think about it: the queen bee secretes a mandibular pheromone that prevents the worker bees from learning through aversive experiences. It's a form of mind control. The scent reduces the likelihood of her young using their stingers; yet another pheromone could equally be used to incite another reaction, couldn't it? It's only when the older bees leave the hive to gather food that they're no longer under the control of the scent, and learn to protect themselves using their stingers.

"So let's say that somehow, someone is using these scents to impel the Thylacosmilus to do his bidding, like the queen bee. That has to be the answer!"

Cutter didn't know whether to laugh or cry; this was no triumph, achieved in the sudden flash of understanding. It only added another layer of doubt. Stephen spoke up again, his voice full of confusion and uncertainty.

"But what? What creature is capable of using the pouch-blades to hunt for it?"

Cutter remained silent for a moment, and a terrifying thought occurred to him.

"What if it's something from another anomaly? And not one that connects to the past."

"Is that possible?"

"Can you think of a better explanation?"

Stephen and Cutter carried Blaine between them.

The SAS man was delirious with the pain of his wounds. He mumbled constantly, his words barely intelligible. Abby walked beside the makeshift stretcher, holding his hand protectively in hers. Strands of short grass stuck to his face where the sweat had condensed on his brow and cheek. She brushed them away.

Suddenly twin beams speared the dark, illuminating every twisted and ugly tree branch, and throwing phantom forms across the canopy of vivid green leaves. The first Land Rover lurched into view, followed by the second and third, and every time one of them crossed the beam it threw the others behind them into near-darkness.

Lucas stood on the driver's side running board, and leaned out to usher them on. His silhouette was emphasised by the light that seemed to stream out from him. Along with Genaro and Nando, he had somehow managed to get the four-wheel driven tyres to bite, forcing it through the craters and over the tangled roots. The old vehicle had negotiated the uneven ground, albeit with some considerable difficulty. The passenger side-mirror had been ripped off by greedy vines and the canvas tarp had been torn away from the back as they squeezed between tree trunks and beneath trailing vines that clawed with grasping thorns.

Their desperate manoeuvres saved the others more than half of the mile-long walk with their burden, and more than double the time.

Now they had to pray it would be enough for Blaine.

Cutter rested a hand on Stephen's shoulder. He held a finger to his nose. Stephen nodded. It was there again, a wrong odour clinging to the air. He breathed it in, embracing the utter wrongness of it. This time it took him a moment to place it, beyond the obvious fish-market reek, then he realised it was subtler — it was the scent of roe. A North Sea smell, and it carried with it trace memories of blasted coastline and rolling waves.

They hadn't shared their theory with any of the others, but now that he had an inkling of how it worked, the sudden materialisation of these inexplicable aromas was a lot less disturbing — if no less alarming.

For it meant they were being hunted on two levels, the primary threat posed by the Thylacosmilus, and the secondary — perhaps more terrifying — idea that those hunters were almost certainly being controlled by some unimaginable overmind.

That there was no animal on the evolutionary chain that was capable of such a feat sent a shiver of dread through Cutter — because there was one word missing from that thought.

Yet.

He couldn't allow himself to give in to the rising sense of panic he felt growing in his gut. Right now, all that mattered was getting Blaine to a hospital, and the rest of the team to safety. Everything else could wait until sunrise.

So Cutter braced the splintered poles of the stretcher against the Land Rover's tailgate and slid it in, then clambered into the cage at the back and used his weight and leverage to man-handle Blaine off it. The soldier grunted as he slid onto the cold metal bed and lay shivering, unable to move for fear of tearing his makeshift stitches.

"It's going to be all right," he said. It was not an easy lie.

Cutter clambered back out of the cage, jumping down to the churned-up ground.

"Get the blankets from the other car," he told Nando. "He's going into shock. We need to keep his body temperature up. Anything you've got in there that can be used to keep him warm."

The reek of roe didn't show any sign of dispersing as the others busied themselves stripping down the emergency camping gear to scavenge anything remotely thermal they could wrap around the shivering Blaine.

Abby clambered into the back of the Land Rover and lay down, pressing herself up close to Blaine to lend him her own body heat. Cutter passed in the blankets and sleeping bags the others brought to him, and helped Abby make him comfortable.

"Just make sure Lucas drives carefully," she said to him.

Cutter said nothing. 'Careful' was a luxury they didn't have if the heightening fragrance was anything to go by. He slapped the side panel and shouted, "Go, go, *go!*"

The vehicle turned awkwardly, like a drunken uncle at a wake, lurching from side to side as its wheels stuck in the rutted earth and then pulled free.

The second vehicle followed the first, as Cutter clambered into the passenger seat of the third, slamming the door. The sound rang out like a shotgun blast in the quiet forest. As the shock of it rustled through the leaves, the beasts came out of the darkness.

There were five of them, yellow eyes caught in the glare of the headlights and turned bloody by the reflection on their retinas. They prowled forward, the huge dark bulk of their bodies pressed low to the dirt as they advanced.

Next to Cutter, in the driver's seat, Nando gunned the engine. It roared to life as he gave it full throttle and slammed the Land Rover into reverse. The car lurched back, the axle dipping as the rear wheel snapped through a thick root and dropped into the rut it left behind. The undercarriage ground against the stone and roots in the dirt, and then the car almost jumped back a foot as it lurched clear of whatever had snared it.

Cutter didn't take his eyes off the five predators moving oh-so-slowly, almost proprietorially, around them, full of menace and raw animalistic power. There was a beautiful feline grace to their movement, but more, as their heads twisted to follow the light and they opened their huge jaws, jowls peeling back on those thick tusk-like teeth. He watched as they inclined their heads, nostrils flaring, and pawed at the dirt. Their fur was slick, and rippled over the musculature as they moved, circling.

It took him a heartbeat to realise what was happening out there.

The first threw back its head and loosed a primal roar. As one, the others answered, the jungle coming alive with their rage.

And then they threw themselves at the Land Rovers, slamming into the side panels and rocking each frame on the chassis. One of the Thylacosmilus leapt up onto the bonnet, leering in through the dirty windscreen as Nando wrestled with the wheel, trying desperately to dislodge the beast. It lashed out with its hugely powerful claws, slashing at the windscreen. The claws grated down the length of the glass, leaving five deep gouges.

As the headlights roved wildly around the grove and the smothering press of trees, Cutter caught a flurry of movement in his peripheral vision. Out of the corner of his eye, it was impossible to say exactly what it was that he had seen lurking in the shadows, only he knew what it *wasn't*.

It was not, by any stretch of even the most warped imagination, a Thylacosmilus.

In truth it wasn't anything he had ever seen before; it was awkward and ungainly, almost like a hybrid of lupine, avian and shadows. Before he could focus on it, however, it was gone, and he could only think that the beast had shown itself deliberately, goading him with its presence.

Nando yanked down hard on the wheel, and accelerated, throwing the Land Rover forward at full throttle. The wheels bit in the dirt. The creature's claws scraped and scratched as it scrabbled for purchase, but the gathering momentum threw it clear.

"Drive," Cutter said, unnecessarily.

Nando Estevez already had his foot flat to the floor.

TWENTY-ONE

The full beam of the Land Rover's headlights speared through the oppressive night.

The creatures had chased them all the way to the open road, then the Land Rovers had managed to pull away from them. They were far behind now. If they were still chasing their prey, no one could see them.

They sat in silence, still in shock over what had happened. In the back seat, directly behind him, Jenny looked at Cutter through the secrecy of the shadows, rocking slightly in his chair like some idiot-savant Rain Man wrestling with whatever it was that haunted him. She was shaking. She had been ever since Blaine had saved Abby's life.

The Land Rover hit a rut in the track and juddered. Jenny pressed her hands up against the ceiling to brace herself as they were thrown about. She felt so far from home, and she couldn't simply pick up her mobile phone, make a call, and put things right. The hospital was more than ninety minutes away, the road about as drivable as a landing strip deep in the heart of a combat zone. And on all sides the darkness was filled with madness.

It didn't matter how much time she spent around Nick Cutter, the world he lived in wasn't the world she was used to. Primordial worms, sabre-toothed cats, velociraptors, these were monsters that had no place in the world she had grown up in. They had no place in *any* world, for that matter. Any modern world.

She found herself watching him again. He was in many ways the father of this little group. They looked to him for wisdom, protection, encouragement and support. They turned to him for answers. In turn he treated them like his children, protective and proud. He was usually the steadying influence, the calm at the core of the enormity that was their role in this insane world of anomalies and truths no one could ever know.

Events seemed to have run away from him though. The strain was in his eyes, if you knew where to look. And she did. His heart yearned for something it couldn't have back, the Claudia in the photograph he still carried in his wallet. She didn't know how she felt about that; she was the paradox in his world of certainties. He demanded so much of himself. When she looked at him she couldn't help but wonder if he were still searching for the other woman.

Was he secretly trying to pull the past apart to find a woman that had never been?

And what if he found her?

What if he found a way to bring his Claudia back? What would happen to Jenny Lewis then? What would happen to her bones and her skin and the thoughts that made up her identity?

Would it be her turn to simply cease to be?

After all, Aristotle had posited that the soul was essentially scientific, not some romanticised religious or spiritual thing, but rather substance. Form and matter joined in biology. The flesh provided the host, but the identity, the soul, that was some holistic other. From this, Aristotle concluded that the soul was part of a collective force that returned to this collective upon the death of an individual soul. He could not bring himself to believe in something created out of nothing.

So then Claudia and Jenny had to be a part of the same collective, created from the same substance, form and matter joined in biology. And one of the basic laws of physics she did remember was that two things could not exist in the same place at the same time — or in this case the same flesh.

The thought came to her unbidden: did Cutter dream of making her disappear? Did he lie awake at night, thinking of the woman she wasn't, and wishing for her to be?

She remembered him calling her by that other name, so sure, alive until she said no and snuffed out whatever spark of hope he had harboured that it might all work out. For all the talk of divergent evolutions and sciences, Cutter was like any other romantic. He desperately wanted to believe in the happy ending.

But then, so did she.

Jenny looked into the dark shadows that were all she could see of his eyes as he stared out into the night, and couldn't bring herself to believe it could ever be so, because when she looked at him she felt something inside herself she couldn't understand, even though she knew full well what it was; a yearning that mirrored his own.

And yet she was getting married, to someone *else*...

It was peculiar. It was more than that. It was as though she had known him for such a very, *very* long time.

A glare that reflected on the glass brought her out of her reverie and back to the here-and-now. She turned to look back even as the headlights of a rapidly approaching SUV lit up the inside of the Land Rover. Jenny scrambled around in her seat, trying to see anything in the blinding light. Beyond the impression of speed, it was impossible. The intensity of the lights grew as the gap between the vehicles closed rapidly.

Then it swept past, disappearing up the road. Two hundred metres away it pulled over.

Jenny turned her eyes to the front in time to see a dark figure step out into the road and throw something in front of the Rover. A thick belt of nails shredded the tires as they drove over it. The rubber detonated, the air exploding out of them, and everything seemed to drop as the weight of the vehicle came down hard on the wheel rims.

The next thing she knew she was being hurled across the back seat by the sudden deceleration as the Land Rover slewed wildly in the road. She slammed up against the glass, cracking the side of her head off the rim. Her vision filmed over redly. She was screaming, Cutter was shouting, the engine squealing and the ruined wheel-rims shrieking. It was an uproar of violence and fear trapped within the claustrophobic confines of the cramped car.

Nando wrestled with the wheel, but the skid became a full slide, all hope of control ripped out from under him by a block of concrete fifty yards down the road from the nail belt. The Rover hit it almost side on, Nando over-compensated, and the vehicle spun wildly out of control. There was a sickening stomach-churning moment of inertia, then the crippled vehicle completed the spin, flipped, and came down on the roof.

The metal frame screamed in protest as the sudden weight crushed down on it, but before the road could completely destroy the frame and crush them all, the Land Rover flipped again, coming down on the passenger side. Then it rolled, spinning out of control on the metal.

Cutter lay with his shoulder and neck pinned against the buckled roof. His chest burned where the seat belt cut into it. He could feel the trickle of blood down the side of his face. His vision blurred as he tried to move. Beside him, Nando groaned.

The Rover had come to a stop on its roof.

He could see Jenny. Without a seat belt to restrain her she had been thrown about viciously as the Land Rover had flipped. She was crushed up against the ceiling, and wasn't moving. There was blood on her cheek from a cut above her eye.

"Is everyone okay?" Cutter said, twisting around as he tried to reach the buckle and spring the mechanism. The blood rushed to his head; he felt it pulsing against his temples and behind his eyes.

Before either of them could answer, flashlights probed the darkness, playing over their faces. Jenny groaned as the light lingered in her eyes. An overwhelming sense of relief surged through Cutter. In those few moments she hadn't answered him worms of dread had burrowed down into his gut. He wouldn't lose her, *not twice*. He refused to.

The flashlight beams crossed, and then came up over his face, fiercely bright in his eyes. He tried to shield them with his hand, but moving only brought on a whole new world of hurt. There were at least three of them; there were that many lights. Why had they been on the road? Why had they thrown the belt of nails? Why had they even been there, out in the middle of nowhere? This road ran back to the reserve centre and out among all points that the rangers travelled to observe the wildlife they protected; it wasn't a shopping route, there were no Sunday drivers out to enjoy the pretty countryside. Which meant that whoever they were, the men behind the torches had to have known who they were ambushing.

All of these things went through Cutter's mind in the blood-swelling silence that preceded a single shocking and sickening sound. breaking glass. The men had turned their torches on the Land Rover's windows, driving them against the surface again and again until the glass shattered, spraying inward.

Cutter twisted wildly around in the prison of his seat, trying to see what was happening. He felt the bite of shards against his face and then he saw the black-gloved hands reaching into the back and grabbing Jenny by the feet and ankles as she kicked and screamed hysterically.

His fingers found the button on the buckle's clasp and pushed it down. For a sickening second he hung there, still trapped by the force of gravity, then he fell, hitting the roof of the car hard. His head took most of his weight from the impact. His vision blurred sickeningly as his eyes filmed over with a wash of blood that turned the night world red.

Then he twisted his body, reaching around into the back of the car. He didn't know what he was doing; he wasn't thinking, he was just grasping, determined not to let Jenny go. Her hands found his. She screamed his name over and over: "Nick! Nick!" as they dragged her out.

He hung on for dear life, for her life, but she slipped between his fingers. He crawled over into the back seat, scrambling toward the broken window, cutting up his hands and knees on the broken glass and not feeling a thing. He couldn't look left or right, his eyes were fixed on Jenny as she was dragged further and further away.

Nando was out cold in the front seat. He had no idea how close the creatures were, so thick was the trailing mist, they could have been twenty feet away, and he never would have known.

She begged him, and that was the worst of it. Frightened, desperately afraid, she begged him over and over.

"Nick! Please God, Nick, don't let me go! *Nick!*"

Her hands slipped from his fingers until he was grasping at empty air. He threw himself forward, trying to worm out through the broken window, to catch her and bring her back.

And then something hit him; a torch, a crowbar, a booted foot, he didn't know. It didn't matter. It took him across the side of the head and the world lurched sickeningly as it faded. Cutter reached out one last time, desperately trying to find her hand in the darkness that consumed his mind.

It wasn't there.

The last thing he heard was her voice, desperately screaming his name.

TWENTY-TWO

Jack Stark drove the ambassador's Escalade into the devouring dark.

He came like an avenging angel in the night.

The engine whined sickly as he grated through the gears and forced it up and down the assault course of tracks that twisted through the oppressive trees. The lights barely touched the night as the rising mist diffused what little illumination they offered. It was almost as though the air had been replaced by a viscous liquid.

He had the co-ordinates written down on a scrap of map, the destination ringed in red.

Stark hit the clutch again, cold fury driving his mind and body.

Chaplin had sold them out to the poachers. A man named Eberhardt had bought them for the not so princely sum of US $50,000. That valued their lives at 6,250 bucks apiece. There wasn't a chance in hell he was going to let Chaplin get away with this.

He hit the accelerator, ramming the gear-stick into place.

It hadn't taken long to get what he needed from the dying man. Most civilians made the mistake of thinking torture worked, but it seldom did.

Almost never, really.

Stick a finger in a bullet hole and wriggle it around, all you do is cause a finite amount of pain. It hurts, no denying that, but the body can process it, can understand it and — most importantly — limit it. The threat is far more potent a tool.

The threat is infinite. He had crouched down beside the dying man and given him the simplest of choices, life or death. The others were dead, and the man's fate lay in Stark's hands. He wouldn't kill him, though. There would be no quick surcease. No going gently into the endless winter night. There would be pain and suffering every inch of the way. It was that simple.

"I could make it painless," he had said, doing exactly what he hated, pressing his finger into the worst of the man's open wounds, "but I won't. It will hurt you to live, or it will hurt you to die, but either way it will hurt. The only thing I will do if you co-operate is call you an ambulance. It's your call."

Eberhardt's man had sung like the proverbial canary.

The German fronted a lucrative business in import and export, bolstering his finances with pretty little rarities. There was a collector out there for everything.

Eberhardt had given them simple enough instructions: silence the boy. No matter what the cost, his story wasn't to be told. Stark could guess why; Cam Bairstow knew the village had been attacked by creatures, and what kind of creatures. His knowledge would bring scientists and worse, tourists, looking for those exotic animals.

Dead, Cam was just another lost student taken by the rainforest. Unfortunate, to be sure, but that was the way it was. Students came to study the environment and the ruins and were rarely prepared for the harsh nature of the Amazon. It was the same in Kenya and Nigeria and Bolivia and all these other exotic places.

And then it hit Stark, the truth beneath everything, the single illuminating fact he had been searching for. The poachers knew *exactly* what the creature was. They had seen it, or been attacked by it, and realised that they had found one of the truly exotic specimens, one so rare that collectors would pay real money for.

The Thylacosmilus was their own personal diamond mine. And they didn't have a clue where it came from.

But now the British government had sent them looking for Cam — so what did that mean?

He had assumed the poachers intended to kidnap and ransom them, just as the so-called freedom fighters would, making demands, listing concessions, but that kind of thinking was dreadfully naive.

No, kidnap-and-ransom would only bring more attention to the thing these people were trying so desperately to hide. So there had to be another answer.

What it came down to was this: as far as the poachers were concerned, Cutter and his team were a thorn they would be better off plucking out of their flesh. They didn't want money — they wanted these intruders dead. Eberhardt's kind were hardly strangers to murder. Their money greased most of the wheels in this godforsaken tin pot 'democracy'. Their money financed the Shining Path, providing guns and ammunition to destabilise the regime, and provided the propaganda machine with grist to pretend the Túpac Amaru Revolutionary Movement were interested in truth and reconciliation.

Eberhardt was, in the most basic of senses, an evil man.

He had offices in Lima and Cuzco as well as bonded warehouse facilities in the main port of Calloa. None of these were of interest to the SAS man. The poachers had to have a base of operations out in the rainforest itself; that was what he was interested in, that and what he could expect to encounter there.

He had taken his phone out of his pocket and dialled the first two digits of the emergency services number, then held it out, inviting the bleeding man to finish dialling.

"All you've got to do is tell me where it is."

"They'll kill me."

"That's supposing you don't bleed to death first," Stark had said almost amicably.

"You don't understand."

"So help me to."

"He owns your man."

"Who?"

"Chaplin. Eberhardt owns Chaplin. Chaplin is his *cabron*," Stark's Spanish was weak, but he knew the word well enough to appreciate the way the bleeding man spat it out; it had several colourful connotations including goat, bastard, and man-whore. None of them was particularly promising, given that Chaplin had taken the team out into the middle of nowhere.

Had he even filed the permits with the authorities? Was there an actual expedition, or was it merely another level of the deception?

Was Chaplin playing his own game, or playing the poacher's? He didn't need to think about it.

A few minutes in the man's company had told him all he needed to know. Stark trusted his instincts when it came to back-stabbing scum like Chaplin. They might have the patter and the smooth looks to go with it, but they were rotten inside, and that rot always broke out eventually.

Chaplin had taken Cutter and the team out into the jungle to die.

The man had nothing to gain from lying and everything to gain from telling the truth. "The co-ordinates for the Río Huepetue compound are Latitude 12° 45' 0 South, Longitude 70° 34' 0 West."

Stark dialled the last of the digits and told the paramedics that they had a dying man up at the ambassador's summer house.

"Thank you," the bleeding man had said.

"I'm not a monster," Stark told him.

"Eberhardt has nine men out at the compound. The front entry is protected by high security, but there is a second way in through the tunnels from an abandoned temple. We use that route occasionally, but it is generally unguarded. Don't walk up to Eberhardt's stronghold waving your gun. He has eyes everywhere." The German gestured weakly upwards, as though at the trees. Stark took the warning to mean that Eberhardt had some pretty hefty surveillance at his disposal.

"You didn't have to warn me."

"You didn't have to make that call. We are even."

"Yes, we are."

He left the man alone with the horrors of the dark, and went in search of the ambassadorial staff. His instincts told him that they were for the most part honest — Cam would likely be safe.

Then he needed some wheels. The garage had been filled with inappropriate cars, high performance sports models or trendy about-towners. Of the seven vehicles, the Escalade was the only one that looked like it might make it out into the rainforest's more remote spots without floundering on the terrible roads. He had been half tempted to fire up the Lotus Elan, just for the sake of it, though. Like women, some cars were made for speed with no consideration for comfort. But they were hellishly good fun to drive hard.

He reached over the seat for the radio, driving with one hand on the wheel and one eye on the road. The radio was tuned in to the military channel, 2112. Holding it to his mouth, he thumbed down the transmitter and spoke for the sixteenth time in sixteen minutes.

"Cutter? Anyone? This is Stark. Come in Cutter. Are you receiving me?"

And for the sixteenth time he was answered by radio silence.

He laid the handset aside for another minute.

They were relatively short distance receivers with a range of about fifty kilometres, further during the hours of darkness. Probably less now, though, with the weather conditions as they were, the insidious low-lying fog crawling about on the roads and through the trees. It was a dirty creature, moving with infinite slowness as it draped itself across the branches and weighed down the thick vines. The words would get clotted in the fog, reducing the range to no more than fifteen klicks.

Balancing the wheel with his thigh, Stark unfolded the map again, cross-referencing the co-ordinates of the hidden entrance to the Río Huepetue compound. He had programmed it into the GPS, but didn't trust the results it was showing. Given his speed, he estimated the location as being considerably further away than the technology indicated.

His gut said the satellite was wrong.

Stark folded the map with one hand, following the creases, and picked up the radio again.

"Cutter? This is Stark. Pick up your damned radio, man! Cutter, do you hear me?"

This time, as he was about to discard the handset, it crackled into life, Cutter's Scottish burr was breaking up badly. It didn't matter.

"Cutter, we've got a problem. I need you to get away from everyone. We need to talk."

"Stark?" For a moment the crackle of static was the only thing on the line, then the Professor's voice came through again. "What the hell are you doing out here?"

"Change of plans, Prof. Let's just say it all came together. Now I'm taking measures to make sure it doesn't all fall apart again."

"They've taken Jenny, Stark. They snatched her right out of my hands."

A low branch lashed across the windscreen. Stark yanked down hard on the wheel with his free hand, swinging the Escalade around a dark lump in the middle of his path.

This road wasn't made for one-handed driving. The wheel bucked in his hand as the Escalade juddered through the potholes and over the broken stones. Dividing his concentration between the road and Cutter was a recipe for disaster. He slowed to a stop.

"Okay, talk to me, Professor. What's going on?"

"We were ambushed as we tried to get Blaine back to the hospital."

"Slow down, Prof. From the top. What happened?"

"Poachers. Military. Shining Path. I've got no bloody idea."

"The *beginning*, Cutter."

Static buzz crackled for a full thirty seconds.

"We found another slaughtered settlement," he said, his voice slower now, his accent thinner. "Chaplin was killed while we tracked the Thylacosmilus that had killed most of the villagers. As we tried to retreat to the vehicles, we were attacked. Blaine was injured protecting Abby."

"Chivalrous idiot," Stark said. "How badly is he hurt?"

"Badly enough," Cutter said. "We got back to the Land Rovers and were heading back to civilisation when this car came out of nowhere. It nearly ran us off the road, then disappeared into the fog. As we caught up to it, a figure threw a belt of nails beneath the wheels of our Land Rover. We lost control and crashed. Nando was hurt, and our attackers came out of the trees then, smashed the windows, and snatched Jenny.

"Everyone else is fine. The rest of our crew were five miles down the road by the time they realised we weren't with them.

"Okay, Prof., Chaplin being dead isn't such a bad thing. Put it this way, it saves me from killing the bastard when I catch up with you guys."

"What do you mean?"

"He sold us out, Cutter. Sir Charles' man on the ground took his thirty pieces of silver and snuggled up nicely in the back pocket of the poachers, notably a guy named Eberhardt — nasty piece of work from Germany. To make a long story short, Eberhardt knows about the creatures. He has to. That's the only thing that explains this. He's looking to profit on trading these supposedly extinct treasures to some greedy collectors, and you guys are slap bang in the middle, threatening to screw everything up for him."

"Are you sure this Eberhardt has got Jenny?"

"I'd bet the farm on it. He's probably using her as bait, to bring you to him, then he's going to kill her, along with the rest of you."

"Oh, *Jesus*. Please tell me you know where she is?" Cutter's voice strained with the need to hope.

"I'm heading there right now," Stark said. "Eberhardt's got a compound in the Río Huepetue region. You leave Miss Lewis to me. I'll bring her home in one piece, you have my word. You do what you have to do your end. I really want to get the hell out of Dodge, and sooner rather than later. The minute I go in there, the crapola is well and truly going to hit the fan.

"When Eberhardt realises we're on to him, things are going to escalate rapidly. Especially given that I fully intend to go in all guns blazing. We aren't exactly in Boreham Wood, Cutter. A full frontal assault is going to blow the lid right off the top of this pressure cooker. These jokers are going to strike back hard and fast. We don't want to be around to give them the chance. That's assuming there are any left when I'm finished with them.

"Right now I'm thinking about a war of total extinction."

"I don't care how many of them you kill," Cutter said. "Just bring her back."

He didn't need to say anything else.

TWENTY-THREE

He checked the co-ordinates on the map a final time. Left with no alternative, the SAS man abandoned the Escalade and continued the journey on foot. As he did, the mist thinned, until it was gone altogether.

There was a reason Sir Charles had selected him for this mission. Before joining the Regiment he had served with the British Army in Brunei and trained with the Gurkhas for seven years, immersing himself in their culture and ethic, learning all there was to know about jungle combat. There was no one more attuned to the environment than him. He didn't talk about it much because there were things he had done, especially in Cambodia, that he never wanted to remember again.

Still, running through the jungle at night brought the memories back to him. The crunch of deadfall beneath his feet was the same crunch he had heard entering the monastery, the rustle of leaves was the same rustle of leaves that he had heard as he ghosted around the outside of the orphanage, all of these sounds were the same sounds he had heard as he approached places of death.

There would be death here today, he knew.

He knew because he brought it with him.

He always did.

Stark moved quickly, running fast and breathing hard as he shuttled from point to point, no more than twenty metres between each, then pressed his back up flat against the tree trunks, scanning the line of trees ahead. He wasn't about to make a mistake when lives were on the line.

The night was still, the chill creeping into his bones as he in turn crept though its dark heart. The ground crunched beneath his feet as he ran, pushing his way through the thick tangle of weeds and creepers that seemed to smother the undergrowth like a spider's web.

He crouched down, close to an imposing shadow-trunk, to check the compass bearings. The compound was no more than two klicks to the east of him, which meant he ought to be running into security right about now. Distant early warning systems were designed primarily to *be* early warnings, not last-minute he's-right-on-top-of-us warnings. Stark pulled the thermal-imaging goggles down over his eyes and scanned the shadows, looking for any heat sources. There were no tell-tale oranges or reds to betray man or beast. He pushed the goggles back and repeated the scan, looking with the naked eye for anything suspicious: cameras, listening devices, tripwires.

Just because he couldn't see them didn't mean they weren't there.

He grunted at his own paranoia. He was beginning to think like those nut-jobs who posted their idiot theories on the Internet: aliens, secret government bases, rifts in time and genetically-engineered dinosaurs roaming the Earth.

He still found it hard to believe the stuff Lester and Cutter had told them during the debriefing in the ARC. It was the stuff you expected from crackpots and cryptozoologists, not serious scientists. And yet...

Just because they're paranoid, delusional muppets doesn't mean they're wrong, Stark thought, pushing himself to his feet and racing — hard, fast, legs and arms pumping as he kept low. He made himself as small as he could, dropping into a crouch twenty yards deeper into the trees. Again he repeated the procedure, then set off once more, aiming for a huge black trunk thirty yards ahead.

As he hit the tree, Stark felt the hairs on the back of his neck begin to prickle. It was an instinctive thing; his soldier's sense. He dropped to one knee and pulled the thermal goggles back down over his eyes. With the world changed to one of hot and cold spots, he swept a quick three-sixty, and midway through the circuit he spied the phosphorescent glare of a man walking cautiously through the undergrowth, directly toward him.

Stark licked his lips.

He had two choices: one, avoid the watcher, which would be easy enough, since he knew exactly where he was and there was plenty of thick cover to mask his passage. Or two, disable him. Stark chose the second. He had no wish to leave a potential enemy at his back. Getting back out meant having a clean run back to the Escalade. A lone sentry prowling the jungle didn't fit into that picture.

Creeping forward, Stark slowed his breathing. He slipped a saw-toothed blade from its boot-sheath and waited, listening to the blunder-ing of the sentry. The man was no more than twenty yards away, his sub-machine gun held lazily down at his side. His boots crunched through the deadfall, making enough noise for a small herd of wildebeest to stampede over his head without him being able to hear it. Stark eased himself slowly to the standing position, keeping the bulk of the tree between him and the approaching sentry.

He counted to sixty, inserting "one thousand" between each integer. *One, one thousand, two, one thousand, three, one thousand...* just to make sure he didn't rush the count and move too soon.

As the sentry passed his hiding place, Stark stepped soundlessly out behind him and clasped a hand across his mouth. Before the man could scream he drew the serrated edge of the blade across his throat. He waited a moment, to make certain the man didn't utter a sound, and stepped back, letting him fall. He bent down to retrieve the sub-machine gun — a compact MP5. He knew the gun well — it was the staple of law enforcement and tactical squads, as well as standard-issue military.

That was the worst thing about the modern world. Death, the great leveller, had found its way into the hands of the bad guys. It was the escalation of killing potential that unnerved him; it wasn't that the villains had never had access to guns — he'd grown up with images of Dick Tracy with his Tommy guns. It was that Desert Eagles, MP5s, CS gas, C5, all of these military grade weapons made for peacekeeping were being used to shatter that same peace. But then, the notion of fighting for peace was an oxymoron.

The dead man had a small short-wave walkie-talkie fastened to his belt. Stark took it from him and headed off toward the compound.

Stark lay in the long grass.

Beyond the chain-link fence he could make out the first of two large buildings, and six prefabricated huts. The larger of the two was probably some sort of storage barn, the other most likely their base of operations.

He saw four main high-power security lights, post-mounted at each of the cardinals, north, south, east and west from the main buildings. No doubt they were rigged up to some sort of motion detectors. There was only one point of ingress, a security gate on the east side manned by a solitary guard who had his head in a paperback book. There were three all-terrain vehicles parked close to the second building, reinforcing the idea that this was the command centre.

Power lines were rigged up overhead, arcing back to a generator located behind the storage barn. As he was looking at the wires, a plan began to ferment in his mind. *What would Rambo do?* he thought grimly. Then he dismissed the idea as near suicidal. Only fools changed their plan mid-execution.

Fools, in his game, had a nasty habit of winding up dead.

He needed to find the back door.

He tried to remember the bleeding German's directions to the ruined temple, and compared them against what he could see in front of him. Using the gate and the barn to orient himself, Stark decided that the way down into the ruin ought to be about 400 yards off to his left, and if the man was to be trusted, it would provide him with a series of tunnels that linked in with the compound's subterranean level.

There's only one way to find out, he thought. Then he set off, keeping low, and grateful for the thick canopy of leaves which kept out most of the moonlight, giving him plenty of darkness to cling to.

The German had been telling the truth.

The spectre of the ruined temple rose up out of the forest like something out of mythology. He could feel the history of the place, the vibrant worship. He could almost taste the vital energies of those poor souls who no doubt had been put to death on this site, in worship of one god or another. He had no way of telling if it was Viracocha, his son Imaymana Viracocha, Inti, Mama Quilla or Manco Capac. This place could have been holy to any of them, or all of them. Peering at it, shrouded in darkness — and at what looked disturbingly like skulls lined up above the main portal — he found himself thinking of supay, the god of death, with his insatiable hungers.

Until the assault, conversations with Cameron had yielded amazing little nuggets of history, facts the average tourist would never bother to uncover. For instance, the Incas had given hundreds of children a year to Supay in the hopes that he would leave them alone. Yet for some reason, the death god never did.

Stark sprinted across the open ground.

He looked over his shoulder once, as he took the last step before disappearing inside. The change in the air was immediate; it went from clear and cold and crisp, to stagnant, stale and syrupy. Five steps beyond the keystone of the arch, and the darkness was absolute.

He pulled the Maglite from his belt and clicked it on. The thin light played over the contours of the passage, fixing them in his mind before he lowered it so the beam only illuminated a small circle around his feet as he strode confidently forward. The floor of the temple was littered with the mulch of the forest and alive with beetles and insects picking over that thick, black muck. There were plenty of tracks in the mulch; enough to suggest that Eberhardt's crew came this way every bit as often as they used the main gate into the compound, which meant he had to be on his guard.

The walkie-talkie he had taken from the sentry crackled to life loudly in the dark, and the sudden burst of noise sent a slither of panic deep into Stark's heart.

"Jorgensen, zurückberichten," the voice demanded in German. Stark's German wasn't particularly fluent but he knew the word: report.

He pushed on, sweeping the beam forward again. Spider's webs clogged the ceiling, draping down over the narrow, twisting passageway. He had paid plenty of attention when they were briefing them about the poisonous spiders of the region, just as any arachnophobe would. There was *Amaxonyan Rectilae*, almost certainly the most poisonous of all venomous creatures in the world; then there was the Murderess, the Brazilian wandering spider, almost ten times more venomous than the Black Widow; and the Panama Blonde. Plenty enough to have the sight of the thick web clot his courage.

Stark baulked. He lowered the thermal goggles, looking for any significant heat sources, then wondered sickly if the spiders weren't cold blooded, like reptiles. He wished to God — Christian or Incan, it didn't matter to him — that Cutter or one of his crew were here to deal with the arachnids.

"Jorgensen, report," the German voice demanded again. Jorgensen was almost certainly the man with whom he had played *The Demon Barber of*

Fleet Street a few minutes earlier. He pressed down on the transmitter and said gruffly in his best German, "All clear."

Fortunately that seemed to convince whoever was listening, and the radio went quiet.

He stared at the thick webs. He really didn't want to push his way through them. A torch was all well and good with light, but what he really wanted was something that would burn. A flame-thrower, hell, even a bottle of deodorant and a lighter would do. Few spiders were flame retardant, after all.

The best he could manage was pulling his shirt up over his head and plunging through the tangled webs. He felt the furry touch of what had to be a spider up against his cheek and flinched, pulling away from it as he tore through its barrier. With the Maglite between his teeth he started to run and didn't stop until he hit a dead-end of cracked and broken stones.

There was nothing to suggest any hidden passage or entrance that led down into the crypts — if the temples of the Incas even *had* crypts.

His skin was clammy.

He dug his fingernails into his palm.

He felt his heart in his throat, his pulse erratic. Cold sweat peppered on his brow and dribbled down his temple to his cheek, merging with the stubble. His breathing was shallow, nostrils flaring as he exhaled. He closed his eyes, focusing on the shallow inhalation, slowing it down, regulating it.

Breathe in. Hold. Count to ten. Breathe out. Count to ten. Breathe in. Hold.

He shivered as he turned to look back the way he had come, seeing the seething shadows that seemed to swarm toward him. Stark tried to remember what the German had said, but he hadn't given any clues. He'd just said that there was a back way in through the tunnels.

He needed to think.

The tracks that traipsed into the temple suggested that the poachers used the hidden entrance pretty frequently. The thick spiders' webs growing across the passageway disputed that truth. The arachnids could spin their elaborate constructions quickly, but not *that* quickly, so logic dictated that he'd taken the road less travelled — and in this case, it was the wrong one. He needed to push his way back through the ruined web and find the place where two passages diverged in the ruin.

He tracked his way back, swallowing down the bile that rose in his throat as the fine filaments of web brushed up against his skin. He didn't dare look left or right. His heart hammered in his chest, trying to burst free of the bones.

It was ridiculous, really; a man capable of snapping the neck of an enemy soldier without a second's thought, scared of a bunch of creepy crawlies.

Poisonous creepy crawlies, he amended.

Then the bulbous body of an enormous spider crossed his path, its furry legs moving through the circle of torchlight. Stark brought his thick-soled desert microlite boot down on its bloated abdomen. The arachnid ruptured.

Stark moved on, back the way he had come, finding the divergent passage he had missed on the way down. It was no surprise that he had; it was little more than a crack between the immense building blocks of the old temple.

He wriggled through, his shoulder blades and chest dragging against both sides of the stone as he forced himself through the gap. It opened up on the other side, leading to a short set of steps carved into the base rock. He followed them down.

The air beneath the surface was old. He was struck by the notion that perhaps a dozen people had breathed this air in 500 years. It was a humbling thought about the nature of time, and his own place as a mote in its eye.

You've been hanging around with Cutter for too long, he thought, chuckling to himself as he shone the light into the deeper darkness, though not far enough that it might give him away. The passage disappeared into the vanishing point, a straight walk on a shallow decline. He clicked off the Maglite and put the thermal goggles on once again. There were no noticeable heat sources, but the cold walls showed up starkly, allowing him to move through the darkness with confidence. He checked to make sure the MP5 was locked and loaded, then moved on down the passage.

If Eberhardt was the kind of anal retentive paranoid most Bond villains were, he probably had a dozen heat-sensitive cameras recessed into the walls, as well as motion sensors, pressure pads set in the floor, and some sort of lethal gas trap waiting to fug up around his face and knock him out cold. These thoughts were hardly reassuring, but in Stark's experience the real world contained few Bond villains.

Most were anaemic little individuals who craved the power money could buy. They didn't have secret schemes of world domination; they watched the Stock Exchange, the Dow Jones and the Hang Seng. They golfed at St Andrews and holidayed in the Maldives. They were, in other words, entirely banal, boring businessmen in suits with two point four children and very little in terms of a flair for the theatrical.

That was the nature of the new evil in the world, it walked the streets of polite respectability, essentially invisible because the gun runners, drug smugglers and crime lords looked just like accountants, computer programmers and government scientists.

He came to a reinforced steel door at the end of the tunnel — most certainly *not* an original feature of the temple. Stark pressed his back up against the old stone and listened at the door. No sounds filtered through.

There was no handle, so he felt about for a latch or pressure point; there had to be a way to open it from this side.

For one sickening moment he thought not, then his fingers found the cracks in the stone around the frame, and in turn the latch that released the door. He eased it open, expecting the slow creak to announce his arrival, but it opened silently on well-greased hinges. On the other side of the door he was presented with more passageway, much like the 100 yards or so of cold stone he had just walked along. There were no turnings. He was actually doing an Alice in reverse and going back *up* the rabbit hole. This was their escape route should the authorities ever raid the compound.

It made sense to have a back door, and the odds of finding a naturally occurring one — or being the beneficiary of an historical one — were slim to non-existent.

He felt out the smooth walls. Every so often he found the rough edges left behind by blasting caps from where the passage had been opened up. It was most definitely man-made, and not too old, either.

He followed it to its end without incident.

TWENTY-FOUR

It took Abby a few minutes to realise she was warming a dead man.

She hadn't noticed the precise moment when Andy Blaine had stopped shivering, or the last sigh that escaped his lips. At least not consciously. She felt the cold of him against her hands, and reached up to his neck to feel for a pulse, knowing even as she did that it wouldn't be there.

He had died to save her.

She felt small then, weighed down by the burden of knowing she had to live for two.

"Damn it," she said. Her eyes stung with unshed tears. She felt a tightness in her chest.

Abby rolled away from the dead man. His blankets were sodden with blood. She looked at his face in the striated darkness, dawn's first blush beginning to filter through the canopy of leaves. He wasn't handsome or heroic to look at, just a normal man, but he was her hero. She placed a soft kiss on his forehead and closed his eyes.

Then she banged on the partition between the cage and the driver's cab, trying to catch their attention. Stephen glanced back at her. He read her face and leaned over, telling Lucas to pull over. The Land Rover slowed to a stop. Abby clambered back out over the tailgate and hugged Lucas.

"I'm sorry," she said, wanting to say so much more — that it was her fault, that she owed him her life — but none of that would come out. So she said all she could say. "I'm so sorry."

Lucas hugged her back. He understood.

"Soldiers die," he said, as though stating some great universal truth. "He fell in the line of duty, saving a beautiful woman. There are worse ways to go."

She shrugged, not convinced but not willing to argue.

After drawing the cover up over Blaine's face, she joined Connor and Genaro up front in the other Land Rover which had pulled over behind them. The back was filled with camping gear.

"Connor? Where's the radio?"

Connor looked like the Wicked Witch of the West, sweat plastered to his scalp, skin pasty-white. All he needed to do to complete the illusion was beg her to help him because he was melting. He passed her the handset — the only one that had survived the mêlée back in the rainforest — and was alarmed to find that it had been turned off the entire time.

Abby radioed Cutter to let him know that Blaine had died before they had made it even halfway back to Cuzco.

That's when she learned about Jenny and the poacher's attack, and the fact that Cutter's Land Rover was out of commission.

"We need you guys to come pick us up. Nando and I aren't far from the ruined temple. A couple of hours walk and it's all done. We'll get the Thylacosmilus back into the Plio-Pleistocene, and then we'll deal with this other thing, whatever it is." She wasn't certain what he meant by the "other thing", but decided to let it slide until later.

"We're coming to collect you, so just wait there," she said. "Connor's got the anomaly detector, and you'll be flailing around in the dark without us. But what makes you think the anomaly is in this ruined temple?"

"It's where it all began," Cutter explained. "Cam and Jaime were first attacked there, and it's where Cam saw the diamonds in the sky."

"But it wasn't there when they went back, was it? That's what Jenny said."

"It's the only place we know for sure there was an anomaly, so it's where we have to start. Maybe it moved; maybe it closed. Connor will be able to tell for certain. If it closed for good we've got no choice but to kill the creatures. If it didn't maybe we can get them home."

"Understood. We're on our way."

They collected Cutter and Nando and drove to the rendezvous point. Both Cutter and the ranger were battered and bruised, wearing the effects of the crash on their faces. Nando had a long gash down his right cheek that seemed to extend his smile all the way to his ear. Cutter had a nasty purple bruise and swelling beneath his left eye, as well as a series of small cuts where the glass had showered across his face.

There were other wounds Abby couldn't see, but knew were there from the way the men carried themselves. The other Land Rover was already waiting, Stephen and Lucas leaning against the vehicle. Both looked the worse for the heat and lack of sleep.

Cutter was already out of the car and talking to the two men as she approached, giving orders. Battered or not, it was good to see him back in control. She had been worried about him. He still appeared haunted, but as much by the lack of sleep as anything else. They had all suffered over the last few days, trying to function off the fumes of alertness.

The sun was edging up over the high peaks, pulling apart the thinnest wisps of mist as it gave the shepherds of the Andes plenty of warning. Even that little hint of sun was enough to take the chill off the morning. In less than an hour it would be unbearable again. The extremes of day and night were unlike anything she had ever experienced.

She checked her watch and wished she hadn't — it told her what she felt in her weary bones. She had been awake for twenty-eight hours straight. And now she was about to trek into the unknown, to face creatures that had already killed so many, and not just faceless villagers. They had lost two members of their team. She stretched, yawning, and knuckled the need for sleep out of her eyes. She looked up at the sky, urging it to wake her up.

By the time she arrived at the other Land Rover, Cutter was already explaining to the assembled group about the theory concerning the strange scents, and their relationship to the unnatural behaviour of the Thylacosmilus. It sounded outrageous, yet it explained so much of what had happened.

"This thing, whatever it is, is far from stupid. It's got a dominant personality. Like men who use dogs to hunt, giving them the scent of their quarry, it has asserted its will on the pack of Thylacosmilus. It's steering them by scent. Back at the settlement you all smelled it, right? Something out of place? Coffee, vanilla, fish, all of these really strong, really pungent odours. It's using pheromones to communicate with the

Thylacosmilus, using them like hounds to track its quarry. And as soon as we go in there, we're going to be its quarry. I can't make myself any clearer. Smell something wrong, something incredibly out of place, and you can bet our predator is nearby, playing master of the hunt."

"What about the poachers?" Lucas asked.

"We'll worry about them when we have to. Hopefully Stark is good to his word, and we won't have to deal with them. Right now I think we've got enough to worry about."

Abby could tell that there was a great deal he wasn't saying — most likely concern for Jenny — but to his credit he focused on their current task.

She looked up toward the peaks, and the outline of the temple visible in the rising sun. Even from ten kilometres away, it was an awe-inspiring sight. She could imagine it all those years ago, the Incas making their pilgrimage to the holy place, watching the sun break free of the clouds to bless the stones with its radiance.

"Cutter?" she said, turning to face him.

"What, Abby?"

"When you say out-of-place smells, do you mean things like sulphur and ammonia?" she said, breathing in so deeply that even the faint traces that lingered brought a tear to her eyes.

Cutter nodded.

"It was here before us. I don't know what the individual odours mean, but I don't think the presence of *any* of them is particularly positive, given what we're dealing with."

Back at the tailgate of the first Land Rover, Lucas cracked the seals on one of the steel coffins and opened it to reveal a high velocity rifle that had been modified to fire tranquilliser darts. Abby had dosed up the ketamine solution, making it potent enough to bring down an elephant. He pocketed a magazine with three extra darts in it, muttering something about feeling like a date rapist.

Connor slapped him on the back and said "Welcome to my world... No, er, that didn't come out right. I mean..."

"Don't worry about it, kid. Let's go find you a date, shall we?" The SAS man grinned despite his obvious distress at the death of his colleague and close friend. The grief would come, Abby was certain, but only when he allowed it, and on his terms.

"You'll need a bigger gun," she said, wandering over to join them as they were gearing up.

Connor tested the anomaly detector, hearing that faint burr of static that said something was definitely active. When they were close enough it would emit that tell-tale interference, pinpointing the anomaly to within about 100 metres. It would be a vital piece of kit, especially if they needed to go underground.

She claimed herself a tranquilliser pistol with a thick grip, and the rest of the group followed suit. It had a two-dart chamber with gas-propulsion. Each dart fired off a separate trigger mechanism and would pierce a hide at thirty metres. She took a pair of thermal-imaging goggles and hung them around her neck.

"Right," Cutter said, "pass me a knife, and then someone give me a hand getting the spare out of the back."

Lucas did as he was asked, handing it over hilt first while Connor and Stephen wrestled with the spare tyre. They heaved it out from beneath the equipment coffin and rolled it toward Cutter. The Professor knelt, driving the blade hilt-deep into the rubber, and hacked his way through it, cutting the tyre into strips.

"Assuming the beast is using pheromones to direct the Thylacosmilus, we've got to inhibit them. Pheromones are essentially saturated hydro-carbon chains. In animals, they're detected by using the vomeronasal organ, which lies between the nose and mouth and is the first stage of the accessory olfactory system. It's how we smell things. Short of wishing a bad case of the flu on the pouch-blades, the next best thing is to intro-duce something into the air that will interfere with their breathing in and responding to the pheromones.

"Burning rubber releases a natural isoprenoid. There are several natural isoprenoids — they're looking into them as pesticides. In Northern California they use a particular isoprenoid formed from the chlorophyl of leaves to block the sex pheromone of moths. Left unchecked, the moths could decimate the forestry up there. So they spray the air in the orchards and around the forests, putting a serious damper on the moth's love life. We're doing the same here. The smell the rubber gives off when it's burning acts as an inhibitor. Get enough of it in the air, and it'll interfere with the pheromones the beast is using to control the Thylacosmilus."

Abby took a bandana from her pocket and fastened it around her forehead to keep her hair back. Beside her stood the two rangers — Nando was checking the batteries in the torches, while Genaro was siphoning off the petrol from one of the three Land Rovers and using it to fill small plastic phials. When he was done he gave one to each of them and said simply, "To light the rubber. It won't burn well without some sort of reagent."

"What exactly can this creature do? I mean with these pheromones? How well can it communicate?" Abby asked.

"I don't know," Cutter said. "This isn't really an exact science. We do know that there are a dozen different types of pheromone at least: aggregation pheromones, arousal ones, primers that trigger some kind of change in the development of events, sex pheromones to lure a mate, while certain insects such as ants use them to mark a trail."

"And to attack?"

"And to attack," Cutter confirmed.

Abby took a flare pistol and slipped it into the waistband of her shorts, and pocketed a lighter. She suggested that the others do the same. All of the gasoline and rubber in the world would be useless without something to light it.

TWENTY-FIVE

Stark heard voices in the dark.

They were speaking low, in urgent whispers.

He pressed himself up against the cold stone of the wall and strained to listen.

Slow, measured footsteps moved toward him, the sound swelling to fill the passageway. Thirty yards from where he lurked, the passage opened out into a brightly lit area. There were three voices that he could distinguish, all male. They were speaking in English, but none of them were native speakers; there was a stilted edge to their words, as though they were filtering them through a second layer of thought processes. One voice had that recognisably sharp Germanic edge to it. The others might have been Italian or Hispanic — it was difficult to say without seeing the speakers.

He had no intention of stepping out into the light.

Not yet.

There was some urgency to their conversation.

He understood why a moment later, when he heard the female voice demanding to talk to their leader.

"The government *will* find out about this, mark my words. You don't want to do this. Let me go now, and I will talk to them for you. I will tell them that you helped me."

They laughed at her, and he understood their arrogance. There was nothing in the threat to frighten them — in this twisted world they had nothing to fear. Eberhardt owned the government.

He almost pitied them the rude awakening they were about to get.

It was so typical of the woman to act as though she was trying to negotiate First Contact. Next she'd be trying to sweet talk them, offering them special dispensations with the British government, promising to grease a few wheels for their boss. Stark couldn't help but admire Jenny Lewis. There was something about her. He could certainly see what drew Cutter like a helpless moth to her flame. Not that the Professor was ever open about it. The man was so uptight around her it was almost funny.

The chatter continued. They seemed to be arguing about what the hell they were supposed to do with her.

Stark had a few suggestions, but he thought it wise to keep them to himself for the moment, at least.

There was movement. They were headed his way.

Stark lowered himself, offering as small a target as he could, then raised the MP5, but didn't yet fire.

The sub-machine gun had a bastard of a kick to it, but considering it could unload eight hundred rounds in a minute, that was no surprise. The magazine had thirty rounds in it. That was more than enough to cut a man in half.

Line 'em up and knock 'em down, he thought, biding his time.

He watched the shadows move across his line of sight.

Still he didn't squeeze the trigger.

His palms were clammy with cold sweat, his body pumping with endorphins. A part of the soldier hated himself for what he was about to do, but another part of him revelled in it. This was what he did. Others built monuments to gods, shot for the moon, found cures to big diseases with little names. Others helped. He killed. It was his gift.

He watched.

He waited.

And then he stepped out, when the voices were closest together. He walked slowly, keeping his pace measured so that his footsteps wouldn't betray him. He turned the corner and unloaded the entire clip in a scything line that cut across the centre of the guardroom in half a second. It was over as quickly as that. Three men whose names he didn't know lay in pools of maroon at his feet, their weapons impotent against the bringer of death.

A heartbeat later, the woman screamed. Then as quickly as she had begun, she stopped.

"Keep quiet," he rasped, his voice carrying across the shocking silence that travelled in the wake of the bullets.

"Who's there?" she called out.

"Stark. Now be *quiet*, unless you want to get us both killed."

This time she did as she was told.

He quickly checked to make sure the three men were as dead as they looked, then double checked the exits to be sure he wasn't in for any unpleasant surprises as he went in search of the woman. There were two more passages that led off the central area, one he assumed went down to whatever they were using for a holding cell, the other up toward the main compound. He found a set of keys on the smallest of the three men and took them.

"Eeny meany," Stark muttered, picking the second of the two corridors. He had a fifty-fifty chance that Jenny waited at the end of the one he chose.

It was all a numbers game. The German had said Eberhardt had nine men at the compound. He'd taken out four, then there was the gate keeper. That meant four more remained. He tossed aside the MP5, drew the Browning, and racked it, chambering a round.

The passage he followed led to a series of cages. It obviously served as some sort of storage pen for the animals they brought in from the forest. He found Jenny hunched up in one of the cages. She looked as though she'd been dragged through Hell kicking and screaming. Her usually coiffured hair was dishevelled and her make-up smeared. There was blood and bruising on the side of her face and her blouse had been torn to bare a badly bruised shoulder. Her skin was covered in cuts and shallow scratches, but none of the physical damage was all that worrying. It was the pain behind her eyes that concerned him the most — the damage that couldn't be seen.

"Come on, Jenny, let's get you out of here, shall we?" Stark said, crouching down beside the door to her cage.

He didn't hear the poacher moving up behind him, until he noticed the haunting snick of the safety being nudged out of place, and the way Jenny's head came up in sudden panic.

Stark threw himself to his left, hit the ground hard on his shoulder and rolled, coming up as the poacher's bullet missed, tearing into the air where his head had been a split-second before.

He squeezed off a single shot, hitting the man squarely in the chest. His eyes flared saucer-wide in shock, then the light that was his life went out. He was dead before he hit the ground.

"Next time a little warning would be nice," he said to Jenny as he fumbled with the lock to her cage, trying each of the various keys he had stolen until the tumblers fell into place and the mechanism clicked open.

He dragged the door of the steel cage open as Jenny crawled forward, and then helped her out. She needed his support to keep her legs from buckling.

"There's three unaccounted for," he said. "If you see anything, don't be afraid to yell, okay? By this time, they know I'm here."

She nodded.

"Good, come on then. We're going home."

"What about the others?"

He knew what she meant. She could play all the mind games her sex liked to play, but when it came right down to it what she was asking was, "What about Cutter?"

"Cutter's going to make sure they finish what they came here for. Right now, my only concern is getting you and Cam Bairstow back to England in one piece."

"And the poachers? Are you just going to leave them to carry on when we're gone?"

He closed his eyes.

He really wished she hadn't said that.

"What would you have me do? Hunt them down and kill them, one at a time?"

"If necessary," Jenny said. There was a coldness to her voice that he found utterly chilling.

"I'm not going to do it," he said. "We didn't come here to solve the illegal trafficking of endangered species, we came here to bring a boy back to his father, and deal with whatever escaped from this rift in... Christ I can't even bring myself to say it, it's so ridiculous."

"I know. I still don't claim to understand it, but I know what I believe, and I believe in Cutter. The rest is icing on the cake," she said, and he knew she meant it. "A multi-billion pound trade, Stark. These aren't good people."

"So that means they deserve to die? That we stand as judge, jury and executioner?" It was absurdly hypocritical to be arguing about it, with four men lying dead between them and the way out. "Deal with Eberhardt when you get home. Freeze his assets. Seize his properties. Bankrupt him. Do whatever it is you do. You've got the power of the entire British government behind you. He doesn't stand a chance.

"But here and now, you don't need to do this. Honestly, you don't. You can go after him and every one of his business associates. He's finished, he just doesn't know it yet. There's no need to stoop to his level. You're better than that. I know you are."

She faltered then. Whatever hurt they had done to her was slipping away as she realised that she didn't have the right to demand their deaths. She wasn't that person. Stark was right, and he could tell that she knew it.

"Take me home," she said weakly.

Slipping her arm around his shoulder, he carried her back toward civilisation.

"You smell terrible," she said, refusing to look down at the bodies as they passed them.

"Next time I come to rescue you, I'll remember to take a shower first," Stark replied.

"Let's hope there won't be a next time, shall we?"

"Sounds like a plan."

TWENTY-SIX

The march over ten kilometres beneath the rising sun felt like a slow journey through Dante's circles of the Inferno.

They made the ascent with precious little water and almost no food, because the majority of their supplies had been left behind in the crashed Land Rover. Still they travelled toward the ruined temple, staring at it on the horizon as though it were the door to Mephistopheles' inner sanctum.

There was no banter. Dry lips and dehydrated thoughts crumbled the words away to silence. When the foliage masked the temple itself from sight, Cutter looked up at the sky whenever he could, fixing their point geographically by triangulating it with the temple mount and another distant peak.

Cam hadn't mentioned the mountain when he'd described finding the temple. Neither had Nando. It was the kind of thing that would have been good to know about.

The straps of his pack cut into his shoulders and the sweat gathered at the base of his spine, runnels dribbling down the backs of his legs as he scuffed through the undergrowth. He squinted up at the sun again. In an hour it would be at its zenith. In an hour they'd either be inside, or flat out on their backs with heat stroke.

He stopped walking. For a moment the grasses around him continued to swish with the subtle ghost of movement, then it came again, a soft ripple of motion in the leaves of some of the dour trees running parallel with them as they climbed.

He breathed deeply, dreading the presence of an unwanted fragrance.

He inhaled the aromas of the rainforest — pollens and the moist air. There wasn't so much as a trace residue of any pungent reek that might have carried the beast's pheromones.

Nevertheless, Cutter listened to the trees.

They weren't alone.

He reached into his pocket for the small strip of rubber he'd cut away from the spare tyre, then stopped as his fingers closed around it. It was a pointless reflex; the beast wasn't using pheromones to control the Thylacosmilus. There were no trail scents laid down for them to follow. No spores that would betray it.

He licked at his dry lips, scanning the shadows that lurked behind the closest trees.

Nothing.

There was nothing he could do but walk on.

The mountain betrayed them.

It was part of the ultimate optical illusion. The temple wasn't on the same peak; rather there was a cleft that opened up into a vast chasm that fell away for hundreds of feet. The perspective of the uphill climb had hidden it from them.

Cutter stood before a fifty-foot-wide rope bridge that spanned the chasm. The ropes were supported on three poles, and fastened in such a way that they formed a 'V', a single rope to shuffle along with two guide ropes to help them balance as they crossed.

He leaned forward to peer down the sheer face of rock to the thin blue line of a river far below. The water no doubt flowed down to feed the Amazon, like a thousand other tributaries this far into the Andes. The thought wasn't exactly comforting.

He leaned back away from the edge.

The ropes showed signs of fraying, but at almost two inches in diameter they would certainly hold the weight of even the heaviest of the group. That wasn't what disturbed Cutter. It was the fact that once they were across the chasm, they were effectively cut off from any chance of escape. Isolated between bare rock and the anomaly, with nowhere to run if things went horribly wrong.

Cutter looked at Nando and Genaro. "Please tell me there's another way?"

"There is," Nando said.

"Thank God for that. Where is it?"

Nando pointed down into the chasm, drawing a line with his finger along the river.

"Well, that's not exactly what I had in mind."

"Then no, there isn't another way. The bridge is safe. It has been here for hundreds of years. No, not the same rope," he said, seeing Cutter's dismay. "We replace it every year or so."

"Why not build a proper bridge then?"

"Perhaps we could build a proper road as well? Or maybe a hotel?" Gone was Nando the cheerful, replaced by Nando the cynical.

Cutter made a rueful face. He had been well and truly chastised.

He tested the rope, watching it ripple like a sine wave across the gap.

Every ten metres or so anchor ropes ran from the guide ropes down to the bottom one, to prevent a huge gap from widening under the weight of passage. It was a relatively simple feat of engineering. Right then he would have killed for a little more stability, though. There was no way they were going to be able to cart all of the equipment over to the other side.

"Who's that trip-trapping over my bridge," Connor chuckled, coming to stand beside him. He paled visibly as he peered down the vertiginous drop. "Yeah, okay, well, I think I'll just stay on this side and offer moral support."

"Thought you might," Cutter said.

"I'm not a coward. I was just thinking, you know, you might want some back-up on this side, in case things go pear-shaped." His face reflected a jumble of thoughts and emotions.

"Of course," Cutter said, his smile taking the sting from the words. "All right, I'm thinking we're going to need to go over one at a time."

"Okay, I'll go first," Connor said, quickly.

"I thought you were going to stay on this side?"

"Yeah, well, I changed my mind," he said. He stepped up, grasped the guide ropes in both hands, and stepped out over the chasm. The rope quivered beneath his feet as he edged forward.

"Careful," Cutter said, needlessly.

"I can't say I like this," Connor called back, having shuffled forward another two feet. There were two inches of worn rope between him and a fatal drop. "Maybe this wasn't such a good idea after all."

"Just keep going, and don't look down," Cutter encouraged. "Stephen, you next."

Stephen nodded, and waited until Connor was twenty metres out, almost to the centre of the chasm. "What do you think?" He nodded toward the rope as Connor's unsteady steps reverberated through its core. The exaggeration was enough that at one point the frayed rope looked like a snake lashing around, about to bite.

"It ought to hold," Cutter said.

Once Connor had reached the other side, Stephen followed. He made considerably faster progress, and quickly reached his goal.

"Abby?" She nodded back at him. "Nando, will you and Genaro bring up the rear? I'm assuming you boys have crossed this bridge a time or two?"

Both rangers nodded. "Once a month, at least," Genaro confirmed.

"Good. Okay, Abby, over you go."

Cutter waited his turn, then stepped out on the rope. He tried to follow his own advice, but with the crisp wind caressing his face and the whistle of it in his ears, it was impossible. He looked down, and immediately regretted it as the rope lurched out from under him. Panicking, he over-compensated, pushing back too far against the movement of the rope beneath him. His foot slid off, and for a moment he was balanced precariously, knuckles white with fear, staring down at a 300-foot drop.

And then he slipped.

His foot dropped off the roll of the rope and he fell, his body plummeting like a stone. The momentum almost tore his arms from their sockets, as he hung out over nothing, arms wide in the classic crucifixion pose.

The rope dug into his crotch.

He could hear them screaming his name, but he couldn't think about anything other than the pain, and holding onto the guide ropes. He *tried* to think, his mind racing. Fire burned through the muscles of his shoulders and across his collarbone as he fought to hold his grip.

He couldn't pull himself up. It was impossible. There was no way he could get his feet back under him and stand, not with the rope whipping and lashing wildly beneath him.

All he could do was let go — in a minute. Less.

There was no way he could hold on.

He felt his palms grease with the cold sweat of fear. His shoulder collapsed, the ball joint wrenching out of place. With a scream of raw terror he dropped another three feet abruptly, the base rope slicing up between his legs so forcefully that it almost flipped him and sent him spinning out into the chasm.

A huge wave of black agony threatened to swarm over him as he wrestled with the ropes, trying to get a better hold. As he twisted, he could see Nando working his way along the rope to try and help him. He had lashed his belt over one of the guide ropes, but even that would offer little in the way of security if Cutter's frantic scrabbling whipped the rope out from under his feet. He was forced to stop.

"Come on! Come on!" Cutter yelled at himself, trying to heave his body even a couple of inches upwards, but the damage to his shoulder made it impossible.

He closed his eyes, trying to gather himself, digging down into a well of courage and strength — and no little fear — that he didn't know he possessed. Behind his eyes he saw her face, her smile, that look in her eyes.

It was cold, the wind cutting into his belly because his shirt had thrust up around his ears, and yet it was still blisteringly hot beneath the naked sun. Sweat greased his straining muscles, tricking down into his ears and into his eyes.

Cutter gritted his teeth against the pain. His breath came in short ragged gasps, his lips curled back from his teeth like some rabid dog straining at the leash. It took everything he had not to simply surrender, to let go and fall.

Raging against the fire in his damaged shoulder, Cutter brought his right leg up slowly, straining against the rope as it tried to get away from him. His arms trembled violently, sending vicious shockwaves down the length of the guide ropes. He managed, somehow, to curl his foot beneath the base rope and hook it around the worn fibres.

And just in time.

His shoulder gave out and he fell with shocking speed, swinging out backwards. Everything in his pockets, his gun, the torch, the strip of cut rubber, the oil, coins, keys, the goggles from the strap around his neck, fell away, spinning out into the nothingness that stretched between him and the ground.

He swung helplessly from his ankle, a huge pendulum suspended over the deepest of pits.

"Hold on, Professor!" Nando cried. Somehow he hadn't lost his balance when the rope had ripped away from under Cutter as he fell back. He rushed along it now with all the alacrity of a blind acrobat.

"There's not much else I can do!" Cutter rasped, trying to haul himself back up, trying not to look down, and trying to do anything but throw up as the world shifted violently beneath his head. Everything was twisting and spinning.

Gritting his teeth, Cutter rocked back, trying to build the momentum he needed to swing forward far enough and snag the rope. It slipped between his fingers. He forced himself to do it again, not daring to look at anything except the part of the rope he was trying to catch, so tantalisingly close and yet just out of reach.

He caught it on the third swing, and hung there, suspended over the chasm by hand and foot.

Cutter's movement had forced Nando to stop again, but now he slipped forward and reached him, leaning down to take his hand.

"Come on Professor," he said between gritted teeth.

There was no way he could clamber back onto the precarious rope. It was all he could do to clasp it with both hands and hook his other foot around it. That would do, though. He could traverse it hand over fist, Nando one step behind him every inch of the way.

He reached the other side, crawling off the bridge and flopping over onto his back. The impact with the hard-packed dirt sent a surge of nausea tearing through him. Cutter rolled over onto his stomach and retched into the long grass, wiping it away with the back of his hand.

TWENTY-SEVEN

The temple of Supay lay in ruins.

The damage had been done long before the Bairstow brothers or any other Westerner had laid eyes on it, dating all the way back to the savagery of the Conquistadors.

"This place is known to my people as the door to Uca Pacha," Nando said, as they approached the weather-beaten arch.

"Why do I get the feeling that doesn't mean 'the door to Paradise'," Cutter said, nursing his injured shoulder.

"It is the door to the Inca Underworld, my friend," Nando told him. It seemed as if their shared peril had begun to heal the sense of betrayal.

"It always is," Cutter responded wryly.

The temple was built on five levels, though the stones at the summit had long since crumbled away to little more than rubble. Above the keystone of the archway, there was a hole set in the stone that was the size of his fist. Nando explained.

"At midday on the solstice the sun will shine directly into the temple through the Eye of the Underworld and open the way to Uca Pacha for the fearless traveller."

"What day is it?" Connor asked.

"Not the solstice," Stephen assured him.

An element of normality had settled down over them after Cutter's near-plunge. The banter felt a little exaggerated, as though they were trying to make up for the scare he'd given them by pretending everything in the Garden of Evil was rosy. He loved them for it.

"Well, there's no point waiting to be invited in," Cutter said. "Coming?"

"Right behind you, Professor," Lucas said.

"Not too close, in case he falls down a hole or something," Connor joked. "You don't want him dragging you down with him."

"Connor, shut up," Cutter said, shaking his head.

"Shutting up now."

Cutter walked under the arch, and into the frigid chill of the temple.

The first thing that hit him was the smell; the bittersweet kiss of spices on the back of his throat; thyme, rosemary, strong herbs that had no place in the dank chill beneath the stone.

"It's here," he said. "Connor, do the honours."

"Will do." Connor took the handheld anomaly detector out of his pocket and turned it on. It immediately responded with a high-pitched ululating static hiss. "We're right on top of it."

"That's what I was afraid of," Cutter said, peering into the darkness. Without his thermal-imaging goggles he was as good as blind. He couldn't very well commandeer one of the other pairs though. Instead, he reached into his pockets for the strip of tyre he'd cut away and spat a curse as he came up empty handed. That, too, was lying at the bottom of the chasm.

"Connor, light the rubber and give it to me. In fact all of you light up, we can try and build a cloud of thick rubber fumes around us as we go deeper in. Who knows how thick a mist we're going to need to interfere with the imperative of the pheromones."

They did as he told them, dousing the strips of rubber in the gasoline, while leaving a long enough piece to hold, and lit them. The air around them quickly turned noxious, the cloying stink of burning rubber obliterating every other scent. Cutter nodded.

"Good, come on," He set off toward the heart room, the centre of the temple where the rituals and worship would have taken place.

They could taste the old blood on the dead air. It was more than merely stale, it was tainted.

The passageways divided into two very different paths; the path of the righteous, and the path of the sinister. On the left the walls were set with death masks and hideous effigies meant to frighten any intruder. The flames flickered across the masks, bringing them to vile life. Cramped as they were in the dank passage, their ragged breathing was amplified by the weird acoustics, and he could have forgiven any of them for thinking some unnatural life lurked still behind those blindly staring faces.

The right-hand passage was no less disturbing for the sounds that drifted up. There was the unmistakeable sound of snakes.

"Supay was the death god, no?" Cutter asked.

"Indeed," Nando said.

"And not only death, he commanded a demon army," Genaro offered.

"Sounds like a right little charmer," Connor said. "Wouldn't want to get on his bad side."

"I think we already have," Cutter observed. Then he held up a hand to shush the others. There was a peculiar high-pitched chittering sound that seemed to swell up around them. It set his flesh to creeping.

"Many of our temples were dedicated to more than one god; they would have chambers within the main body of the temple given over to Cocomama to ensure the health of the devotees, or to Ekkeko to ensure wealth and prosperity for those the temple served, and Inti, for his warming love without which all would fail. It was only on the solstices that this place opened into our ancestor's Hell."

"Well, that's something, at least," Connor said.

They edged slowly down the left-hand passage, deeper into the swallowing darkness. Cutter felt something crunch under his feet, and lowered the burning rubber to better light it. The dirt floor of the temple swarmed with the seething shapes of cockroaches and beetles.

"Oh, God," Abby said, behind him.

He felt the insects swarming over his boots now that he stood still, then the ticklish creep of them against his calves as they began to climb. Instinctively, he reached down with the hand that was holding the burning rubber to brush them off; the heat of the flame singed the hairs to which the insects clung, as well as their thickened carapaces.

Connor muttered a curse under his breath.

"Come on," Cutter said, walking through the heaving mass of bugs toward the arch that led to the next chamber.

As he crossed the threshold Cutter was surprised to find that the ground was clear of cockroaches and the other bugs that had infested the passage they had just left. It was almost as though something kept them from crossing over into the next room.

"It's clear," he called, urging the others to follow as quickly as possible. As he looked back, the flickering light revealed black writhing masses of centipedes and millipedes, army ants, black-carapaced beetles, beetles with mottled shells, larvae, enormous crickets and so many other insects it made his skin crawl. This was the most intensely claustrophobic place he had been in his life — and it was alive.

This new chamber was circular, an antechamber perhaps for the heart of the temple. The walls were marked with deeply scored engravings of phalluses and other signs of fertility. It seemed a curious juxtaposition to the other engravings he had noted alongside the death masks. But then, death and life, it was all cyclical. Why shouldn't the bringer of death also be revered as one capable of providing life. The turn of the calendar was the death of one year and the birth of the new.

The others gathered in the chamber, the lights of the burning rubber conjuring those demons Genaro had talked of back on the surface.

The walls, he saw, as he reached out to touch them, were flaked with a fine layer that might have been gold; such was the state of decay it was impossible to tell. There were three archways that led out of this prayer chamber. Two led into a bigger room lined with vegetable fibre and clay tower-shaped sarcophagi, while the third opened into the vast central chamber that was the heart of the ruined temple; the one room dedicated solely to death. Uca Pacha.

Cutter crossed the threshold.

A peculiar chill prickled his bare skin. By some trick of the geology this one room was considerably colder than those around it, as though they insulated it from the heat of the outside world, completely and utterly.

Ahead of him, in the oily flickering light, he saw dark shapes lined up on either side of what must once have been the sacrificial stone of the altar of Supay. Yellow eyes stared back at him. In the centre, as though bound to the altar itself, glittered the diamonds in the sky that Cam had promised.

The anomaly was failing.

A bluish tinge marred the imperfections of light as they hung frozen in the air. It was breathtaking in its geometry, every angle reflecting and refracting the flickering lights they bore, as well as carrying fractured daylight from the other side, across millennia.

"I really hope you've got a plan," Connor said, almost stumbling into the back of him as he saw the muscular silhouettes of the five Thylacosmilus facing him.

"I was *planning* on playing it by ear," Cutter said.

"Now you tell us," Connor said. "One of these days you'll give me a gun, and we'll all be so much happier."

"But not today," Cutter said, his laconic Scottish accent accentuating his amusement.

"So what's your ear telling you to do, Professor?" Lucas said. He'd shouldered the high-velocity tranquilliser and was drawing a bead on the central pouch-blade. If needs be, Cutter had no doubt the SAS man could take it between the eyes in a heartbeat. It wasn't just training. Lucas, like Stark, and like Blaine, was a different beast. He was an explosive violence pent up in human form, just waiting to be unleashed.

"Can you smell anything?"

"Only rubber."

"Good."

"They don't seem to be doing anything — it's like they're waiting for the word to attack."

"That's exactly what's happening," Cutter said. "Only it's not a word, it's a trigger pheromone. Abby, Stephen, on my word I want you and Lucas to take your shot. Abby, you left, Stephen you right. Lucas take the one in the middle."

"Right between the eyes," the SAS man promised. There was a sharp hiss of compressed gas as he chambered the ketamine dart.

"That still leaves two of them. Nando and Genaro, ready?" They nodded. "One shot, take them down and drag their bodies through the anomaly before it fails."

"Got you," Nando replied.

Cutter tossed the shrivelled strip of rubber into the centre of the heart chamber, throwing shadows up against the far walls. "Build a pyre," he said. One by one the others tossed their scraps of rubber onto the fire until it was a small blaze reeking of toxic fumes that clogged up the dank air and brought tears to their eyes. The eyes of the creatures smouldered through the flames and the fumes, fixed on them.

"What's to say we'll be immune to the pheromones?" Lucas asked.

"Nothing," Cutter said. "So we better make sure these inhibitors work."

"Jesus, you could have mentioned this before."

"Would it have helped?"

"No," the SAS man admitted.

"I didn't think so."

"But maybe we could have stripped more than one tyre?"

"And walked back a hundred miles or more through the rainforest, with no food or water? Not the best idea."

"Where's the smell, Daddy?" Connor asked, voicing what had been on Cutter's mind ever since they had stepped into the heart chamber.

Then Cutter wasn't wondering anymore.

Out of the darkness came the embodiment of the hook-beaked god, Pacha Kamaq the Earth-Maker.

And then the Thylacosmilus sprang forward, sabre teeth bared, guttural roars tearing from their throats as they answered the unheard command to kill.

Lucas fired first, the yellow dart driving home deep inside the open mouth of the pouch-blade as it lunged toward him.

Two more darts launched simultaneously, one just missing its intended victim, the other flying high and wide, clattering off the stones of the temple wall.

A huge Thylacosmilus powered across the fire, the fumes rafting up over its face and into its lungs.

Lucas didn't need asking; he took a second shot, landing the ketamine tranquilliser two inches above the marsupial's heart. It went down over the smouldering rubber, extinguishing what was left of its flames, plunging them into darkness.

The remaining beasts sprang straight toward Connor and Abby, those eight-inch teeth bared to rend flesh from bone as they impacted. Lucas hurled the tranq gun aside and dropped to one knee, pulling his service SIG-Sauer from the holster strapped to his ankle, and squeezed off six shots in a split second. The muzzle flare lit the chamber. He didn't have time to worry about the niceties of evolution. The bullets clustered in the side of the first Thylacosmilus' skull in a tight grouping that shattered through blood and bone into the primitive part of the animal's brain. It was dead before it finished skidding across the hard-packed dirt of the temple floor.

Lights began to flash as members of the group located their torches.

He didn't see the hook-beaked beast until it was too late.

The beak opened, and a bloated red thing came squirming out of it; a worm. The oleaginous worm-tongue coiled out and fastened on the side of Lucas' face. The millions of tiny teeth that formed the end of the proboscis dug into his skin, burrowing quickly beneath the surface. Blood leaked across the back of his eyes as pain exploded through his skull.

His finger clenched reflexively around the trigger of his gun, discharging the remaining nine rounds blindly as the worm ate.

Bullets ricocheted off the stone as Lucas went down. The SAS man was dead, but that didn't stop the beast from feeding. The bullets dug into the soft stone, causing the frame to shift as the weight pressing from above redistributed across the broken stones.

Cutter cast about frantically for something to stop it. He was reduced to trying to follow the wildly roving beams of the Maglites as the fight became a slaughter. Screams filled the darkness. More shots. One of the torch beams fell, rolling away across the floor.

Cutter stood in the centre of it, frozen.

The isoprenoids had failed; the beast had retained control of his hunting dogs. But it should have worked. *It should have.* Yet there were so many different constructions of the carbon chains, so many different ways the building blocks of life could be assembled. There was no way he could know what combination would block out the pheromones the beast used to command the Thylacosmilus. It was random.

Chance.

"Cutter!" Abby screamed. She was unarmed now, the dart gun knocked from her hand by the charge of one of the pouch-blades. Stephen was at her side, trying desperately to fend off the raging predator with the butt of his empty rifle.

We're going to die, Cutter thought sickly.

Nando and Genaro ran together, side by side, straight at the creature that had Abby and Stephen pinned down. Their screams became a war cry as they charged, their torches swooping and slashing through the thick dark. Nando struck the back of the Thylacosmilus, causing the great beast to rear violently and turn on him, huge fangs bared.

Connor brandished his torch as though he believed he could stove the creature's skull in with it. He was backed up against the wall — *Back to back with the sarcophagi in the other room*, Cutter thought, trying to banish the death and dying from his mind.

He needed to think.

It was all there. He shook his head, trying to think straight.

No it isn't, Cutter realised, *it isn't random at all. It isn't chance. It's the building blocks of life!* And the thought revolted him. He struggled to rationalise what he had to do, to tell himself that it was the only way. Lucas had already given his life for them; he was a soldier, he would willingly give his flesh as well, if it meant they might survive.

One of the creatures was dead, two were fighting the hallucinatory effects of the tranquillisers, while the last two fought with fury, snarling and snapping as they drove the team back.

As the Thylacosmilus reared up before him, Nando fired a dart, missing the mark by some distance.

It was all happening with such horrifying speed around him. Cutter could barely think or react before the patterns of death changed again, but there was no indecision this time.

These were his friends, his responsibility.

He would not fail them. Not now, not ever again.

"Abby!" he yelled, knowing it had to be done. *Dear God, forgive me*, he thought. She turned to look at him.

"The flare gun!" he yelled, holding his hand out. She threw it to him. He caught it and turned on the hook-beaked creature that was feasting on Lucas. He aimed the flare gun, but not at the creature.

He wanted to. He wanted to launch a blazing flare right into the middle of its face, but he didn't.

He aimed the muzzle down at the corpse, praying to God he remembered which pocket Lucas had put the small petrol phial in. *Right*, Cutter reasoned. *Lucas was right handed, he'd put it in his right pocket. That was his dominant side.*

Before he could change his mind, he fired the phosphorescent flare at the dead man's side.

For a moment the heart chamber filled with a deathly silence that stretched on too long for Cutter to think it was going to work — and then he heard the soft crump of the flare's heat, melting through the casing and releasing the petrol. As the flammable liquid seeped out across his clothes, it caught and went up in a brilliant blazing flame.

Within seconds Lucas' body was a beacon.

The fire drove the Thylacosmilus back, but more — the fire broke down the carbons in Lucas' body, the roaring flames carrying the isoprenoids locked within the dead man's mortal remains, releasing them into the air, thickening and clotting in the lungs of everyone trapped within the chamber.

The intensity of the flames coupled with the sheer volume of the chemicals being released effectively isolated every last shred of control the hook-beaked creature had over the prehistoric animals.

It meant that the iron hand with which the creature had ruled them was broken. Natural instinct, a fear of fire and burning, took over. The beasts turned tail, looking for somewhere to flee.

The only option was the opening that existed within the glittering shards of the anomaly, and another time.

Hook-beak didn't wait. The vile creature reeled in his worm-like feeder and scurried toward the collapsing portal.

Cutter watched it flee, hands on his knees, stinging tears flowing from his eyes.

All he could think was that they had faced a god, the hook-beaked god of the Incas: Pacha Kamaq the Earth-Maker.

"Was that...?" Connor said, obviously thinking the same thing.

"I don't understand what happened," Abby said. She avoided looking down at the burning man, Cutter noticed. The shock would catch up with all of the other griefs she had been trying to swallow down, though. After all she had been forced to witness that day, after so much death had surrounded them, it had to catch up.

But later.

"Isoprenoids," Connor said. "I was listening, even if you weren't. Saturated carbon chain. What are we if we aren't carbon?"

She nodded, still looking unsure.

"Come on, give me a hand with these before the anomaly collapses," Cutter said, struggling with his ruined shoulder to drag the first of the huge black marsupials toward the glittering prize.

"Do you think there are any more of them out there?"

He shook his head.

"No. Hook-beak had dominated them and was using them like hounds to do his bidding. They were all here, to protect him."

"And now they're gone."

"And so is he."

"But where did he come from? I mean? What *was* it?"

Cutter shrugged, and his shoulder reminded him not to do it again. He didn't have the answer.

"The future of evolution? Maybe he was a bird, using pheromones to control weak-willed animals. Who knows? It isn't where it came from that's important, it's where it went."

"But we know that. He went into the past. Didn't he?"

Cutter didn't answer. Instead he asked another question.

"What did it look like to you, Nando? Genaro?"

The two men stared at each other, each badly shaken by what had just happened.

"Pacha Kamaq," Nando said. "But it couldn't have been, could it? I mean, those old stories... they're just stories. The gods never really walked the Earth."

"But perhaps they will one day," Cutter said.

It was the only answer he had.

TWENTY-EIGHT

Lester sat in the closest thing to darkness his office allowed. Even with the lighting subdued it was still almost day-bright, thanks to the intense spots illuminating the loading bay area and all along the ramp.

He closed his eyes, pinching at the bridge of his nose. Life was never, ever, as simple or straightforward as he tried to make it. Just this once it would be nice to say, "Keep it low key," and for Cutter and his crew to manage to do just that.

The man was a maverick, unpredictable and so annoyingly self-righteous when he thought he was in the right. 'Bone-headed' was the phrase that sprung to mind. Still, he did have a habit of getting things done.

Lester folded his hands behind his head.

"Let me get this straight — you allowed a creature from the future to escape into the past? Now, isn't that precisely what we've been trying to avoid for the last, oh I don't know, forever?"

"It couldn't be helped," Cutter said. No, *I'm sorry Lester, I screwed up.* No, *I promise you, Lester, it won't happen again.*

"So what, pray tell, are we looking at here? Worst case scenario, lay it out straight."

"Worst case," Cutter said, leaning forward, "we've irrevocably changed the course of evolution. Altered the ages of man beyond recognition, wiped out great minds and all of their great creations, changed the immune systems of man and animal, and maybe created a god."

"What?" Lester opened his eyes then, and rocked forward in his chair. "Please tell me you are joking. Very funny, Cutter, I have to say. *Much* better than making up a name and pretending one of our team members has disappeared."

"It's no joke," Cutter said. His eyes were cold.

"Please explain, then, in words of two syllables or less, if possible."

"It's really very simple," Cutter said. "The future predator bore an uncanny resemblance to the mythical figure of Pacha Kamaq, the god the Incas called Earth Shaker."

Lester leaned forward, resting his elbows on the desk in front of him, and put his head in his hands. For a moment he didn't say a word. He simply sat there. Then he looked up.

"What part of creating a god seemed like a good idea, Cutter?"

"It wasn't exactly part of the plan, Lester."

Still no *sorry*. Lester inhaled slowly, that single breath the only sound in the room. He shook his head.

"We lost two good men out there in what was clearly reckless endangerment. And now this? Carelessly allowing an unknown creature to escape into the Plio-Pleistocene. 'Not part of the plan' is, frankly, not good enough. What do you have to say for yourself, Professor?"

"Don't be ridiculous, man. Look at what we've learned here," Cutter protested. "We can't simply close our eyes to this stuff. Everything's changed, in just a matter of days. Everything we *thought* we knew, we don't know anymore. Anomalies are opening overseas, Lester. They could open at any time, in any place. Places that are out of range of our detection devices. We're the only ones —"

Lester cut him off.

"Yes, thank you. We are the only ones. I seem to have heard that before. Jenny, what do you have to say for yourself? You've been awfully quiet."

She looked at the faces around the room, at Abby and Connor, Stephen and Cutter. They weren't the same people with whom she had travelled to Peru. The experience had changed them all. She couldn't exactly claim that it had brought them closer, and neither had it driven them apart, but they had lived through things together.

Abby had held a man in her arms while he died. That wasn't something she would ever forget. Cutter had been forced to burn a man who had become a friend. Even though by doing so he had saved all of their lives, there was no way something like that couldn't affect him.

She had been dragged screaming out of a broken window into the mist, and locked up in a cage like an animal waiting for the slaughter. Connor, Stephen, all of them, had walked through the valley of death in the shadow of the Thylacosmilus. Something like that changed you. It took the excitement of their job and mutated it into something horrible and deadly.

How many more people would have to die because of the anomalies and the corruption they had come across?

She didn't believe for a minute that the dying was done. It would go on as long as anomalies opened rifts in time and space, and let the creatures through. And one day it *would* be one of them dying, not just soldiers who had been seconded to the team. They all knew it. Peru had proved that much beyond a shadow of a doubt.

That was why she was quiet. It was why they all were.

"Cutter's right."

"Now *there's* a surprise," Lester said acerbically. "Do tell me, I'd love to hear how. That's what I live for, after all. Tell me more of the brilliance of the good Professor, do. I shall save it as yet another entry for my memoires."

"Now we know that the phenomenon isn't limited to the British Isles, that opens up a whole new can of worms. Judging from the kind of corrupt officials we encountered, wanting us dead and buried and dumped in an open grave in deepest darkest Peru, it throws open the potential for a whole slew of political disasters."

"My little ray of sunshine." Just the thought of the diplomatic nightmares that were unfolding in front of him, and the fact that he'd be reliant upon Cutter and the others to try and avert them, did not exactly set his heart a-flutter. "I think I need a couple of aspirin, I've got a migraine coming on. Out you go. Leave." He dismissed them.

The door sighed shut as it closed behind Jenny, Cutter, and the rest of the team.

It could easily have been the sound of Lester's heart.

THE END

ACKNOWLEDGMENTS

Nothing can survive in a vacuum, and as the song goes, no one can exist all alone. This book couldn't have happened without a few good men and women, so, my thanks go out to Dan Abnett, he knows why, to Cath Trechman, and yep, she knows why too (though for everyone else's benefit, it is all about patience and insight. Every good book needs an even better editor)... to Adrian Hodges and Tim Haines (come on, everyone can work out why they're getting the hearty slap on the back — they created the show, without them dinos wouldn't be roaming the earth, and what fun would that be?)... to Marie for coffee and cuddles and coping with the sleepless nights having a writer in her life entails... to Roddy Frame for music to write by, and to each and every person who has beavered away behind the scenes making this book possible: particularly the designer Martin Stiff, proofreaders, sales reps and marketing and publicity, all the guys you never think about when you sit down to write the first word, and forget when you crack open the spine and read the first page — so to the unsung majority who do what they do, my heartfelt thanks. But most of all, to you, for picking this book up off the shelf. Without you it's all rather pointless after all.

This book was brought to you by the letter S.

PRIMEVAL
THE LOST ISLAND
PAUL KEARNEY

A trawler is torn to pieces by a mysterious creature off the Irish coast; meanwhile Connor's anomaly detector goes off the charts. Half a dozen rifts in time have appeared... all on one deserted — yet politically contentious — island.

The team battles through a deadly storm to reach the island, only to find themselves powerless against the great creatures roaming free across the landscape. In fear of their lives they seek refuge inside a sunlit anomaly — watching helplessly as it winks out behind them, marooning them in the past. Back in the present Lester and Jenny must fight to control an escalating political catastrophe as the British, Irish and French governments all struggle to take control of the island.

www.titanbooks.com

PRIMEVAL
EXTINCTION EVENT
DAN ABNETT

When an Entelodon goes on the rampage down Oxford Street causing untold damage and loss of life, Cutter decides a new approach to tackling the anomalies is needed. And when a mysterious Russian scientist arrives at the ARC, he thinks he might have found the answer...

When Cutter, Abby and Connor go missing, Stephen and Jenny must work together in a desperate attempt to uncover the mystery of their disappearance and track them down.

Meanwhile, kidnapped and smuggled into Siberia, the remaining members of the team are faced with an anomaly disaster on an epic scale...

www.titanbooks.com